Keeping
Faith

by
N.L. Quatrano and D.K. Ludas

Published 2021 by Two Stone Lions Press
Printed in the United States of America
ISBN 13: 978-1-62390-085-4
E-ISBN: 978-1-62390-084-7

Cover photo: Sue Ortiz

For information, address:
Two Stone Lions Press
1202 Old Agateville Road
Hillsboro GA 31038

Two Stone Lions Press is a division of Salt Run Publishing LLC

Dear Readers,

We're so excited to share Keeping Faith with you at long last. Our precious publisher has been a tremendous blessing to us in this long journey, always showering encouragement on us, always assuring us she would wait until the story was right. We are as honored to be part of the Two Stone Lions family today as when Merciful Blessings was published in 2018.

Without exception, exceedingly difficult things occurred to everyone in 2020. Even though this series takes place ten years earlier than present day, Faith's challenges are large, and her journey may look and sound like some of yours. Maybe your challenges are even larger or not as daunting. What's important is how we react to those hills and valleys and it always will be the most important factor.

Sometimes the darkness is overwhelming, the hurts so big, the uncertainty so vast that we can't pray for help or hope for deliverance. And that's why the Lord made us all to be part of a community, be it family or friends. This life isn't meant to be traveled without a network.

We personally know about keeping faith for each other, our families, our communities, our church, and our world. And we encourage you to pray for others, too. Let's help each other to remember that the Lord hears every cry and every prayer. He always provides the answers. The key is to listen – and remember that He knows the right timing for those answers.

We hope you'll enjoy Keeping Faith and thanks for emailing us your encouragement, too. If you'd like, please write a review, or send us an email. Stay safe and we will pray for your joy and peace no matter the circumstances.

N. L. Quatrano   D. K. Ludas

D.K. Ludas & N.L. Quatrano

D.K. Ludas and N.L. Quatrano are experienced short mystery story writers. They've been friends a good long time, too. Well, more like sisters than friends, really. They've been in Romance Writers of America and Sisters in Crime and Mystery Writers. They're still with Sisters in Crime. Ludas in Central New Jersey and Quatrano in Northeast Florida.

When they first brainstormed this series, they just loved the idea that smart, independent women of faith could have their ups and downs, face their demons, find their common bond and then band together to defeat their enemy.

About the only thing more important to both writers than families and friendship is their faith in the Lord. It is central in their lives. They glorify Him for the fever He instilled in them to write, the guidance to write what will serve Him, and their relationship with each other.

It is their prayer that you'll be entertained and encouraged by the Amazing Grace Series. Both ladies enjoy hearing from readers, and would love to know what you thought of this book.

Dedication

We dedicate *Keeping Faith* to our wonderful writing organizations, Liberty State Fiction Writers, Sisters in Crime, and Florida Writers Association. The knowledge, encouragement, and friends in these groups continue to inspire us to keep writing our stories.

CONTENTS

"Be strong and courageous. Do not be afraid or terrified because of them, for the Lord your God goes with you; He will never leave you nor forsake you."
Deuteronomy. 31:6

CHAPTER ONE

Celebration

I can barely stand another minute of not being home with my boys, sleeping in my own bed, going to church with my family on Sunday morning . . ..

Faith Blessing-Walker, just released from the rehab center where she'd spent the last three months recovering from a knife attack, was so excited to get home her whole body tingled.

As Hope, her sister, made the turn into the circular drive that led to the front of the old farmhouse, Faith smiled from ear to ear to see her mother's roses now colorful and healthy when they'd been all but dead a few months back. Home.

Now, sitting in her wheelchair, she hoped her sister wouldn't dump her in the freshly mulched garden at the foot of the new ramp that led to the front porch. Who'd painted it Key West Pink?

"Hold on tight, Faith!" Hope said with a laugh.

"Hey!" Faith yelled, flapping her arms. "Take it easy. You almost pushed me out of this thing."

"Relax, honey. Your big sister is in control here. I've got you covered–from all angles."

Safely on the porch, Faith almost pinched herself to be sure it was real. *Home!* She was finally back home to the house where she was born and raised. Where her sons waited for her. She stretched to turn the key in the front door and pushed it open to face a gang of friends and family members.

"Welcome home, Faith!" they bellowed in unison.

Faith gazed around the room. *Oh, my goodness.* Tears filled her eyes as she grabbed Hope's arm. "This is... so... I'm so happy to be home," she sobbed.

Her guests rushed to hug and kiss her. Her boys stood to the side with broad smiles on their faces. Of course, they'd known all about this little surprise, she was sure. She winked at them through her tears.

Hope leaned down to hug her. "Everyone wanted to welcome you home. Probably half the town of Merciful is here. Not everyone got to visit you in Gainesville, so here they are. They want you to know they care."

"I wish Grace were here. Does she know I'm home?"

Hope nodded. "She'd have been here if she could, but even a Colonel doesn't tell the Army what to do. She'll be back as soon as she can."

Faith inclined her head, then wheeled away from Hope and into the crowded living room.

Hope wiped a tear from her eye and walked into the kitchen. She leaned on the granite countertop island to catch her breath, but the memories flooded back.

"No tears here today." Margaret Ann Butler, Hope's best friend, marched into the kitchen. "Why are you crying today of all days?" She reached for the tissue box on the counter and pushed it toward Hope.

Hope wiped her face, then turned to finish replenishing the vegetable platter. "It's just that I still struggle with what she's had to suffer because of me."

Margaret hugged her friend. "No, she suffered because of a lunatic with a knife. Something I learned in my years as a cop is that the bad guys do the bad stuff, and we aren't responsible for that. Now, that day is in the past. Leave it there. The Lord and the Law have already dealt with all that. We only have happy days, now."

She swept the platter into her ample arms and lifted her chin toward the dining room. "Come on! It's time for eating, drinking, and some merrymaking." And so, Margaret Ann and Hope, side by side with arms full, pushed through the opening into the dining room.

"There you two are." Faith motioned for Hope and Margaret Ann to adjust something on her wheelchair. "May I have everyone's attention please?" Faith yelled. "I have something important to share."

On either side of her, Hope and Margaret Ann locked the chair, lifted the footrests out of the way, and took a step to the side.

"One. Two... three," they counted – and Faith stood on her own. Cheers filled the room.

A smile took over her face. "Thanks. It's been a long road to recovery and three grueling months in rehab, but I'm up on my feet. Now watch this."

She took one step forward. More cheers, applause, and whistles engulfed the room. "In a few months, I'll be as good as new," she declared.

Hope patted her sister's shoulder. "She sure will be. Gracious, we'll have her driving a rig real soon."

Unassisted, Faith dropped back into her wheelchair, fumbled to release the locks, and then rolled to the buffet table. "Time to party!" she yelled.

Hope sauntered to her beau, Eddie Highspring, and wrapped

her arms around his waist. "Need any help?" she whispered.

Eddie shook his head and finished filling the remaining champagne flutes. "There you are." He placed the empty bottle down and gently placed a kiss on her forehead. "Time to toast." Eddie released her. "Let's pass out the champagne."

They handed every adult a glass. She held her glass high, blinking back tears furiously, and said, "To my little sister, Faith. Welcome back!" She squeezed Faith's hand. "God Bless You!"

"Amen," echoed through the house as glasses clinked and chimed.

While Faith sipped her champagne, her twin boys, Jeremiah and Isiah, bent down and hugged her.

"How are you feeling?" Jeremiah asked.

"Much better now that I'm home with the two of you." She ran her hand across their heads and kissed their cheeks. "Thanks for visiting me so much. Aunt Hope tells me you were a great help to her around here while I was laid up."

"Yeah. We helped out as much as we could," Isiah grinned. "Aunt Hope is a bit stricter than you, Mom."

"Oh, you don't have to tell me about your Aunt Hope being strict with teenagers. When your Aunt Grace and I were in high school, she was on us like bees on honeysuckle."

Hope interrupted Faith's conversation with her sons. "Just as I thought,' she said, sniffing the boys' champagne flutes. "Neither of you is twenty-one, and no alcohol is served to minors in this house." She replaced the champagne flutes in their hands with new ones. "Here, these have sparkling cider in them."

The boys' faces turned pink. "Gee, thanks, Aunt Hope," they moaned in unison.

Hope tugged Isiah's ears. "You're most welcome. No nephews of mine will be getting into any trouble under my watch."

Faith giggled. "You go, girl. It seems like old times at the Blessing household." She wheeled back to the buffet table and made herself a plate. A gentle hand squeezed her shoulder.

"Hello, Faith."

Her stomach felt like she'd just hatched butterflies there. *Oh my, I'd know that voice anywhere.* Faith looked up and smiled. "Scott." She grabbed his hand. "How good of you to come today."

Scott Byrnes, the first EMT on the scene to rescue Faith at the shop, had made it a point to keep checking on her ever since. "I wouldn't have missed this celebration." He knelt beside her. "I'm so glad you're home. You look wonderful."

"Thanks," Faith said, noticing the heat in her face that would turn her beet red in a second. "A little make-up works wonders."

"You don't need any make-up. You're a natural beauty."

"Honey, make-up is every woman's secret." She patted her cheeks. "A little dab here and there covers a multitude of sins." *And maybe he won't notice that I blush. Gads.*

"No sins on this face," Scott teased as he tweaked her cheek. "Perhaps a dab here and there would cover these freckles," he said, pointing to his own face.

Faith stared at him. "I never really thanked you properly for saving my life, Scott Byrnes." She held his face in her hands and brushed his lips with hers. "Thanks," she whispered.

"That's what EMT's do." Scott held her hands. "Saving you was doubly rewarding since you were a beautiful damsel in distress to boot."

"So, if I'd been ugly, you wouldn't have tried as hard?" she asked with a wink, freeing her hands to steady the meal that balanced on her lap.

"No, of course not. That's not what I meant." He glanced across the room and then met her gaze and held it. "I can think of a way you could properly thank me."

Faith picked up a piece of broccoli from her plate and nibbled on it. "How?"

"Go out with me. Like, on a date."

Oh, no. Faith frowned. "Go out? Where? I can't get around much, yet." She fanned her arms out over the wheelchair.

Scott grinned. "You would be out with an EMT. I can handle a wheelchair, right? Second, you won't be in that chair forever. And third, a girl must eat. You have to build up your strength again. So. How about dinner Friday night?"

Oh my, Lord. Breathe. It's just dinner, right? She glanced around the room though she had no idea what she was looking for: another sigh and a forced smile. *I'm divorced, not dead–though it's been a long while....*

"Okay, sure. Why not?" She nodded. "Yes, I'd love to go to dinner on Friday. I'll need a break from the house and PT by then, I'm sure."

"Good! It's a date then." Scott checked his watch. "I'm on call and have to put in a few hours at the squad, so I've got to get going. If you need a ride to your physical therapy sessions or doctor appointments, just give me a call. If I'm not on duty, I can take you or arrange the Medi-Bus service for you."

"I might take you up on the ride, we'll see. This week Hope, Eddie, and Margaret Ann have adjusted their schedules so they can take me. Hope and Eddie are teaching my boys to drive, so before long, they can take me if I'm not independent by that time." She looked up. "Lord, help me when they're driving."

"He will. Believe me. Well, duty calls." Scott started toward the tall parlor doors. "Can I call you tomorrow?"

"Of course, you can." She looked around for a place to park her plate. "Let me show you out." Faith rolled to a tray table and slid her food beside the empty glasses sitting there. "Oh, wait – don't you want some dinner to take with you? There's plenty."

He shook his head. "I'm fine, don't worry. And you eat now — I know where the door is." He looked at her for a long moment. "Goodbye, Faith. Take care." He leaned over and kissed her.

She returned the kiss and held him for a moment. "Thank you for everything, Scott. I'm excited about dinner on Friday night."

"Me too."

She wheeled the chair beside him anyway. The front door chimed just as Scott opened it. "Registered letter for Hope Blessing," the mailman said.

"I'm her sister. I'll sign it." Faith scribbled her signature on the line and handed the board back to the postman. He tore off the green receipt and gave her the letter.

Scott waved to her, then followed the postman down the front steps. "Back to the party," she mumbled and wheeled back to the dining room area and looked around.

"Eddie, where's Hope?"

Eddie pointed toward the kitchen, and Faith wheeled herself through the large opening. Hope and Margaret Ann stood at the long black granite island, placing pastries on platters.

"Hey, Sis, a registered letter came for you. Here you go." Faith held it out. Just a year ago, registered letters meant they were one step short of bankruptcy, but not so now.

Hope placed a mini cream puff on the tray and wiped her hands with the kitchen towel. "Oh, gracious. Not another bill collector, I hope. I thought we were past the days of registered letters."

"Well, open it up and see what's up," Margaret Ann said. "I'll finish here."

Hope removed her apron, wiped her hands, and left the kitchen, letter in hand. She tapped Eddie on the shoulder — a shoulder she knew now she could lean on. "Come to the office with me," she whispered.

Eddie grinned. "My pleasure."

****

Eddie closed the office door behind them. Hope grabbed her glasses from a front jeans pocket, placed them on her nose, and picked up the envelope. "Lone Star Oil Company. West Virginia," she read from the return address. She opened it and pulled out the neatly typed page and read the contents.

She frowned and handed it to him. "What in Sam Hill is this about?"

Eddie read the letter and gave it back to Hope. "I think we better sit down."

They sat across from each other at the desk. "Several years ago, your dad had some extra cash he wanted to invest. At the time, my advice was to invest in oil. This letter states you and your sisters' own several shares of a land lease by the Lone Star Oil Company of Texas. He must have bought some land and then leased it to them – or someone."

Hope's brows arched as high as a new gusher spewing oil. "Do you mean we're rich?"

"Hold on. I'm not saying that," he said with a laugh. He held out his hand as if he was stopping traffic. "I have to make some inquiries and do some research. But I would say you could be quite comfortable if conditions are right – but we don't know that yet. This looks like a land lease agreement in West Virginia. If the lease is producing, there could be royalty money coming in."

Hope leaped out of her chair. "Well, I'm going right out to that party and announce this. After the year we've had around here, this is going to help a lot!"

Eddie grabbed her forearm and shook his head. "Please don't do that yet, babe."

Her smile faded quickly. "Why not?"

"Like I just told you, let me make some inquiries, first. Let me contact them, find out what he owned, what the lease is paying, and all of that. You could have a new income stream — or not. Could be there are back taxes due which could wipe out any profits. We don't know. Why get everyone all excited if it's not what you think?"

Hope bent down and kissed the top of Eddie's head. "All right, I'll hold off, but can I tell my sisters?"

He gave her a lazy smile that reached his eyes. "Sure. How about we tell them together? But not until after the party."

Hope sighed, then shrugged. "I'll go along with that, Counselor."

He kissed her thoroughly, then released her, but held onto the lapels of her white blouse. "Do we have to go back to the party right now?" he whispered.

****

It was nearly nine o'clock when the last guest was gone, and the kitchen was clean and orderly again. The refrigerator had enough leftovers to keep them fed for the rest of the week.

With the pocket doors tucked away and the office open to the hallway, Faith, Hope, Eddie, and the twins settled into the old room with the fresh wallpaper and floor-to-ceiling windows.

Faith's boys stood on either side of their mother like sentinels, their faces uncharacteristically stern. Her near-death had aged everyone in the family, including them.

"So, what's up?" Faith asked, covering her yawn with the back of her hand. Hope looked at Eddie, who nodded.

"We received a letter today from an oil company. It looks like Daddy owns or has shares of some land that now belong to us," she explained.

"You're kidding me," Faith chirped. "After all we've been through, there was money all along to get us solvent?" She looked hard at Eddie. "Did you know?"

He shook his head. "It wasn't on the inventory list he gave me. I do remember mentioning investing in natural resources before I was even his attorney but didn't know he'd done it."

Jerimiah stuffed his hands into his jeans pockets. "How much is it worth?"

"I have no idea, young man," Eddie said. "I told your Aunt Hope that I'd check on it first thing on Monday. Could be a good deal of money or nothing at all."

Faith noticed the glance the boys gave one another. "What's up with you two?" Assuming the pose of angels, they straightened their shoulders and donned wide smiles.

"We're just happy for you, Mom. We're going for more cake. See you later."

As teens, they seemed to be non-stop eating machines. And she understood the look they'd shared. She and her twin, Grace, had conveyed thoughts to each other with a similar look many times during their teen years. She eyed them carefully, but they held her gaze without wavering. Either they were telling the truth, or they'd learned how to cover a lie well from their father – her ex-husband.

"Do not make a mess in that kitchen, do you hear me?" she called to their retreating backs.

CHAPTER TWO

Home on the Range

The dusty red pickup rolled up the circular Blue Bonnet Farm driveway. Beauregard Walker parked, climbed out of the truck, and limped toward the farmhouse. Gads, the bumps and bruises were getting harder and harder to take in stride.

"Beau!" Edna Anne Walker hugged her son as he entered the kitchen. "What happened to your face?" She caressed the gouges on his cheek. "Let me get you an ice pack to take the swelling down in that eye."

She went to the freezer, grabbed a hand full of ice cubes, and placed them in a plastic bag. Familiar with the routine, she pulled out the meat mallet and crushed it until it was malleable.

Beau took a seat at the kitchen table and held the cold pack to his eye while he closed the other one. It was good to be around his people.

Anne handed her son the ice bag and went back to the stove. "How many eggs can I scramble up for you, son?"

"Good morning, my love." Bill Walker kissed the back of his wife's neck and hugged her waist as he swiped a slice of bacon from the plate.

Anne pushed his hand away with a light slap, then put a hand on her hip. "Now stop stealing the bacon, Russell William Walker!" She brushed his cheek with her lips. "Look who's joining us for breakfast."

Bill walked to the table. "Good morning, Beau." He shook his son's hand. "Looks like the rodeo was a little rough this time."

Beau nodded. "Yeah, you know how the circuit is, Dad." His cell phone chimed. He gazed at it, grabbed it from the table, and walked toward the door. He raised his index finger to signal to his father that he'd be right back.

Bill stared at his son. "Are you sure those are rodeo scrapes and bruises?"

Beau nodded and let the screen door slam shut. He paced on the wrap-around porch to talk on his phone.

Bill took his seat at the kitchen table. "I wonder what that's all about."

"I'm not sure." Annie cracked six eggs into the pan and scrambled. "He hasn't been the same since the boys joined Faith in Florida."

The kitchen door opened, and Beau walked back in. He was hungry and there wasn't anyone home at his place to make breakfast or anything else.

"Just in time. You know how cross your mom gets if she serves cold eggs," Bill said.

"Sorry. That was an important call. I had to take it."

Annie served the plates of food and sat down. "Was it the twins? How are they? We miss them so much."

"No, not the twins, Mom." Beau shoveled a forkful of eggs into his mouth. "It was a business call."

"What kind of business, son?" Bill asked.

"Ya know, rodeo stuff."

"Yeah, I know all about that rodeo stuff, son, and I'm concerned. We need your help full time here at the ranch."

Beau grinned. "No need to worry about me, Dad. I understand, and I'm working on that."

"That's what worries me, boy." Bill sipped his mug of coffee.

"Worries me, too," Annie said.

Beau took another bite of eggs, followed with a large mouthful of sourdough biscuit, then washed it all down with coffee. He reached across the table and placed his large hand on his mother's slender wrist.

"No need for either of you to worry. But I've been rodeoing a long time. I've got a few rides to finish, stuff to sell off, and then I'll settle down to ranching full time, I promise."

Bill looked at his son a moment, then ate more of his breakfast. "How's that leg healing on Dyno? No infection?"

Beau pulled his hand away from his mother and picked up his coffee but didn't look at his dad. "He's doing fine. Better than I am." He laughed. "I've got to drop off some money at the vet for his bill, though. I'll get that done today." If he didn't, his father would know all about it before the week was out.

He cleared his plate and got up for more coffee. "Anyone else need a refill?" he asked, waving the pot. His parents shook their heads.

"How's Sherri doing?" his mother asked. "Haven't seen much of her in a few weeks. Why don't you two come on over for Sunday dinner? We've got some spring lamb in. I'll make some chops and my butter cake for dessert."

Beau smiled at her. "Sounds nice, Mom. I'll ask her. It seems she's always too busy for family stuff, though. She's over in Dallas this week, shopping with her friend, Dee." *I hope.*

Bill pushed back his chair and picked up his plate, then took it to the counter. "Gotta watch the bills, son. You don't need to get back into the mess you had after Faith left. And we can't keep bailing you out. Farm needs new wells this year. Going to cost a good penny, even if we do the work."

13

"I know, Dad," Beau said, his tone irritated. "I'm fifty-five, not fifteen. I told you, we're good on the cash side, so stop worrying. I learned my lesson."

Annie got to her feet and moved to Bill's side. "We're your folks, Beau. We'll never quit worrying. Now, go on and get on with your day. And let me know about dinner by Friday, okay?"

"Sure will, Mom. Thanks for the breakfast. I should hear from the boys today. I'll tell them you send your love."

****

Beau idled at the end of the three-quarter-mile driveway just inside the gates to the Blue Bonnet Farm. He dialed Sherri's number for the third time that morning, and again it went to voicemail.

"Honey, call me. I have no idea where you are or who you're with, but the Visa company called again. You told me you paid that bill. Call me as soon as you can."

He'd been betting on that credit line to pay the veterinarian for fixing up his horse. Despite what he'd told his father, he was leaking money like a sieve. But this time, he didn't know where it was going. A man in his fifties shouldn't have to keep running to his father for money.

Sure, when he'd been married to Faith, he'd spent every dime and then some, always sure the pot of gold was at the end of the next rodeo. Or dice game. And, after nearly twelve years, she'd had enough. But he'd learned some things. He didn't gamble and he spent less. Why were they still so cash-poor all the time?

The only explanation was that Sherri had a spending problem. He didn't see a lot of new clothes and her car was only a year old, but he'd nearly paid that off. His truck was pushing ten years and ran great, so he kept it going. The horse sales weren't off the charts, but he was selling quality stock regularly. They should have money in the bank, but he'd found out that morning they didn't have much.

Before he pulled out onto the road, his phone rang. He glanced at the screen and saw a familiar number. "Hey, Jimmy. How's the agent game doing?"

"Not too bad, Beau. Hey, I've got a moneymaker for you over in Ft. Worth next week if you're interested. Not a huge payout, but with two rides, you can probably pick up a grand. You interested?"

"I don't know. I'm getting too old for this game, buddy. But I need the money. I won't have Dyno – he's still healing up where that steer got him last month."

"Not a problem. This ride is as much a show event as a rodeo. Fundraiser for Cook's Children's Hospital."

"Sure, count me in. I'll head back to my ranch and pull a flashy horse. When are we due for check-in?"

"Next Friday by noon. I'll cover the entry fee, right?"

"Please. And thanks, Jimmy. I'm going to miss you when I get out."

"Yeah, yeah," Jimmy said with a chuckle. "Rodeo bums don't retire—they die, buddy. Or end up in jail," he said with a laugh. "See you next week."

Beau put the truck into drive and headed down the road. His ranch was only four miles from his parents' spread, where world-class rodeo bulls were bred, raised, and sold for top dollar. His own stock and trade was breeding reliable cutting horses, and he'd had a good year so far – so why were they broke? He'd have to call the vet and make an excuse on that promised payment. Blast.

As he drove toward home, he wondered if maybe his new wife would be there waiting for him with nothing but an apron on.

"Dream on, Beauregard Walker, dream on."

****

"Sherri Walker, when are you leaving that broke down cowboy so we can get the hell out of Texas?" His long fingers traced lazy circles on the white sheet that covered her left hip and little else.

Her long lashes fluttered open, and she gazed at him with her deep blue eyes. "I've told you before, lover, I'll let you know. I'll know when the time is right, so don't push me."

She swung her long legs over the edge of the bed, stood, and walked to the bathroom door before turning back to him. "Why don't you be a dear and go get us some coffee? I'll get freshened up."

He laid on his back and glared at the ceiling. He hated Texas. He hated Beau Walker with his swagger and his money and his damned good luck. He could hear Sherri humming in the shower, and he smiled as he got out of the rumpled bed and pulled on his jeans.

Well, Earl Foster had something that Beauregard Walker didn't. Her name might be Walker right now, but before that cowboy figured out what's up, her name would be Foster. And then Earl would be calling the shots.

CHAPTER THREE

Bad Penny

"Keep going. Keep going. Come right to me – now – Faith!"

"I can't go anymore." She slumped over the bars sobbing. "It's too hard for me, Scott. I just can't do this." *I've never been the strong one, have I, Lord? You made Hope and Grace strong, but not me. How will I do this?*

The physical therapist came around in front of her. She put her hand on Faith's shoulder. "It's just a little way to reach Scott. Focus on getting to him, one step at a time, okay? Tell you what. I'll stand right behind you. You have to try to get those legs walking again. Push through the pain, or you may not walk again, and I know you don't want that. I won't let you fall and get hurt, I promise."

Scott opened his arms. "I know you can do it. I want to give you the biggest hug you ever had. Won't you try it again? For me? For your boys?"

She rested her arms on the bar and took a deep breath. *Lord, I do want to walk again. I want to dance with this man, ride with my sons again. They all believe in me, why can't I believe in myself? Please – help me to be strong.*

Faith wiped the sweat from her face, then looked at him. She straightened, lifted herself on the bars, and placed her right foot on the floor. Keeping her eyes fixed on Scott's, she set her left foot in front of the right one. She went pale with the pain in her arms and her back. By the third step, the sweat was running down her back like a swollen river.

I've got to believe I'll walk again. She clamped the inside of her bottom lip in her teeth. *I will do this.* Left foot down, right foot up. *This is so freaking hard.* Left foot down, right foot up. Right foot down, left foot up. Six whole steps. *Scott is so close I can smell his Old Spice–*

"You did it!" Scott shouted as he lifted her off the end of the bar. "You did it!" He placed her back on her feet and kissed her.

His smile made her heart almost burst with pride. Faith held on to his neck and buried her head in his chest. "With your help and the grace of God," she whispered. "I'm so dizzy I feel sick to my stomach."

The therapist tucked the wheelchair behind Faith's knees, and she collapsed into it. "You rest for a while. Put your head between those knees until the dizziness passes."

"Thanks. Both of you," Faith rasped. "Water?"

Scott dashed to the dispenser, brought back a cup of cold water, and held it for her so she didn't shake it all into her lap. Then she leaned forward for a few minutes, eyes closed, willing the nausea away. *The Lord is my shepherd, I shall not want.* She straightened up and smiled at the man in front of her, kneeling with a worried frown on his face. Her heart skipped a beat when she saw the immense pride in his eyes, along with a shimmer of tears.

She cleared her throat and squared her shoulders. "Let's set up my next appointment."

The therapist motioned for them to come to her desk. "I think you should rest tomorrow. Your arms and legs will be quite sore. After all, you haven't used them in this capacity for quite some time. I think you should come back again on Wednesday, and then on Friday. We'll try that for this week."

Faith rubbed her aching palms along the top of her thighs. "I guess that will be all right. I'll arrange it with my drivers, but I'll call you if I can't get a ride–"

"That's not a problem," Scott interrupted. "I've arranged for flexible hours, so I can always drive you here and pick you up if I can't stay. I want to do this."

Again, she looked into his eyes and saw his honesty. She smiled. Faith looked at the therapist. "What time?"

"Plan on being here for two hours at a time, okay? We'll do some heat and stretching on the table. Then we'll do some strengthening exercises on you, and then you'll walk the bar the rest of the time." The therapist thumbed through the appointment book. "I can give you a standing nine a.m. appointment." She looked up at Scott. "Will that work?"

Scott winked at Faith. "Perfectly." He pocketed the appointment cards. "Let's go hit the Blue Gill and celebrate, okay? I promise to have you back to the offfice before the boys get home from school."

****

After they'd gotten settled at the table and ordered their iced teas, Faith reached over and took Scott's hand in hers. She gazed into gray eyes, then glanced at the tattoo peeking out below his rolled shirt sleeve just above his wrist. *How did I get so lucky to meet such a man now that I can't even walk? Or is it all an illusion?*

"I swear, as happy as I am to finally be walking some, I can't believe how long it's taking for me to get back to my old self. The rehab just feels endless at this point," she said.

Scott's thumb rubbed across her knuckles. "Hey, the doctors said your spine was nicked when that lunatic stabbed you with that Bowie knife. Learning to walk takes time – just be patient. You'll get there."

"Are you sure about this?" she asked softly. "You're a good man – and you've been a good friend all these months, but I'm not your responsibility. You don't need to give up your personal life to truck me around, you know."

The waiter delivered their drinks and told them lunch would be out shortly. Scott thanked him, then turned back to Faith.

"I'm not a man who does things he doesn't want to do. A part of me fell in love with you the day I learned that you'd survive that madman's attack. Before that, I was terrified to let myself do anything but pray for your recovery. But my heart tells me that if you're ready, I'm ready to see if what we have is a forever-thing."

Okay, it's now or never. Can I do this? Running out of the restaurant is not a viable option.

She freed her hand, then pulled her drink over and took a long sip. Her heart was beating loud enough for the bartender to hear it.

"Have you ever had a 'forever' thing?" she asked.

He took a long drink himself. "I have. It was an extraordinary relationship. One I'll cherish forever."

Faith sat back and looked at him for a long minute. "I'm not sure I believe in forever, Scott. My 'forevers' aren't all that long, it seems."

"Why do you say that? Even if your first marriage didn't work out, you know about the kind of love that has staying power. I've seen you with your sisters – that's an amazing relationship."

She shrugged, then nodded. "It is, but it wasn't always the relationship that it is now. When my mom died, Hope got stuck raising Gracie and me, and we didn't make it easy. We've only come back into her life in the past year since our father died. Her reward for giving up so much for us was our ingratitude. Our mother didn't live to see us become adults, see what I mean? Short term. It's like God is telling me to make my moments count because I may not have the people I love for very long."

His smile faded. "Yes, well, I understand about that kind of disappointment, for sure. My parents are both alive and aging well. They live with my sister Sarah and her clan up in Asheville, North Carolina." He rolled his sleeves up a bit further and showed Faith the cross and dove tattooed on his forearm. The name *Megan* was on one of the dove's outstretched wings.

She waited for his explanation.

"When I was thirty and finishing up with an advanced degree in certified financial planning, I met a woman five years younger than me, and I fell head over heels for her. Bright, funny, and had a smile that lit up a five-mile area." He took another drink of tea before he looked back at Faith.

"Long story short, we had pretty much a story-book life for about five years. We loved to do a lot of the same outdoor things, so we spent a good deal of time together. We worked for different firms, but both of us were CPAs, so even during tax season, when the pressure was on, we knew how to laugh the stress away. But one night, Megan was driving home late from the office – it was April 14th, and she'd stayed to file extensions for her clients – and she got hit head-on by a drunk driver. She died before I could get to the hospital."

"Oh, Scott . . ." Faith shook her head, almost too shocked to speak. The pain radiated off him as he relived what must have been the most horrible night of his life. She swallowed around the lump in her throat.

He shook his head as though to pull himself back from that night. "It was the end of me forever. I was sure of that. The first year or so, I functioned, but just barely. And to be honest, the grief still comes out of nowhere sometimes, but not as often as it once did. Come the following January, I sold the house and quit the firm. I wanted to do something with my life that counted for something. I enrolled in a program for EMT training. I couldn't help Megan, but maybe I could help someone else's 'Megan.'"

The waiter came by with Faith's shrimp po'boy and his fried fish sandwich, asked if everything was all right. They ordered fresh drinks and extra lemons, and off he went.

"I'm so sorry for your loss, Scott. My story isn't nearly as devastating. I married a rodeo cowboy who was charming and sweet and loved me to the moon – for a while. When I got pregnant with the boys, he resumed entertaining the rodeo bunnies while on the road, and I stayed home. When the boys turned twelve, I decided I'd had enough. We were constantly broke, he was always gone, and I hated the cheating the worst. The last time I called him on it, we had a huge fight, and he lost it. I had broken bones with that one. I filed for divorce and opened up my welding shop."

He looked at her for a long time, then took her hand in his. "He must have gotten his brains rattled too many times. That's the only reason I can think of that might explain behavior like that. I can't think of any justification for hitting you. Even once."

Faith blushed and pulled her hand out of his and picked up her fork. "Okay, Scott Byrnes, let's just see where this all goes. No pressure. For now, let's eat!"

****

It was two-fifteen when Scott wheeled Faith up the ramp to the Amazing Grace Trucking Company office and opened the door. Hope, with a phone to her ear, motioned for them to come in. When she put down the phone, she tucked a renegade lock of hair behind her ear and stretched.

"Lots of new orders are coming in. So how did therapy go today?"

"Just great! I took six whole steps." Faith reached for Scott's hand. "It was hard as anything, but Scott wouldn't let me quit, and I got it done." She turned her reddened palms upward so Hope could see the developing blisters.

Hope ran around from behind the desk and hugged her. "I'm so happy for you. I knew you could do it. We'll soak those palms, but you'll develop tough skin there. Grace phoned earlier to see how you were doing."

"Lordy, I miss her. How is she? When is she coming home?"

"Just as soon as her paperwork is approved, she's out and on her way back. It sounds like it may be just another week or so. You know how Army red tape is – and she warned us, remember?"

Scott leaned over to Faith. "Faith was a hero today! You did a great job, hon. I've got to run now, though. I'll check on you later." He kissed her forehead. Before he closed the door, he stopped and looked over his shoulder. "Nice to see you, Hope."

When his footsteps could no longer be heard, Hope poked

Faith in the arm. "Do I see sparks between you two?" She winked. "Think it will get serious? He seems like a nice guy and you deserve a nice guy."

Faith thought a moment. *And I once thought Beau was a nice guy, too.* She nodded. "Yes, I do, and yes, he is. We're going to see where it goes. We didn't make any real plans but to date and see where it leads. But I'm happy about it. I wasn't sure how much heart I had left in me after I left Beau, but I like where life with Scott and the boys could lead. As long as I can keep the fear at bay, anyway."

Hope sat down in the chair next to her. "That's great news. I'm happy for you, for sure. Just take your time, okay? I was there too, remember? But keep asking the Lord to help you trust again, baby. He will. Life is hard enough without living with fear."

I know the words, it's the doing that's hard. Faith put on her happy-woman smile. "Yes, ma'am. Speaking of taking plenty of time, when are you and Eddie getting married? Can I be a flower girl?"

"Faith Walker, you bite your tongue! Who said anything about me getting married again?"

"Oh, come on. He's always been the love of your life, and he's paid pretty dearly for his mistakes, hasn't he? I mean, having to live even one day with Betty Jo must have been pure misery, don't you think? You fall off the horse, and you have to get back on."

Hope jumped to her feet, her face bright pink. "What's gotten into you today? Has Eddie been talking to you? I'm just not sure, that's all. It's not about him – it's about me. I'll let you know if I need a flower girl or matron of honor."

Faith tugged at her sister's hand. "Hey, it's that trust thing, right? I'm sorry, but you need to get on with your life, Hope. Don't you think that Gracie and I want to see you get your happily ever after, too? We love you, that's all."

Hope sighed. "I love you, too. Now how about we get this office caught up a bit. Before you know it, the boys will be home."

"Where are they? I was expecting them about now," Faith

said.

"The Reverend needed some help at the youth center, so when he called to ask if they could work with some of the boys after school, I said okay. I'm sorry — now that you're home, you should be making those calls. Forgive me for overstepping."

Faith waved the air. "That's fine with me. They enjoy being with the other kids, and that makes me happy. Most teens would hate the idea of moving in their junior year of high school, but the boys have friends here already, so it's not as hard as it could have been."

Hope breathed a sigh of relief. "Good. They'll call when they're ready to come home, so let's just get these invoices in the mail and call it a day."

Faith had just stamped the last envelope when a heavy door slammed in the yard. "You expecting someone? That sounded like a pickup truck."

Hope shook her head and got up to look out the window. "Oh, my Lord . . ."

"What in the world?" Faith said, turning her wheelchair to face Hope.

"Come over here by the desk," Hope hissed. She reached into the right-hand drawer, pulled out her revolver, and settled it in her lap. Heavy footsteps climbed the stairs.

"Should we call–" Faith whispered.

The door opened. *What the hell does he want? It can't be anything good.* Faith felt her blood pressure rise and though her heart might jump out of her chest.

"Hello, Sugar," the tall man with the blackened eye drawled, his gaze fixed on Faith. "So, what's this I hear? Things are turning around for you, eh? You're almost able to walk now?"

Faith stared at him. No wonder he enjoyed riding bulls and getting bucked off broncos. He was not only full of himself–he was obviously stupid. She looked at her sister.

"Give me that gun, Hope," she said evenly, never taking her eyes off the man in front of her. He needed to leave and now or she was going to scream like a banshee.

"Now, honey, no need for a gun. Is that any way to act toward your husband – the father of your children?"

"Don't you dare talk to me about being my husband. You weren't ever much of a husband, Beauregard Walker. And you've got a new wife – where is she? Waiting for you in the truck? Magic wore off that marriage too, you pitiful excuse of a man?"

"Whoa, Faith. What kind of Christian woman are you, talking like that? What happened to forgiving us our sins? And loving until death do we part?"

What? Is he for real? She blinked at him and felt the heat in her face. "I'm a Christian work in progress, I guess. I could arrange for you to be dead if that's what it will take to get you out of my life, though. We've been divorced for years in case you weren't paying attention. You're remarried for three and a half of those. What the hell do you want?"

"I came to check on you, that's all. Losing you was a big mistake, and I'm sorry. I thought that maybe you and me could talk about the future. However, my timing might be off. Maybe not today."

She hated how her laugh sounded to her own ears – half hysteria and half madness. *He was always one for understatement unless it was about his bank account or winning purses.* "You are full of bull, Beau. What do you really want?"

He shook his head, his baby blue eyes open wide in an attempt to look innocent. "I'm telling you honest. I came with good intentions. One, to see my boys and the other to try to help you recover. I rode in my last rodeo on Friday. I'll be starting over."

Hope sucked in a breath but didn't say a word. She held the gun in her lap.

"I know you all too well," Faith snickered. "You have ulterior motives behind everything you do. It may be nice for our boys to see you regularly, but it's not nice for me."

Beau's dimples creviced a mile wide. "I know, my being near you would always get to you." He ran long fingers through his wavy hair.

Faith picked up the glass paperweight holding down the stack of work orders on the desk tray and hurled it at him. He ducked, but the paperweight hit the paneled wall and shattered into thousands of tiny slivers.

"Get over yourself, Beau. You're a two-bit Texas gigolo." She shook her head. "It always amazed me how something like you could come from such a refined family like the Walker Ranchers of Texas."

He hung his head. "Yeah. I guess I'm just no good, Faith. That's why you married me and had my sons."

Faith laughed. "Well, I was a fool. Did you ever not cheat on me? No – don't answer that. But what would possess you to think I'd ever consider coming back? You are done, son."

Hope stood. "That's quite enough." She handed Faith the revolver, went to the closet, pulled out a dustpan and broom, and shoved them into Beau's big hands. "Clean up your mess."

"Why should I clean it up? I didn't throw it."

Hope went right up to his face and shoved her index finger into his shoulder. "Listen to me. You provoked her to do that. And as a matter of fact, I think you've worn out your welcome here. I suggest you get yourself a hotel room – maybe in Louisiana."

His eyes opened wide. He accepted the broom and swept the glass pieces into the dustpan and dumped them into the trash can. The two women watched in silence.

"There. All cleaned up." He handed the broom and dustpan back to Hope. "Anything else I can do around here?" he drawled.

"Leave," said Faith.

CHAPTER FOUR

What's the Deal?

Faith and Hope worked together in the kitchen, getting dinner ready. The mid-September breeze was still warm, but there was a cooling side to it, too. With the door to the back porch open to the kitchen, they could hear Jeremiah and Isiah out by the paddock with the horses.

"How are you going to tell the boys that Beau was here today? He'll be back, you know. He's relentless about getting what he wants," Hope said as she viciously tore the lettuce into tiny pieces.

Faith placed the dinner plates in her lap. Poor lettuce. "Let's say grace like we usually do and get the updates on everyone's day. I'll tell them then." She sighed. "They're going to want him to stay, but he absolutely cannot stay here. We don't need the stress he brings along."

"Agreed," said Hope. "Here, take the silverware with you, too. I'll get the glasses and drinks – be right behind you."

Faith had mastered her wheelchair and quickly set the table, thanks to the rearranging Eddie and her sons had done on the long, screened porch. She wheeled to the low ramp and watched as Hope placed the glasses and napkins just so on the table. Her sister's habits gave her away. The constant rearranging of the same small item meant Hope was upset – more upset than her words or tone let on.

Will Hope ever get over all the betrayals? Eddie had been the love of her universe when they were in high school, but he married Betty Jo Clark right after graduation, the woman who almost cost Hope everything. Then Matthew Kane asked her to marry him, and Hope settled in to be a preacher's wife, but he died of a heart attack in Betty Jo's bed one fateful night. How much could one heart take before it decided, no more?

A car door slammed, and Faith heard the boys stampeding toward the front drive of the house, yelling as their long legs carried them like gazelles.

"Mr. Highspring, how are you?" they called in unison. "Are you . . ." their conversation faded when they rounded the front of the house.

Hope let out a sigh. "I was almost afraid it would be Beau."

Faith tried to laugh like she didn't care, but her stomach was in a knot, and she couldn't. She didn't need or want Beau in her life. The fact that he was here was far more than a mere annoyance, but she walked a fine line. She'd never forced her boys to choose between her and their father—but she'd have to make sure her boundaries didn't get crossed.

"I know. Especially when the boys took off like that, but I doubt he'll be back tonight. He's not entirely sure that I won't shoot him."

Hope hugged her. "Well, fear has its place. Let's get dinner out here. We've got some hungry men to feed."

Faith looked at her. "The twins really are more men than boys, aren't they? I'm going to have to work on remembering that."

"I know, I am, too. But we'll get it all figured out, together," said Hope as she followed Faith up the little ramp into the kitchen.

****

After the blessing was said and everyone had roast chicken, dumplings, and greens on their plate, the conversation was light until the initial hunger was satisfied. *This is the best part of our meals,* Faith thought as she gazed at her family. *Being together, no complaints, no arguments, a perfect moment of peace.* She smiled and thanked the Lord for it all.

"Hey, Mom. How did your therapy go today?" Isiah asked when he'd washed down a mouthful of food with sweet tea.

Faith put down her fork and pumped her fist in the air. "I was out of that chair and stepping out like a dancer!"

"Really?" exclaimed Jeremiah. "That is so cool! Bet you'll be glad to get out of that thing, Mom. Maybe we can go riding soon. Dad's going to bring Tempe out to be with Magellan and Magda."

Isiah poked his brother in the ribs. "We were supposed to ask first, you idiot." He looked at Faith and Hope. "Can we have her come, Aunt Hope? Mom?"

"Let me think about it, okay?" Faith said. *Why aren't Magellan and Magda good enough?*

She smiled at the boys. "How is the work at the youth center coming along?"

"Reverend Jackson says we'll be done by Friday. Tomorrow we start painting the walls. We can finish up with him, right, Mom?"

"Of course. I'm sure he's counting on your help. Have you heard from your father?" she asked, just before she forked some greens into her mouth.

"We called him the night of the party, but we haven't talked to him this week. We'll have to call and tell him you're walking now," Jeremiah said.

She wondered if they knew Beau was right here in Merciful

this afternoon. She also wondered how much she wanted Beau to know about her recovery or anything else in her personal life.

In the long silence, Eddie glanced at Faith. "How many steps did you take today?"

She smiled. "Six or seven. And it took forever." *The most painful thing since childbirth,* Faith thought as she gazed at her sons' faces. But, hopefully, just as worth all that screaming pain.

"It's a start," she said with a shrug. The therapist says it will be about a month, and I'll be out of this chair for good. In the meantime, I'm to walk some every day using the walker instead." She pointed her fork at Jeremiah. "I won't be riding any time soon, though."

He smiled at her. "We saw a movie in school about horse therapy farms and all the work they're doing with disabled people. Maybe we can get you a special saddle to keep you on the horse."

She wrinkled her nose. "I've got a perfectly good saddle, thank you, J. And we'll just see who the better rider is when I get better, how about that?"

With a mouthful of food, he nodded at her, his eyes bright. He gave her a thumbs up. Her spirits soared.

She looked at Eddie. "Did you have court today?"

He shook his head. "No, but I have a friend over in Putnam County area who is in a bit of a bind, so Jack and I drove over there to see what we could do for him today."

"Well, if it's a criminal case, Jack is the best guy in the world to help him. I hope it works out," Hope said. "He sure kept me from getting railroaded on Betty Jo's death."

"He is the best, which is why I called him for you," Eddie said.

"Boys, how was school?" Faith asked.

They each speared another hunk of chicken before Jeremiah spoke. "Good. The teacher was talking to us about working on our two-year degrees while we do our senior year. I told her I didn't know if we were staying, though. Maybe we're going back to Texas with Dad?" he asked quietly.

Faith pushed her plate aside and placed her glass of tea in front of her. She traced the beads of sweat on the outside of the glass with her index finger. "I think we have to talk about all that, don't we? Our trucking business is stable, and I'll be well enough to go back to my welding business in a few months. To be honest, I haven't thought that far out. I hoped you'd want to finish your junior year here, at least. You'll be driving in another month, and then life will change for you both."

"When you get that oil money, can you buy us each a truck?" Jeremiah blurted out.

Eddie laughed. "Afraid there isn't much oil money, fellas." He patted the envelope beside him on the bench. "Your grandpa was one of ten owners on that property, and he had some quarterly royalties that went into an account for you boys, but it's only paying a few dollars each quarter. There's probably enough saved to buy one good used truck. You'll have to share it."

Hope moaned, then addressed the twins. "Your grandfather probably meant that money for college or trade school."

"Besides, what makes you think you don't need to earn your own money to buy a truck?" Faith asked the boys with her brows raised. *They are not going to grow up like their father, thinking everything they want they should have.*

The boys shared a look and went back to eating what remained on their plates. Faith watched them. Something was up. She didn't press, though. She knew they wouldn't give it up, no matter how she cajoled or threatened them. She and Grace would have died rather than tell on one another when they were growing up. But what was that look all about?

"Do you boys have plans for when you graduate?" asked Eddie.

"Nothing solid, sir. Jeremiah wants to be a rodeo clown. I'd like to be a rancher and raise livestock like G'daddy."

Faith nearly choked on her greens at the idea of one of her

sons being chased around a ring by angry bulls and horses, but she said nothing. It would probably pass. *Please, God.*

When they were done eating, they asked to be excused.

"Take your plates into the kitchen, please," Faith reminded them. "Then go groom and feed the horses and get their stalls ready. Florida Fish and Wildlife is reporting coyote activity, so we'll be putting them in at night for a while."

"Yes, ma'am," they replied in unison. Isiah walked around the table and picked up everyone else's empty plates as well, and they disappeared into the kitchen for two minutes, then raced each other past the adults and out the back door without even touching the steps. The wooden screen door banged like a shot behind them.

"And be sure to latch the barn door properly," she called after them.

In the warm silence, Faith watched them bumping shoulders and laughing as they ran toward the barn and paddocks. In a month, they'd be sixteen, driving and making much bigger decisions than ever before. And bigger mistakes, too. All she could do was hope they'd learned strong character traits. Well, and rely on the good Lord to walk with them along the way.

"You didn't tell them, Faith," Hope said softly.

Faith shook her head. She'd opted for a peaceful dinner instead of one loaded with questions she couldn't answer.

"Tell them what?" Eddie asked, a frown forming between his eyes.

Faith drank the last of her tea and looked at him. "Beau was here this afternoon."

"Their father? What did he want? Is he a threat?" Eddie fired away. Hope put out her hand in his direction, her signal to slow down.

"I don't know what he wants," Faith said. "I know what he *said* he wanted, but he's a liar, so hard to tell what the real motivation is. I wonder if the boys told him about our oil field?"

Hope burst out with a laugh. "Well, if they did, and that's

a good possibility, he deserves the disappointment. As soon as he learns there's no windfall here, he'll mosey on back to Texas and Sherri."

Eddie had his notebook and pen out. "Why not give me the names of the whole clan, and I'll have them checked out?"

"Beau's folks are wonderful people. They wouldn't be part of anything shady, even if it involved their son. But I think this is a good idea. I know nothing about Sherri Walker," Faith said.

"Do you know her maiden name?" he asked as he wrote.

"Duncan. I remember because that's the name of the actress who played Peter Pan – Sandy Duncan. It was ironic to me because Beau is exactly the man who never grew up."

"All right, we'll just start with the major players. I'll keep you posted," Eddie said as he put his notebook back in his shirt pocket.

****

The boys came into the library shortly before eleven. Faith looked up from her book and marveled at their height, already five feet eleven inches tall. Isiah leaned over the back of her chair.

"What are you reading?" he asked. She showed him the cover. "Heaven is for Real – well, of course, it is," he said. "I find that a comforting thought, to be honest."

She put the book down and looked at him, his brown hair falling over hazel eyes more green than brown. "What makes you say that?" She patted the sofa next to her, and he came around and sat, stretching his long legs out in front of him.

It had been far too long since she'd talked about meaningful things with her sons and what they thought about life – or death for that matter – hadn't been among their discussions since the Easter service when they'd turned ten. And that conversation had been more about how someone could come back from being dead than the actual living and dying part.

He shrugged. "When you were all cut up by that crazy man,

Dad wanted us to know you could die. I was terrified, Mom, but part of me was okay because I knew you'd go to Heaven. I didn't want you to go, of course, but I figured if Heaven is a place with no pain or suffering, if you had to leave us to go there, that was okay." He looked at her closely. "Did you see a tunnel of light or anything like that?"

Oh Lord, how frightened they must have been, she thought, all those months keeping these thoughts and fears inside. She'd been so consumed with getting well she never guessed. She shook her head and swallowed hard.

"Nope. Scott Byrnes and his partner got me on the stretcher, and that's all I remember – the light in the ceiling of the ambulance. I woke up in the hospital emergency room, and then they put me right back out and took me to surgery – or so I'm told. I don't remember any lights or angels or anything like that."

Jeremiah sat in the armchair near the big desk and watched them. "Dad just wanted us to be prepared. That's all. We didn't really think you were going to die."

"Well," she said with a laugh, "I'm delighted to hear that. Any more questions about this? We haven't talked about it, have we?"

Isiah wrapped his lanky arm around her shoulders. "I didn't even want to think about it, but with you getting better every day, it's not so scary now. I wondered about your experience, though."

"Whatever you want to know, you just ask me, okay? If I can answer, I will." She shifted to look at Jeremiah better. "Your father stopped here today," she said.

Isiah leaped off the sofa like he was on fire while Jeremiah just looked at her as though she'd announced rain for tomorrow's forecast. *He knows all about it.*

"When was he here? Why didn't he wait for us to get home so we could see him?" Isiah shifted from one foot to the other in an awkward dance step.

"Mom probably told him to leave, idiot," Jeremiah said. "She doesn't want him here. Right, Mom?" he nearly sneered.

"I did ask him to leave, J. I don't know what his plans are, but I'm hoping they don't include uprooting you from school in the middle of the year to return you to Texas. I'm sure he'll be back to see you in a day or so. He knew I was pretty angry about him just dropping in on us."

"Was your boyfriend here?" he asked.

Isiah flinched. "Jeremiah! Stop."

Jeremiah got to his feet, his expression shooting daggers at his brother. "No. Was Scott here?"

Faith sighed. Suddenly she was so tired she struggled to keep her eyes open. Maybe this was partly why she'd never even considered dating after the divorce. "No, he wasn't here. Scott and I don't know where our relationship is going, but just today, we decided to spend some time with each other and figure it out. He's a good man, and I like him a lot. But that's between Scott and me. And," she said, looking Jeremiah in the eyes, "you will show respect to him just as you do everyone else. Right?"

He held her gaze, and she saw the defiance go out of his eyes. "Yes, ma'am. But Dad says–"

"Your father says a lot of things," Faith interrupted. "But he and I are in the past. He's got a new wife and a new life. You are my happiness, boys. I will never be sorry to have had you and to be your mom, but I won't ever go back to your father. And I've never told you anything else, have I?"

"His new wife is weird," Isiah said. "She's nice to us and everything, but she's no farm woman. She freaks out about dirt and blood. Even Dad doesn't think she's going to stay much longer."

"I'm sorry about all of that–for your father and you. I want you to stay with me, you know that, but I also know how much you love the ranch and your grandparents, too. Let's not make any decisions tonight, okay? School is good, I'm getting stronger, and your birthdays will be here in a few weeks. Let's just take our time, okay?"

Again, the twins shared that glance. "Sure, Mom. Good night." They each kissed her on a cheek and left her with her book and the quiet.

She pictured her father in this room long after all had gone to bed, praying for those in his care. She couldn't kneel on the floor as her father had, but she could sure pray.

Lord, please help my boys to know how much they are loved, how wonderful they are, how precious they are to you and me. Keep them safe from all evil, always. In the name of your son, amen.

CHAPTER FIVE

Everyone's Got Baggage

Faith had slept well once she'd gotten to sleep, but the conversation with her sons weighed on her mind. Isiah never wanted to anger his father, but he was protective of her. Jeremiah was much more bonded with Beau and he blamed Faith for the divorce. She worried that the bond the boys shared as twins might be damaged by whatever Beau had planned. Is there anything I can do about this?

She had the coffee on and was sitting at the kitchen counter lost in thought when Hope came downstairs just after dawn.

"Wow, you're up early, Sis. It's Saturday. And you managed the coffee, too? Everything all right?"

"Worried about the boys. We had quite a chat after you went up to bed last night. They are young men in so many ways, yet in others, they're still kids. I wish I could make life easier on them. I thought they'd come to terms with the divorce, but Jeremiah's very angry with me."

Hope poured her coffee and sat down next to her. "I guess we all come to terms with our losses in our own time. We learned in Healing Ministry training that divorce almost always forces the kids to find someone to blame. Could be Mom, could be the dad or could be themselves.

"Maybe J's not mad at you, but that's just how it sounds. We wish we could see inside their heads, but we can't. If Beau has laid the blame on you, then J would be struggling. They love you both, but in a way, they have to choose who to forgive, give allegiance to, that sort of thing."

"The boys remember that last year – they were what, almost twelve?" Faith sighed. "They spent more time at their grandparents' ranch than ours. It was not Beau's most charming year. Let's just leave it at that." I don't even want them to know what he was doing or with whom. Maybe they'll never have to know.

Hope nodded but didn't say anything else.

Faith looked at her. It dawned on her at that moment that though Hope had no children, she'd raised two hard-headed, rebellious girls. "Were we this hard for you after Mom died?"

"You and Grace were devastated," Hope said with a shrug. "Hurt, angry, and then Daddy couldn't cope either—and we all floundered. But it wasn't a time of angry words as much as it was more a time of no words. Sure, you got tired of me bossing you around and let me know it at the top of your lungs once in a while, but for the most part, we all went into our own corners and tried to get through it. I considered dropping out my senior year, but Eddie kept telling me it would all work out, just not to give up.

"But I think it doesn't matter why kids aren't happy with their adults, raising or guiding them can't be done without reliance on Father God. It's just too hard. If there is anything that I've learned, it's that. Maybe just keep being willing to listen to them, they'll work it out with you. And we'll keep them in our prayers."

Faith struggled to her feet carefully and lowered herself

into the wheelchair, balancing her empty coffee mug in her lap. Wheeling herself to the coffee pot on the counter near the stove, she placed the cup on the counter and then pulled herself upright only to be lifted off her feet from behind.

"Mom! You're getting so much stronger!" Jeremiah hugged her. "I'm so proud of you. You never give up."

Faith's heart swelled with love for her conflicted son, and she swallowed hard before she found her voice. "Well, I've got to get ready for that horse race, don't I? By this time next week, I'll be done with this wheelchair—around the house, at least."

"Wow! That's really great." He cleared his throat and looked at her. "I'm sorry about last night. Isiah said I was a real jerk." He put her carefully back on her feet but kept a hand on her elbow.

She blinked furiously as she poured her coffee. Then she turned, reached up, and stroked his cheek. "I appreciate your apology, but I'm tougher than I look. I'm glad you spoke your mind, J. Keep doing that, okay? Keeping communication open is the key to keeping the family healthy."

He was quiet a moment. "Can I get you anything before I leave?" he asked.

"No, I'm good. Put the horses out in the paddock and make sure the barn is closed up, that's all."

Hope walked in and stopped him at the door. "But what about some breakfast? And where are you off to? Where's your brother?"

"He was looking for a missing boot, but he'll be right down. Reverend Shawn is picking us up at seven-thirty. We're going to work at the new teen center."

"I can scramble some eggs for you boys, first. It will only take two minutes."

"No, thanks, Aunt Hope. Miss Margaret Ann is doing a breakfast casserole and biscuits and gravy for the volunteers. She'd be upset if we didn't eat."

Hope winked at him. "She sure would be!"

Isiah bounced through the kitchen doorway and hugged Hope before wrapping his arm around his mother. "We'll be okay. We get paid in food."

"Lord help the church, then," Faith said with a smile. "They'll be taking up an extra collection to cover the expense."

"Funny, Mom," said Isiah. "But true. We're growing young men! We need to eat." The doorbell rang. "I'll get it," said Jeremiah. "It's probably the Reverend."

When he returned, Shawn Jackson was one step behind him. "We've got to let the horses out, and we'll be right back," Jeremiah said over his shoulder. "Then we'll be ready to go."

"That's fine, boys. Take your time, I'll be right here," Reverend Jackson said. Then he turned to Faith. "I just thought I'd check on you for a minute. How are you doing with your therapy?"

When the back-porch door slammed behind the boys, Faith wrestled herself to her feet and demonstrated with halting, painful steps, never letting go of the countertop.

"I'm doing well," she said when she'd gotten back into the chair and wiped little beads of sweat from her forehead. "Still some work to do, though. Thanks so much for keeping the boys occupied and out of trouble."

He grinned and bowed. "It's my pleasure. They're good kids and great helpers, too. I think they've cut our work in half. We could be doing the ribbon-cutting next week if the county will come out and do inspections."

"Wow, that's great news. Just have them call for a ride home, so you don't have to stop what you're doing to run them back here. Hope and I will ride over to pick them up."

"No problem, we'll work it out. You ladies have a terrific day, and we'll see you in church, right?"

Hope and Faith nodded in unison and waved as the boys dashed through the kitchen doorway ahead of the pastor. "Whew. What a lot of energy," Faith said, wheeling herself onto the back porch. "Darn, I forgot to ask them if they told their father about the oil lease."

"Don't worry about it. If they did, we'll know soon enough." Hope got to her feet and wrapped her arms around her sister. "You are an amazing woman, and I'm proud of you. You're a great mom, a great sister, and I'm going to make us some breakfast, okay?"

****

Faith watched Hope and Magda canter around the paddock for the third time. The breeze was steady but sweat still trickled down the center of her back as she watched them from the shade of the porch.

She remembered the day that Magda was born. Anticipating the big event, Faith had made the barn her first stop every day after school. She and Grace had just gotten home from school when she found the mare out in the birthing stall pushing hard. Faith had run all the way back to the house to get Hope and Grace.

But their help was not needed and Magda's mother, Cherokee Woman, delivered a fine filly all on her own, despite being nearly fifteen years old at the time. Faith never forgot the wonder and awe of watching that new life come into the world and how tender Cherokee was with the tiny, slimy, spindly-legged creature. Magda was the first foal on the farm.

She smiled at the memories. Hope always had a graceful form when on horseback, and it was no wonder that she'd won so many ribbons and trophies over the years. Magda was a stunning black and white paint that stood almost fifteen hands tall. She had a sweet disposition that matched with Isiah's easygoing personality, so it wasn't surprising that they took to each other so well.

She saw Hope wave to someone and then heard footsteps crunching on the gravel. Scott pulled open the wooden screen door and strode up onto the porch.

"Hey, there. Imagine meeting you here," he said with a

boyish grin.

Faith laughed. "Hey there yourself. Nice to see you. What's on your to-do list today?"

"Just dropped in to see if you want to take a drive."

Faith shrugged. "Where to?"

"How about a ride along the river? We can catch some lunch at one of the outdoor cafes."

"Why not? Sounds like fun."

She called out the back porch to Hope, who was putting Magda through some tight reigning exercises. Before Faith rolled to the kitchen door, Hope and Magda had easily jumped the paddock fence and galloped to the house.

She reigned in the paint a few feet away from the screen. "You two have fun. If the boys call before you get back, I'll get them. I'm done out here for now – it's just too humid to do much more. I'll work Magellan after dinner."

"You keep an eye out for Beau, okay? I don't want him sneaking up on you. Keep the doors locked."

"Not to worry, I'll be careful. Eddie will be here shortly anyway. We're going to paint the office today."

Faith shuffled through the kitchen, the dining room, and into the front hallway, where she grabbed her purse from the side table and hooked it on the walker. She looked back over her shoulder at Scott. "So, what are you waiting for?

He scurried to the foyer, wrapped his arms around her, and kissed her deep. Faith's knees buckled, but not from her injuries. The kiss surged through her body like lightning through a metal rod.

"Ready to go?" Scott asked, holding their embrace as he gazed into her face.

"Ready," she whispered. She leaned into her walker as they left the house. Scott helped her into his SUV, then scurried to the driver's side.

"Settled in?" Scott asked, buckling his seat belt.

Faith stared at him, beaming, remembering the jolt his

kiss sent through her. "Yup." She felt like a teenager with her first crush. *Whoa there, girl.*

Scott looked at her, a puzzled look on his face. "What's got you so happy?"

"Oh, I'm just thinking of how great it feels to be going someplace other than the doctor's office or physical therapy."

"Good." Scott winked. "I'd like to take you on more excursions like this."

"Sounds good to me." Faith smiled. "Although I do hope to be working full time very soon. It's been hard on Hope. She's had to work double duty even with leasing the beauty shop. She's put in so many hours at Amazing Grace with Grace gone and me laid up."

"When is Grace due back?"

"We're waiting for an update call, but she usually calls on Sunday, so we should hear tomorrow," Faith said. "Her papers were approved last week. She's just waiting for a formal discharge date. She's all packed and ready to go. And she mentioned that she's got a surprise for us."

"She's a strong woman. I suspect you'll be happy to have her back here," Scott said as they got onto the I75 ramp going north.

"Hope and I will be, but I hope she'll be happy, too. Grace is—well—complicated. She's moved around a lot, and I wonder if she'll be okay setting down roots. I wonder what she'll do to stay busy, you know? She won't have to drive all the time."

"I'll bet she has a plan from what you've told me about the Colonel," he said with a smile. "Have you been back to the beauty shop, yet?"

No, and it may be a while before I do, Faith thought as she looked out the window. She shook her head and then glanced at him.

He checked the rearview mirror and pulled into the middle lane. "Does Hope miss it, do you think?"

"She misses the people a lot, but Dixie is amazing. I think

Hope would like to sell the business to her someday. The lease arrangement seems to be working out for them both right now, though. Hope will be there on Tuesday doing cuts while Dixie drives down to Tampa to see her daughter at college."

"That's good," Scott said with a nod. He glanced at her. "Please let me know if I can help out in any way. Maybe I can help in the office and free her up. One thing about being an EMT, we learn how to do paperwork really well."

She laughed and realized how good it felt. She felt her shoulders relax for the first time in days. She looked at him. "You're doing quite enough by getting me to rehab when I need a ride. That's a big commitment right there."

His smile deepened the dimples on either side of his face. "I'm happy to oblige, ma'am."

****

He parked the car at the Riverside Café. "Would you like to dine indoors or outdoors, Madam?"

"Outdoors would be terrific."

He opened Faith's door and helped her out of the van, gently placing another kiss on her lips. She used the door handle to steady herself as he got the walker from behind her seat and locked the legs into place.

It won't be long before I don't need you anymore, walker!

****

The hostess led them to the patio and seated them at a white wicker table under a green umbrella. "The waitress will be right over to take your drink order." She placed two menus on the table. "Enjoy your lunch."

A teenage girl dressed in a green uniform appeared. "Hi folks, what can I get you to drink?"

"Faith, would you like a cocktail or a soft drink?" Scott asked.

"I'll just have a lemonade."

He looked at the waitress. "Two, please."

They'd studied the menus for a few minutes when the waitress appeared with their drinks. "Ready to order?" she asked, pad and pen in hand.

"Salmon Caesar salad for me," Faith ordered.

Scott handed back the menus. "I'll have a crab salad sandwich."

The waitress jotted their orders and left.

Faith gazed out at the boats jetting by on the shimmering water. "This is a beautiful area. Living in inland Texas so many years, I'd forgotten the beauty of the river." She inhaled deeply.

"You're right," Scott said. "Sometimes, when you see things or have them your whole life, you begin to take them for granted. I'm guilty of that." He cleared his throat. "Texas has a lot of lakes, though. I've been fishing there a few times."

"That's true, but somehow, we never made the time for those trips. Texas is only second to Florida for powerboat sales, by the way. I just read that in a boat magazine at physical therapy last week. Who'd have thought that?" She placed her elbow on the table and rested her chin in her palm, gazing at the water flowing by. "It's so serene. I could sit here all day," she said.

Scott took her hand. "And I could watch you all day." He waited a long minute. "Faith, I want to talk a little about – us."

Oh, dear Lord, she thought, what now? She refused to react. If he'd changed his mind about dating, she'd survive. *Not happily, but I'll survive.* She swallowed. "Hmm . . . and what would that be?"

"I'm not interested in seeing anyone but you."

She let out the breath she'd been holding. "Well, it isn't as though I'd be giving up much to date you exclusively, you know. But you . . . ." She squeezed his hand with hers and then pulled it away. "I have baggage, you know. Twin teenage boys and a crazy ex-husband who has suddenly turned up in my life."

"I know about your baggage. As for the twins, I've gotten to know Jeremiah and Isiah a little. They're great kids. I'd like

45

to know them better. I think in time we'd get along fine. As for Beau, I deal with guys like him all the time—they're a dime a dozen. He's not a problem for me." He glanced away. "Unless you've still got feelings for him."

He was quiet a long moment as he looked out at the water. Then he gazed back at her, his jaw set. "So, what's your answer?"

Faith felt the lighting surge through her again as she looked into his eyes. "Scott, you've been a wonderful friend to my family and me. You saved my life. My head tells me this could only lead to trouble for you. But my heart tells me it's so right."

"So, follow your heart," he said just before he leaned across the table and kissed her.

"Yes," she sighed.

****

Hope noticed the red pick-up truck pull into the long driveway. "Oh, hell, here comes trouble," she muttered through clenched teeth. *Should've locked that door like Faith told me to.*

Beau Walker strutted into the office, carrying a bouquet of flowers. "Are those for me, Beau? Or are you throwing petals at a wedding?"

Beau snickered. "You think you're so funny, Hope. Come to think of it you were never funny. No, they're not for you. Where's Faith?"

"She's out for the afternoon." Hope busied herself with the ledger in front of her, ignoring him.

Beau parked himself into the leather easy chair. "I'll just wait then."

Hope slammed the ledger shut. "Not here! How many times do I have to tell you, you're not welcome here? You're just a heap of trouble that my sister doesn't need." She stood and put her hands on her hips. "And just what are you still doing here in Florida? Don't you have a ranch or something to run in Texas? What about your wife? Don't you miss her?"

"Like I told Faith, I made a big mistake when I left her and the boys. Sherri's history."

"Ha. I'll bet she dumped you!" Hope said.

Beau ignored her comment and checked his watch. "When do you expect Faith back?"

Hope leaned on the mahogany desk. "I said, I don't know. So why don't you just leave?"

Before he could form an answer, Scott's vehicle pulled into the driveway. Hope rushed out of the office to greet them, leaving Beau to fend for himself.

Scott helped Faith out of the van.

Hope hugged her and whispered, "Beau is in the office. Why don't you two go up to the house?"

"Crap. We had such a nice lunch, too. Now I'll have heartburn." She looked at the truck. "Are you alone? Where is Eddie?"

"He had a client emergency. He'll be over later." She glanced behind her. "Yes, that's Beau's truck."

As though summoned by negative thoughts, Beau strode up behind Hope, still clutching the flowers.

"Just what are you doing here?" Faith hissed.

Beau smiled, seemingly undeterred. "I'm here to see you. You're looking mighty nice." He handed Faith the bouquet.

Faith dropped them like they were on fire. "What are those for?"

Beau looked at Scott and Hope. "I'd like a private moment with my wife, please."

"Ex-wife!" Faith and Hope shouted in unison.

"Please, Faith, I just want to talk to you for a minute."

"Make it quick. I don't have much to say to you. Well, actually, I do, but I'm trying to be a Christian woman here. You do not make it easy."

Hope and Scott leaned against the side of his Chevy.

Beau and Faith moved toward the back porch. "I was wondering if you would like to go to dinner tonight and celebrate with me?"

"Celebrate?" Faith frowned. "Celebrate what?"

"I got a job. So, I'll be staying here permanently."

Faith twirled her index finger in the air. "Wow. Yippee! Just the news I've longed to hear."

"You dating that guy?" He indicated Scott with a shrug.

"Beau Walker, whatever I do and whoever I choose to do it with, is none of your damned business. And, by the way, won't your stripper-wife miss you if you stay here in Florida? What about your folks?"

Beau placed his hand on Faith's shoulder. "She's history, darlin'. Like I told you, it was a big mistake. The biggest mistake I made in my life was lettin' you leave, hon."

"Get your hand off me now!" He'd never put his hands on her again—that was a vow she'd made when she left him.

Beau jerked his hand off Faith's shoulder. "Sorry. I'll keep my hands to myself, but it's tough. I just want to hold you like I used to."

Faith rolled her eyes. "Well, I don't. Our only conversations will be about our boys. Other than that, I don't want anything to do with you."

"I'm a changed man. Can't you come to dinner with me? I'll show you how I've changed. I can be the man you want me to be."

"No. Not tonight, not ever. Where's this job of yours?"

"I'll be driving for Logix. It's steady work and benefits for you and the boys."

"I don't want or need your benefits. Haven't for years. The boys will need coverage, though. That's the least you can do for them. So, I'm glad about that." She sighed and shook her head. "Look, Beau. I'm happy you have a job so you can stop mooching off your parents, but I won't go to dinner with you tonight or any other night. Why not just take the boys? They'd be delighted."

"Where are they?"

"They're at the new teen center. At the church in town. Maybe you could pick them up and surprise them. Or do they already know you're here?" She wanted to know if their father's visit and alleged relocation was one of the secrets they were keeping because if it was, she and they were going to have a serious talk.

Beau kicked some pebbles with the toe of his black dress boots. "No, I haven't talked to them yet."

"Well then, they'll be surprised to see you, right? Now, if you'll excuse me, it's rude to leave guests standing in the driveway."

"Faith, I gave up a lot to be here for you. For the boys. Cut me a little slack, will you?"

She turned away from him, then stopped, turned back. "I cut you slack for many years, Beauregard Walker. I'm over you, over us, and over all the lies and fantasies. Best thing you can do is go home and make up with Sherri because I wouldn't come back to you if my life depended on it."

Without another word, she rejoined Hope and Scott, with Beau only a few feet behind her. Thankfully, he kept his mouth shut.

"Beau's going to pick up the boys from the rec center and take them to dinner," Faith announced.

Scott walked around the red pick-up. He looked at Beau. "You've been busy. New truck?"

"No. Not that it's any of your business," Beau growled.

"I thought you had a blue truck with Texas license plates the other day."

"Yeah. This is a loaner. I hit a sandstorm on the way out here. Did a lot of damage to the paint, so it's being painted." He raised his chin a fraction. His posture was a surefire challenge.

Scott nodded. "Interesting account."

Beau glared at Scott, and for a long minute, Faith could

almost see the testosterone waves in the air.

"Time for me to go," Beau said. He hopped into his truck and glanced out at Faith. "I'll get the boys and have them home at a decent hour." He pulled out of the driveway and sped away.

CHAPTER SIX

Vanishing Act

Beau pulled into the new rec center parking lot. He parked his truck and walked into the building. He strolled around and looked at the ongoing construction.

"Can I help you?" a man asked.

"I'm Beau Walker. Jeremiah and Isiah are my sons."

The man extended his hand. "Shawn Jackson, pastor here. You have two fine boys there, Mr. Walker. They've been a huge help to us on this project."

Beau accepted his hand. "Thanks." He craned his neck, searching the place. "I'm here to pick them up and take them to dinner."

"I'm sorry. You missed them. They left here about forty minutes ago. Should be home by now."

"Okay, thanks, Reverend. Do you know who picked them up? I just left Hope and Faith at the farm. They both said the boys were here."

Shawn shook his head. "No, I don't know who collected them.

One of the boys got a call, and a few minutes later, they were cleaned up and ready to go. I told them I'd see them tomorrow in church."

"Well, I'll just go back to the farm and wait for them."

Beau hopped back into his pickup, pulled out his cell, and dialed Faith. "Hey, it's me. Reverend Jackson told me the boys left an while ago. Did they come home?"

"They aren't here, Beau," Faith answered. "You didn't pass them walking on the road, right?"

"No, I didn't see anyone walking or driving all the way here." He drummed his fingers on the dashboard. "Do they have friends who drive? Maybe they went home with some friends."

Faith was silent for a long moment. "It's not like them not to call here first. Where the heck can they be? They were expecting one of us to pick them up this afternoon. What's going on?"

"Hey, I have no idea. I'm the new guy in town. They do have friends, right?" he asked with more than a hint of sarcasm. "They're probably out having fun." Had Faith forgotten that all teens wanted to have fun?

"Come on back here, and we'll decide what to do," she said, then hung up.

****

They'd driven about ten minutes. Something was wrong.

"Hey, mister, where's Sherri? What did you do to her? Where are we going?" Isiah asked the man in the front seat. For some reason, he was having trouble getting the words out straight.

He glanced over at Jeremiah, who was almost asleep beside him, his eyes closed, his head nodding.

He looked at the water bottle in his hand, then at Jeremiah's, which was empty. The only explanation was that they'd been drugged. They'd left the Merciful town limits a few minutes ago. Or maybe longer. Why wasn't he sure?

He pulled at the door handle, but the door wouldn't open. He leaned forward to demand the driver stop and let them out, but the passenger in the black cowboy hat met his nose with a hard, quick fist.

Isiah slammed back in the seat, clutching his face, fighting the tears because it hurt so much. Through blurry eyes, he saw blood running between his fingers. They were in big trouble, but he had no idea why. Why hadn't J told Reverend Jackson about Sherri's call?

He worked his bandana out of his back pocket and wiped his eyes, then held it firmly against his nose. With his other hand, he poured the water that remained in his bottle onto the floor. If he drank the rest, they'd both be out cold.

Then he closed his eyes. When the bleeding stopped, he'd pretend to sleep, though his face throbbed something fierce. He'd have to figure out how to get them out of this mess.

****

"What do you mean they're missing?" Faith snapped at Beau for the sixth time in ten minutes. "How did you lose our sons?"

"Don't yell at me. I didn't lose them. They were working with that Jackson guy when they got a call from someone, and then they cleaned up, told him they'd see him tomorrow at church, and walked out the door. Or at least that was his story. He said he doesn't know who picked them up."

Oh my God, please, keep my boys safe. She fought for control. "What time did you get there?"

"Told you all this, Faith. Around four-thirty. Introduced myself to the Reverend, and he told me they'd already left. Then I called here."

"Okay. You need to call every school and church friend you can and see if the boys just went off with friends," Eddie said. "Beau, you and I are going back to the center. Maybe one of the other volunteers saw the vehicle that picked them up."

The two men left through the front door, and Faith reached into the pocket on her wheelchair for her cell phone. She took a deep breath and glanced at Hope. "We have that list in the kitchen. Let's get calling."

****

Everyone was gathered in the kitchen two hours later. Shawn Jackson, Margaret Ann, and half a dozen other church families had come to help after Eddie and Beau's visit to the center.

Faith looked at them all. "I've called most of their school friends. So far, no one seems to know anything. Only two didn't call me back yet. I'm going to call them again in a few minutes."

Reverend Jackson shook his head. "We've searched the property here and a good part of the preserve, too. We even looked all around the church grounds just in case they might have gotten turned around out there. Not a sign of them, though."

Beau's complexion was almost grey. "Neither boy is answering their cell phone. Goes right to voicemail. I just do not understand this at all. J is supposed to keep his phone on at all times."

The room was quiet except for Margaret Ann's movements at the counter, where she put on a pot of coffee.

She turned and looked hard at Beau. "I was in the Atlanta Police Department for fifteen years as a sworn officer. Five of those years, I commanded the early response for missing kids. And you know, in 90% of those cases, a parent was involved in their disappearance. Now we got a lot of those kids back, but they'd run away because of something going on with a parent. For the record, I know that Faith had nothing to do with this, so that leaves you, sir."

Faith sucked in her breath. "Oh, my lord, Margaret Ann. Maybe this is about me. Jeremiah hasn't been all that happy with me since I got home. The past month he's made that clear. Maybe he's decided he's a big enough man now to leave home."

"He was just venting, Faith," Hope said as she reached her sister's side. She knelt beside the chair and looked into Faith's eyes. "This isn't a runaway situation. Nothing's gone, not even his favorite hat. The Stetson his father gave him—would he leave without that, at least?"

Faith shook her head. "I don't think so, but Lord, I just don't know anything. I'm scared to death."

Margaret Ann looked again at Beau. "You up and leave Texas in a hurry, get your truck painted, set up residence in a new state leaving behind your business, your parents and your wife, and you aren't running from somebody?"

Beau looked at her. "You have no idea what you're talking about. That cop psychology crap isn't worth a dime on me, sister. I came here to put my family back together, plain and simple."

"And now half of it has gone missing," Hope hissed.

Faith listened to the verbal barrage around her and thought she'd scream herself unconscious if they didn't all shut up. Where was Grace when she needed her? She'd keep this mess under control. Faith just wanted her boys home. Right now.

"Shut up!" she yelled. The room went quiet.

"Margaret Ann, what do we do now?" Faith asked.

"Call those last two boys and make sure Isiah and Jeremiah aren't there. It's past time to call the sheriff's office."

Eddie agreed. "They've got far more resources and experience with this stuff than we do. We've done all we can do here, and it's been over two hours."

Faith wiped the tears from her face with her sleeve and pulled out her cell phone to make those calls. *Please, God, please let them be with those boys.*

After the second call was answered, it was evident to everyone in the room that the boys were not at either of those homes, either. "Thanks, Mrs. Palesio. Yes, I'll let you know."

The fear she'd had in the beauty shop with the knife-wielding psycho last spring was nothing compared to the fear that cut off her oxygen right now. She struggled to get a deep breath, but it was almost impossible. *All right, then shorter breaths will have to do.* Wherever her boys were, she couldn't be of any help if she lost control.

With fingers that shook like a small tree in a windstorm,

Faith pushed 911. "Alachua County Sheriff's Department. What is your emergency?"

"My twin sons are missing. We went to pick them up from church, and someone else had picked them up, but everyone who would have done that is here at the house," she said on a sob.

"Ma'am," the dispatcher began. "Stay calm for me, okay? How old are your sons?"

"Fifteen. They'll be sixteen in a few weeks—on October 29th."

"Have you asked their friends? Looked all around the property?"

"Yes, we've called their friends, and no one has seen them or called them today. They've been missing for over two hours. We've looked everywhere we can think of. Please, can you send someone to help us find them?"

"Yes, ma'am, let me get some basic information, and I'll have a deputy on the way to you in a matter of minutes."

Faith struggled to listen carefully to the questions and focus on answering them calmly and correctly. When she finished the call, she put down her head and cried.

Hope was listening in the doorway and moved to console her. She put Faith's cell phone back in the wheelchair pocket.

"It's going to be okay, honey. We'll find them safe and sound. We're gonna pray and believe, and they'll be home soon."

She let Hope hold her in her arms like a heartbroken child as she sobbed. What would she do if Isiah and Jeremiah didn't come back?

****

Faith recognized the deputy when he came through the door and removed his hat. Deputy Taylor had been one of the many who'd responded when she'd been stabbed in the beauty shop. His smile was kind when he sat across from her on the back porch.

"We've got our K9 unit on the way to the church center, too. So while we're waiting for them to come and collect some of the boys' clothing, I need to get information, okay? The more I get and understand, the more help we can be. Do you need anything before we get started?"

She shook her head, teeth clenched. *I need my boys home. Safe. I need their father to go away. Far.* "No, let's get going so you can find them."

Hope set two glasses of sweet tea on the table in front of them and returned to the kitchen.

Faith gazed out at the paddock while she answered the deputy's questions. After forty-five minutes, she noticed the K9 officer with a bloodhound down near the garages. *How will I find them? I'm exhausted already.*

"I'm sorry, but the boys didn't disappear from here. They were are the church. Why is the dog here?"

"The officer is just verifying that the scent on the shirts your sister gave us is going to track. If not, we take another piece of clothing, that's all. They're getting ready to pull out now. I understand your husband is here from Texas, is that right?" he asked.

"My ex-husband. We've been divorced for a little over four years. He arrived yesterday to visit with them. He was supposed to pick them up at the church and take them to dinner."

"Are either of you remarried?"

"I'm not, but Beau remarried about three years ago. His wife's name is Sherri, and they live in Texas." She sighed. "But of course, you know what. You just said that. I'm sorry. I feel like I'm losing my mind."

"I'm sure you do, and I am sorry for all the questions. We're about done." His phone buzzed, and he glanced at it, then answered it. "Are you sure? Okay, I'll ask. Thanks."

Taylor glanced at his notes and then looked at Faith. "Your ex's truck has a Florida registration on it. If he lives in Texas, why did he register his truck in Florida yesterday?"

She shook her head. "I don't know. He babbled something about wanting to get back together, but that's not it. My guess is he's running—or hiding—from someone."

"Could that someone be capable of taking your boys?" he asked quietly.

She had to take a drink to swallow past the lump in her throat. *If that rat is the reason the boys are missing, I'll never forgive him. I might even kill him myself.*

"I just don't know the answer to that. He had serious gambling and mistress habits when we were married. Lord only knows what he's into now. It could be possible, I guess. He'd never endanger them deliberately, though."

"And you are one-hundred percent sure they didn't run away?" the deputy asked as he put his notebook and recorder away.

She looked at him and shook her head. "I'm not sure of anything. Jeremiah isn't happy with me as I rebuild my life, but Isiah is doing fine. And this morning before they left, Jeremiah and I were on good terms." She felt a tear run down her face and hated that she couldn't keep them at bay. "Please find them and bring them home."

Deputy Taylor got to his feet and picked up his hat. "We're going to do our very best, Faith. Look out there—the dog has their scent from the tee shirts. There's a good strong scent and no rain in the forecast. They'll be heading out for the church now. You stay by the phone and let me know if you hear anything at all, right?" He handed her his business card.

She took the card and clutched it in her fist.

He put his hand on her shoulder. "You just sit here a little bit while we get organized out front. It's going to be a chaotic scene, but we know what we're doing—it'll just take a lot of us to get it done," he said with a smile. "I'll send Hope in to sit with you."

"Thank you," she whispered to his back as he walked through the kitchen doorway. *Father God, you saved me and gave me those beautiful boys. I'm begging you not to take them away from me now. I'll never survive it.*

CHAPTER SEVEN

Hostages

Isiah lay on the hard, dirty, wood floor and listened hard. He recognized the croak of a bullfrog not far off. Then some cicadas. Evening sounds? Then he thought he heard a coyote way off. But nothing that made him believe their captors were close by.

"Jeremiah," Isiah whispered. His throat felt like it was on fire, his face hurt like he'd been kicked by a horse, and he couldn't move his hands or his feet. He swallowed hard partly to fight the nausea and tried again. "Jeremiah!" He was having trouble seeing in the dim light. Dawn or dusk?

It was only a moment or two before his brother responded. "Ohh, what happened?" He coughed. "I feel awful. Where are you?"

"Shhh. Keep super quiet. I'm on the floor by the bed. I'm trussed up like a dogged calf." He laughed. It was good to know that his twin was alive, anyway. "I don't feel so good myself."

"Are you okay? Where are we? What the hell's going on?"

Isiah gently shook his head though his brother couldn't see it. "I don't know. The two guys that picked us up at the road by the church drugged the water they gave us, I'm thinking. You guzzled yours and were out cold before we got out of Merciful. I think I got my nose busted when I told them to let us out."

"Oh, no! I'm sorry I got us into this mess. I was just so excited when Sherri texted to say she and Dad were taking us to dinner that I didn't even think something was wrong. But what do these guys want with us?"

"I have no idea. It can't be anything good. And if they want money from Dad, then we'd better find our own way out of this 'cause he never has any."

Jeremiah sighed heavily before he replied. "That's the sad truth. Dad would give his life for us, but if he has to come up with money, we're in trouble." He thought a moment and then added, "I wonder if Sherri's okay."

"Listen, Mom and Dad, and Aunt Hope will be looking for us. But I don't know how much time we have because I don't know what's going on." He didn't add how scared he was that they were going to die. Kids vanished every day, and no one ever saw them again. He choked on the thought and bit his lip to stay quiet. How he wished they were back home on the Blessing farm with their mom.

"What can you see from up there?" Isiah asked quietly.

"There's a window to my right. And a doorway behind us. Maybe it's a bathroom." He cleared his throat. "And the door to the closet, maybe."

Isiah heard the bed rustle as Jeremiah moved around. "Hey, J, can you get your hands or feet loose?"

"Working on it now, but my hands are really tight. Think I can get my feet loose, though. How about you?"

"My hands are tied up so tight they're almost numb. Working on getting my boots off so I can slip these ties. Lordy, my face hurts so bad I'm trying not to cry or throw up."

Jeremiah laughed softly. "Cry if you want to, brother. Who's gonna know? Just keep working on getting loose."

****

Sherri lifted her coffee cup and gazed over the rim at Earl. Seven was way too early to not only be up but dressed and eating breakfast, too.

"The ransom note should be arriving in Merciful shortly. I'll be glad when we've got our money, and this is over."

He took a long pull on his sweet tea. "Well, the ketamine did its job. The boys were still sleeping like babies when we left them an hour ago. Old Beau will freak out, call his father, and get the money, and then we'll be heading to points south. As in South America, here we come."

She smiled at him but, for a long moment, wondered if she dared trust him. Was he so eager to make this kidnapping work to hurt Beau or because he desperately wanted to be with her? Nearly a million dollars each was a lot of money, but would it be enough for Earl?

"Did you get food and water for the boys? They can eat up a storm, I can tell you," she said.

Earl's laugh was more of a bark. "They slept through the night, honey. Denny is doing breakfast right now. Even told him to get ice for the big mouth's busted nose. But honestly, we ain't investing much in those boys. We can't just let 'em loose, and you know that. No sense in giving the gators too good a meal."

She controlled the shudder that ran through her. The boys were a pain in her butt sometimes, but she didn't want them dead. They didn't deserve that. She kept her voice level though she was mad enough to spit nails.

"Busted nose? And how did that happen?" She took a deep breath and put down her cup. Then she looked around to be sure they wouldn't be overheard. "We talked about this, Earl. If those boys are harmed in any way, we won't get our money. Beau and his father will never stop hunting us down if anything happens to those boys, and I don't want to live that way. Denny is the only one they see, and he wears his bandana so they can't identify anyone. You and I stay away from there, and they don't know we're even involved. I've got the storage unit reserved. We get the money, and you dope them again, then we leave them in the unit. By the time they wake up, we're long gone."

He motioned to the truck stop waitress for the check and tossed a five-dollar bill on the table for the tip. "We'll see, Sherri darlin'. Don't worry about it. You and me are in this for the long haul now, so you just be a good girl, and it'll all be fine. You let me do the worryin'."

She reached for her purse, careful not to show how angry she was. Suddenly she could see this whole thing working out to be anything but fine.

****

Isiah had worked his hands against the duct tape so long that his wrists burned, but he felt it finally give a little. He had to pee, and his nose was bleeding again. *I can't give up, or we may not get out of this.*

Jeremiah had just moaned that he thought he could free his feet by wiggling out of his socks since his sneakers were a bit big when Isiah heard an outer door slam.

He leaned against the side of the bed, where he'd worked himself into a sitting position. He hissed at Jeremiah to be still.

Someone was walking around in another room of what was probably once a fishing or hunting cabin. Isiah held his breath when he saw the doorknob turn.

A tall, skinny man with a cowboy hat on, a tarnished Ft. Worth Rodeo buckle, and a bandana around his face walked into the room. He had a McDonald's sack in one arm, and Isiah could smell the sandwiches through the bag. *How can I be hungry at a time like this?*

"Here's your breakfast, boys. Bathroom's in there," he said, nodding towards the door. "One at a time, I'm gonna undo your hands and feet. The other one stays tied up. You try something stupid, and I kill the other one. Do you understand me?"

Isiah nodded. He knew Jeremiah had, too.

The cowboy jerked Isiah to his feet. "You first."

The blood rushed into Isiah's face and feet at the same time, and he cried out in pain. *Oh God, I'm going to throw up.* If the man noticed the wear on the tape that held Isiah's hands, he didn't say anything. When he pulled out a Bowie knife the size of a machete, Jeremiah gasped.

"Easy there, boy. Just gonna cut him loose, that's all."

The gun the man wore on his side wasn't a small compact one like his Aunt Hope had. It looked more like the .45 that so many Texans wore with great pride. Isiah mentally cataloged its exact location and breathed a sigh of relief when his hands were freed.

He dashed into the bathroom without a word and prayed that Jeremiah wouldn't do anything stupid before he got back. As he washed his hands and splashed lukewarm water on his face, he glanced in the ruined mirror and got a glimpse of the damage done to it. His left eye was half-closed, and his right one already sported a dark purple ring around it. His nose was swollen to twice its normal size. *I'd sure like to return the favor,* he thought before dragging himself back into the bedroom.

Jeremiah was on his feet but still bound hand and foot. The cowboy waved the barrel of the gun toward the bed and motioned for Isiah to sit. He did. Cowboy pulled out black zip ties and retied Isiah's ankles, then tied his hands in front of him. He handed him an egg sandwich still in the wrapper, tossed two bottles of water at him, dumped the hash browns in the bag, and tossed it on the bed.

"Eat, boy. Then drink your water. All of it."

He freed Jeremiah and watched him go into the little bathroom. Isiah busied himself with unwrapping the eggs and taking a bite, refusing to give in to the terror picking at his brain. Out of the side of his right eye, he could see the gun pointed at his head. If he made a move, this guy would kill him before Jeremiah could do anything. They'd have to bide their time. And pray.

****

"Faith, where are you?" a big voice boomed through the quiet house.

From where she was dozing in the swing on the back porch, safely tucked into the crook of Scott's shoulder, Faith jumped. Scott moved her to the side. Getting to his feet, he blocked the doorway between the porch and the kitchen.

A large man, probably in his late seventies, nearly filled the opening. "Son, I'm a friend so you can stand down."

Faith almost cried with relief. *Thank you, Lord.* "Scott, this is Bill Walker, Beau's father. And one of my best friends. Bill, this is Scott Byrnes."

The two men shook hands, and Scott stepped aside. "It's almost four a.m. Can I get you something to eat or drink? I think the whole town was here with food, so there's plenty," Scott said.

The big man smiled. "Nothing right now, but thanks for the offer."

Bill took Faith's small hands in his large ones. "I got here as soon as I could get a pilot and plane in the air. I am so sorry about all of this, and I promise you we'll get the boys back before you know it."

Faith began to cry. "What if they want something ridiculous? Like two million dollars, Bill? Not even you can come up with that kind of money."

"You have no idea what I'm capable of, young lady. Those grandsons of mine mean the world to me. So, do you. And Beau is certainly capable of some king-sized mistakes, but I love him, too. We'll get whatever money's needed. Don't you worry."

Scott cleared his throat. "I'll just go check on Eddie. Be back in a few minutes." He looked at Faith. "Need your sweater?"

She rubbed her arms to warm them. "I think it's in the

dining room. Thanks." She patted the swing seat now vacant beside her and motioned to her former father-in-law.

"Come and sit for a minute. Not much we can do at this time of night anyway. Where is Annie?"

He gently settled in and stretched his arm along the back of the seat behind her. "She'll be along tomorrow. How are you?"

"Eight hours ago, I thought I was well on my way to putting my life back together. I'm learning to walk again, dating a nice man, and the boys are pretty happy here. As bad as it was to be knifed by that maniac, this is the worst nightmare I can imagine for any mother."

She looked out at the dark pasture and paddocks between the house and the horse barn and could feel her heart breaking into such tiny pieces that it was hard to get her breath. Her boys were out there somewhere and needed her, but she couldn't help them. Were they still alive?

She gasped at the thought and looked at her former father-in-law. "I don't want to hate Beau, Bill. I really don't. But right now, I do. What do I do with that? How will I ever forgive him for this?"

He was silent for several minutes, using one leg to push them ever so slightly back and forth. Then, he cleared his throat. "Maybe you just ask the Lord to help you keep an open mind, honey. Beau's sure it's about money. He told me when he called me that he hadn't borrowed money to gamble in years, and I believe him. I checked around with my sources and Beau's clean, according to them. He hasn't won a lot on the circuit of late, though. He just rode in a charity rodeo last week, but I think Sherri is his new spending habit. It may not be Beau's fault the way you think, so maybe just be open to that idea. Hate's a terrible companion, Faith. You don't need that one on your heart, believe me."

She laid her head against his chest and sighed. "Well, for tonight, I'll just let it be because I've got no energy to do anything else. I'm exhausted, Bill." She wondered if anything would ever be right again. "The fear is killing me."

He wrapped an arm around her and squeezed a little. "I know, honey. Just rest a few minutes. I'll be right here. And when your young man gets back, I'll make some calls, and then we'll get some sleep for a few hours. In the morning, I'll meet with all these law people and make a plan."

****

Faith dozed in Scott's arms. She cried until she slept, then she slept until the nightmare woke her—her boys were calling her, but she couldn't find them.

At the first pinking of the dawn sky, Hope made fresh coffee and brewed jugs of sweet tea while Faith and Scott baked several breakfast casseroles. It helped everyone to be busy.

Faith, Hope, Scott, Eddie, and some of the Alachua County Command Center Team were at the dining room table when the ransom note arrived in a Fed Ex Express delivery envelope at seven-thirty.

The deputy that accepted the envelope thanked the driver, shut the door, and handed it over to the Lieutenant.

They photographed the heavy cardboard, dusted it for prints, and then tore the perforated strip back and opened it. A neatly typed note was inside. It was processed the same way the envelope was, then slipped into a plastic sleeve.

"This was what we were waiting for, Ms. Walker."

She stopped her chair beside the Lieutenant and reached for it. Her head throbbed, and her hands shook. No matter how she tried, she couldn't seem to calm down. She dropped her head. Lord, please give me strength. Taking a deep breath, she read aloud. It was short and to the point.

Beau owes us big time. If you don't pay $2 million by midnight on Sunday, we'll consider the boys as payment in full – they'll be auctioned off to the highest bidder. No cops. No marked bills. Nothing larger than $50. We'll be in touch Sunday morning with instructions.

"I can't come up with this kind of money – not even if I had a month, let alone a day and a half," she sobbed.

Hope knelt beside her. "Listen to me, honey. We've been in tough spots before, right? We're going to keep our faith and ask for all the help we can get. Don't go giving up, okay? You don't give up."

Faith looked through her tears. "I'm afraid you'll have to believe enough for us both, Hope. I just don't think that I can."

Eddie knelt on the other side of her wheelchair. "We're going to get those boys back safe and sound. Now dry those tears, and let's put our heads together and figure out what we can do to get this ball rolling. We've all got friends, and if we call enough of them, we'll raise the money we need, I'm sure of it." He patted her wrist. "The authorities don't advise paying, but we'll be ready if that's how you want to go."

Faith nodded as she looked at him. "Where's Beau?"

"The commander sent him to his hotel last night," Eddie replied. He took her hand in his. "I read people for a living. He may be the cause of this Faith, but he's not part of it. He'll do everything he can to bring Isiah and Jeremiah back safe."

I believe that, but I'd still like to shoot him. If he'd only given up the women and the gambling, this wouldn't be happening at all, so it is his fault. "Until I have to speak to him, I'd rather not. I'm so upset and mad right now I don't know what I'd say to him that wouldn't make things worse."

Deputy Taylor joined their group. "The note doesn't give us any instructions or location information to leave the money, so they'll be calling you. We'll insist on speaking with the boys to make sure they have them, and they're okay. Our team in the Center has the communications tracing set up for both cell phone and the house phone. Since this seems to be about Beau, we expect the call to come in on his cell phone, but we need yours just in case. I'll bring it back to you when we've got it synchronized."

Faith reached beneath her left hip, pulled out her cell phone and handed it to Taylor. "You know they said no cops, right? Have I killed the boys already?"

He shook his head. "They have to know you'd have called us when the boys disappeared. Maybe they think they're smarter than you and us, that's all. And that's a good thing. They'll make a mistake, and we'll be right there."

"I hope so," Faith whispered as she wheeled her chair toward the kitchen. She needed a good cry, and it wasn't going to be in the dining room with an audience.

CHAPTER EIGHT

Running on Empty

"Annie, we're so glad you're here," Hope said, holding Faith's former mother-in-law in her arms. She glanced at the younger woman with her. "Mary Lou? You must have driven all night. Thanks so much for coming. Let me make you something to eat. We've got so much food we could feed half of Alachua County, I think."

Mary Lou pulled off her sweater and draped it over her purse on the bench in the hallway. "I need the bathroom, and then I want to see my sister-in-law."

Hope pointed up the stairs. "You're welcome to go lie down upstairs, honey. You look done in."

"I will after I see Faith. I just need to hug her first." Mary Lou vanished along the hallway toward the small half-bath under the staircase.

"Can you eat a little?" Hope asked Annie again.

"I'm not sure that I can, but I'll try. We stopped on the

way, of course, but I couldn't force anything down. Will you join me?"

"Sure. Come into the kitchen. The note arrived this morning just as we were going to have breakfast, so most of that was untouched. Is Bill outside with Beau?" Hope asked.

"I don't think so, but he did say he'd seen him last night. I think Bill is probably with Faith. Or he's found the barn." Her smile was tired.

Hope led the way to the food. When Annie settled herself on the stool at the counter, she pointed toward the porch. "There he is. I can't see him, but I can hear his voice."

"I hope you three will stay here with us. There's plenty of room. The boys have Faith and Grace's old rooms, but we've got the bunkhouse set up and the guest apartment in the barn."

Annie nodded. "Thank you. We'd like to be as close to the situation as possible, but we don't want to put anyone out. How is Grace?"

"Wishing she were here, but she was sent to Germany for a week before they finalize her discharge. The Army wants every minute of her thirty years, I guess. She called twice last night, and she's wiring funds this morning."

"Bill said the ransom note was for two million dollars?" Annie picked up a can of ginger ale and poured it into a glass.

"A staggering sum for us," Hope said. "We've had a miraculous year in getting the trucking company almost out of debt and saving the farm, but it took us a year, and all of that only amounted to three-quarters of a million dollars. We'd sell it all in a second if we could."

She turned to Annie and placed a small plate of spicy egg casserole and a bowl of cut fruit in front of her.

"It's a lot of money for anyone, Hope. But money can't replace those we love, a fact that our son is sadly coming to terms with. Bill and I are blessed to have very influential friends, so thankfully, this may not be the most impossible thing we've ever faced."

Hope nibbled on a cracker and sipped at her coffee. "Well, perhaps we can find the boys before the money even has to be paid. The deputies mentioned that it happens more these days because of the technology available. I sure hope they're right. I can't imagine how scared those boys must be."

Annie's smile was frail, and the dark circles under her eyes betrayed her concern. "We've got to rely on the Lord to keep them safe, protect them from too much fear, and show them the way to get home. He won't let anything happen to them."

Hope sighed. "Amen to that."

"Faith must hate Beau with a passion, now," Annie said quietly.

"Probably so," Hope replied. "But she's needed to let go of all that stuff for years, and she hasn't done it. The Lord has a way of forcing our hand, so we'll learn to forgive - even the stuff that seems impossible to forgive. But we are not going to think for a minute that Jeremiah and Isiah won't be returned safely."

Faith crossed through the doorway with Bill behind her and looked from one woman to the other. Annie knelt beside the wheelchair and took Faith in her arms. Then she let her go and stood.

Faith reached for Annie's hand. The woman was once her mother-in-law but always her friend, first. "I'm so glad you came. And none of us is going to entertain any thought other than the boys are fine and will be home before we know it. I hope that's clear," Faith said evenly. "Do you know where Beau is?"

"My brother is at his hotel, though not because he wants to be," Mary Lou said as she strode through the doorway.

"Lou!" cried Faith just before the tall, dark-haired woman

bent to kiss her on the cheek with a squeeze. "I didn't know you were coming, too."

"What? Why wouldn't I be here with my family? Not sure what I can do, but just say the word, and I'm willing. Besides, Mom can't fly right now, so we drove out."

Faith looked at Annie. "Is everything all right? You used to pilot planes...."

Annie shushed her. "Nothing to worry about, but I'm getting up in years. Been having some clotting issues, so no flying for a while for me."

"Do you just want to kill my brother now?" Mary Lou asked softly.

Faith shook her head. *What good would that do? Will it bring my boys back? Will it make any of this go away?* She'd do it readily enough if it would, but she knew it wouldn't.

"I did when we first got the note. But now I'm plain terrified, and I can't waste any energy at all on Beau. I'm too tired to hate him. Now, do I hate the people who took my boys? Absolutely."

Mary Lou poured a cup of coffee and picked a piece of melon from her mother's plate. "Well, I want to kill him. If he stays away from here, maybe he'll live a little longer."

"I appreciate that," Faith said with a half-smile, "but Beau should be here if he wants to be. Isiah and Jeremiah are his boys, too."

Annie looked at her and then glanced at Hope. "I'm sure he'll be back here before long, and he'll only wait that long out of respect for his father."

Faith shook her head. "I'm glad that he respects someone."

Scott came into the kitchen and leaned against the door jamb. "Can I do anything for anyone? Eddie's in the Command Center with Bill Walker, so I thought I'd come back here. They don't need me out there." He ran his hand through his hair, sending the dark curls everywhere. "I feel so damned helpless."

Annie approached him, stuck out her hand, and introduced herself. "I'm pleased to meet you, young man. Thank you for taking such good care of our Faith."

He nodded and returned the handshake. "I'm used to being able to help – not being unable to do anything at all."

"Do you pray, Mr. Byrnes?" Annie asked.

"Yes, ma'am, I do. And I'm praying with all I got. But I'm a man of action, too."

"Of course you are. However, prayer is not only a noun. It's a verb as well. So you are, in actuality, in action when you pray – and believe."

He placed his hands gently on Faith's shoulders. "And the Lord said, 'Be still and know that I am God,' right?"

Faith placed her hand on his. "I don't see any choice at this precise moment, so maybe we try to rest. I've got a horrific headache."

Scott bent to give her a kiss. "I'm going to stretch out on the porch for a couple of hours. If anyone needs me, come get me. I wake up easy."

****

The next morning, around eight-thirty, a silver crew cab pickup bounced along the rough dirt road and parked next to Denny's rented Jeep. He was whittling a tiny rifle out of a piece of wood, but he looked up and said nothing until the tall man got out of the truck.

"Mornin' Earl," he said quietly. "What are you doing here? I thought you weren't supposed to come out here."

Earl shrugged and handed over a steaming cup of coffee in a paper cup with a lid on it. "Just checkin' in, that's all. Everything all right?"

Denny put down the piece of wood but not his knife. He sipped the coffee. "They're fine. Give 'em a heavy dose at night. Sleeping, still. I was just getting ready to go to the truck stop to get some breakfast. Thanks for the coffee."

"You just stay here and watch those kids. We can't afford to lose them yet. I'm bettin' today Beau will want to talk to them – so I've brought you a phone." He reached into the front pocket of his jeans and pulled out a flip phone. "We'll call you, and you have them call Beau, talk for a couple of seconds, then you toss the phone in the swamp. The boys, too. Then get outta here. I'll be in touch."

Denny was quiet and sipped his coffee, thinking. He hadn't signed up to kill kids. And when would he get paid if they all split up? "I thought the plan was we get the money, lock 'em up, and then go our separate ways. Something changed?"

Earl glared at him. "That was her plan, not mine." He looked out into the tall pines, then smiled at Denny. "Yeah, plans are always subject to change, you know that. You figure a horse to go left he goes right – happens all the time, right? Nobody understands zig-zagging like a rodeo clown, buddy." He clapped a firm hand on Denny's shoulder. "How long will they sleep?"

Denny shrugged. "Another couple of hours, probably. Made 'em drink the water again around eleven-thirty, so they've had a good amount."

Earl began to walk back toward his truck. "As long as they're tied good, go eat and get back here before they wake up. We're going to have a busy day, I suspect."

Denny waited until the taillights of the truck were out of sight and resumed his whittling. He heard those blasted church bells way off in the distance and wished they'd play a different song. Amazing Grace. His mom's favorite. The words "a wretch like me" made him think of Earl. If dumping those boys in the swamp didn't bother Earl, that SOB wouldn't think twice about skipping town with the money. Or eliminating his partners.

74

He stopped cutting on the wood. Today was Saturday. Why the bells? He'd lost track in the deep woods and swamp. He'd be darned glad to be rid of the smells and the bugs. He closed the knife and tucked it into his shirt pocket.

As he listened to the last notes of Amazing Grace fade into the damp morning air, he got to his feet. He wasn't killing no kids, and he wasn't going to stick around and get himself killed by Earl's greed.

Maybe it was exactly the right song, after all.

****

At noon, Beau's cell phone rang, and he jumped out of his chair at the sound. His boys! Finally, they would get this over with, and Jeremiah and Isiah would be home safe and sound.

He looked at the sergeant and waited for the signal like he'd been told. On the third ring, he answered it.

"Hello?"

"Got the money, Beau?" the distorted voice asked.

He could picture a sneer on that face and wanted to wipe it off with his fists. He took a deep breath. He glanced at the script the sheriff's team had given him. "We're working on it, but we don't have all of it yet. But you aren't getting any of it unless I can talk to the boys. Both of them."

He clenched his fist and listened carefully, but he didn't hear a thing. He battled back the urge to ask if they were still on the line. The hostage negotiator had warned him about that. Just wait.

The caller was brief. "They'll call you back later."

The line went dead, and Beau looked at the sergeant. The tech winced. "A payphone – maybe off I75. I'm pretty sure the truck stops still have some of those."

Faith, Hope, and Eddie looked at one another. Truckstop? They knew truckers and lots of them.

Hope looked at Faith. "Let's make some calls and get our guys out looking for them."

****

"Jeremiah?" Isiah whispered. He'd heard a door slam outside the cabin.

"Yeah, I heard it," said Jeremiah.

"Think we can take him? There's only one of him and two of us."

"I don't know about you, but I'm not sure I can stand up, let alone whoop someone. My head's always spinning with whatever he's giving us."

Isiah sighed. "I know. Me, too. Let's spill the water instead of drinking it."

"But he may kill us if we aren't drugged 'cause he can't chance us getting away."

"Crap, I didn't think of that. Well, I'm going to try and pour mine inside my shirt and see if that works – at least I won't drink as much."

"Just be careful," Jeremiah hissed. "He's here."

Denny returned to the cabin with breakfast for the boys and more water. He got his bandana in place, pulled his hat down low, and unlocked the door.

"Good morning, boys. You slept good, I know." He laughed. "Here's your breakfast, but let's get you cleaned up first, right?"

The boys knew the routine and held out their hands to be cut free, one at a time. He re-tied them and put their breakfast bag on the bed. He'd brought coffee, too.

"Thanks for the food, mister," said Isiah around a mouthful of ham biscuit. He put it down on the wrapper and reached for the coffee. Even black, it was so good he almost cried. He was more scared than he'd ever been in his life, but maybe the coffee would help him wake up.

Their captor didn't reply, just stood by the door watching them eat. *Hell, they're just kids.* Not rude. Not mouthy. Just kids unlucky enough to have Beau Walker for their pa.

"I'll be back in a couple of hours for your bathroom break. You stay quiet and don't make any fuss, and you'll get to talk to your father today. You make a fuss, and you don't. You die."

For effect, he stood at the door for a long minute, watching the boys for a reaction. He noted the fear in their eyes and knew at least for the next few hours, they'd be fine.

And he'd have time to figure out his plan.

****

Denny was stretched out on the worn-down porch of the cabin, his hat pulled down over his eyes and resting on the bridge of his nose when the new cell phone vibrated. He opened it. A text message, just like Earl promised. Looked like it was showtime.

The word "NOW" was followed by a phone number. He got to his feet and went back inside. He opened the door and the boys looked at him. They were scared but they were alert. Good.

He flipped the phone open, punched in the number Earl gave him, and pressed the speaker button. The ring sounded like a clanging bell in the silence.

"Hello?" a deep male voice answered.

"Dad, hey, Dad, it's us! You gotta get us out of here," Isiah blurted.

Denny pulled his gun out of the holster and pointed it at Jeremiah as he looked at Isiah. Just as he did, he could hear the distant church bells playing again.

"Are you boys all right?" asked Beau.

Denny ended the call and shut the phone. Then he dropped

it on the floor and smashed it with the heel of his boot. He returned in a moment with two bottles of water.

"Drink."

CHAPTER NINE

Closing In

"Isiah sounded terrified," cried Faith.

That she could speak at all seemed a miracle—she could barely even breathe. Her words broke the silence that hung over the Command Center when the call terminated so abruptly. Scott placed his hand on her knee but stayed quiet. She guessed he was praying, and she was thankful that he could. She wasn't sure she had a prayer left in her. *Why did God let this happen to them? To me.* He's supposed to be a loving God, isn't He?

Lieutenant Weston spoke with the communications tech, then turned back to Faith and Beau. "The call pinged off a cell tower. It's a start. A seventy-mile radius is far better than hundreds. And there's some noise on the call that may help us pinpoint it better."

"What is it?" Faith asked.

Weston shook his head. "Not sure. Some kind of music. It's not close, though. It'll take a little time to place it electronically."

"Get Eddie and Hope in here. The one thing we don't have

is time. They might know what it is if you don't." She felt like she was losing her mind. *Have to focus. My boys are alive, and that's what counts.* Everything else could be handled. But what if they didn't stay alive? She began to tremble, and Scott placed his hand on her shoulder.

"They're going to be all right, Faith. Remember that. We've got to believe that." She leaned forward, and his reassuring hand dropped away.

Weston got on his radio and gave an order. A minute later, a knock sounded on the Command Center door, and Eddie and Hope climbed aboard the customized RV.

"What's happening?" Hope asked a little breathlessly. "Did you talk to the boys?"

Faith wrung her hands in her lap. "For a second, yes. Isiah was terrified, but alive. The call was short, but there's a sound on the tape that the team is hoping we can identify."

"Let's have a listen," said Eddie, moving close to the comm panel. The tech handed them both a headset and then played the digital recording.

"Again," Hope said. She poked Eddie in the shoulder. "Newberry?"

He tilted his head to the side. The tech played it again. Eddie nodded slowly. "I think that's it. The little evangelical church in Newberry plays Amazing Grace on the weekends at nine, noon, three, and then six at night. Workers and kids in the area know the time by that chime."

Lt. Weston said to a sergeant standing nearby, "Verify and get the sheriff's office and FHP on the move to that area." In an instant, the center exploded into action as information and orders were gathered and issued like a well-choreographed routine.

The technician reached out for the lieutenant's arm. "Church music verified, sir. It is Amazing Grace."

The tall officer allowed himself a crooked smile as he exhaled and rolled his eyes heavenward. "It certainly is."

Faith stood near the folding chair, leaning on Hope. What was taking them so long to call back? Did something happen? Oh Lord, what if they changed their minds? What if it wasn't about the money? What if . . ..

The second call came in nearly ten minutes after the call from the boys, and she almost collapsed with relief, then covered her mouth with her fingertips.

The distorted voice filled the air. "You have the money? Cause you only got one chance to do this, and it better be right."

Beau's big hand shook as he held the phone. His expression said he'd be only too happy to break the neck of the caller. The lieutenant held up a cue card that read, STAY CALM. BREATHE.

"We're still working on the money, but we'll have it by morning. What time and where do you want to make the exchange?" Beau asked, lips pursed, eyes closed as if in prayer.

"No exchange. You leave the money. We'll let you know where to get the boys."

Beau went white as a sheet, and Lieutenant Weston shook his head as if to say, "No way."

"That doesn't work for me," Beau said evenly. "No boys, no money."

There was a second of hesitation and Faith, Hope, Eddie, and the men in the center held their collective breath.

"That's my line, Beau. No money, no boys. How about I let you think about that a bit? I'll call you later tonight. Let me know then if you changed your mind."

The call ended, but the comm tech had a gleam in his eye. "That was a payphone call, Lieutenant. Not too many of those still working in Florida. If I can get a list of them in the general area of Newberry, maybe we can figure out where they are."

"You get that list and do it now. Any trouble with the phone company, you let me know." He turned to Beau, Faith, Hope, and Eddie. "Go on inside and relax if you can. I'll come on in when I've got some of the plans mapped out. We've got cars already rolling. We'll get them."

Beau looked as though a mule had kicked the air out of him. "I pray to God that I haven't just killed my sons," he whispered.

Tears rolled down Faith's face as she sat in stunned silence, watching him. "Me, too," she said. Scott had her hands in his, his eyes fixed on her face.

Weston shook his head. "They'll call back. They didn't go through all this trouble to not get their money."

Before he stepped out of the unit, Beau asked, "What if it isn't about the money?" Lieutenant Weston stared at him. The silence was answer enough.

****

Isiah woke to the sound of the church music playing again. He'd heard it earlier, but it hadn't registered on him. He thought about his Aunt Grace and wished she were around. She was a colonel in the U.S. Army, and she would find them for sure. But she wasn't even in the country according to his mom, though she'd be coming to Merciful in less than ten days. He hoped he'd be alive to see her again.

The room wasn't really dark, but it was warm. Meant the sun was still up though it had to be midafternoon, or maybe he'd slept until dinner time. His stomach rumbled, and he figured maybe that was it.

"Hey, J, you okay up there?" he asked. He didn't get a reply. "J? You awake?"

He felt the bed move at his back. "I think so. Give me a minute."

Isiah shook his head. He knew from experience–getting his brother up to get to school–that he wasn't someone who woke up fast. It took a whole lot of minutes. "Sure, I'm not going anywhere," he said.

"Very funny. How's your face?"

"Doesn't hurt so bad if I don't move too fast."

"Listen, we need to get out of here. We got to be out of time on this deal, don't you think?"

"I do. I don't think Cowboy drugged us as much the last time. I don't have a headache, but my mouth is still awful dry. Maybe they need us awake to return us to Mom and Dad."

"Or to walk us to the swamp to shoot us," Jeremiah said.

"You always look on the bright side, J," Isiah said. "But you have a point." He worked his wrists a bit against the heavy zip ties. "I'm not tied as tight, either. I might be able to slip these. And," he grunted as he concentrated on wriggling his foot out of his boot, "I think I can get my feet loose, too."

"Okay, then do it, big brother. I'm almost out of my sneaker. Not too good on the hands, though."

They worked in silence for a few minutes, trying to be quiet in case their guard was close enough to hear them. With freed hands, they could take him before he knew what hit him but tied up like a Thanksgiving turkey, they didn't stand a chance.

"He must have come back in and changed the ties. I couldn't even feel my fingers after he left," Jeremiah said softly.

"I don't care how, when, or why. I'll be happy to get the hell out of here," Isiah said. "Got it. Boot is off, and the other one will be soon."

Jeremiah managed to wriggle his right foot out of the sock and then the other one. He got to his feet at the side of the bed and reached down to help Isiah to stand. "Well, we can run at least."

Isiah nodded, then grimaced as he pulled his wrist free of the tie. "And we can hit if needed, too."

"I can't get my hands free, Ike," he said, using the nickname he used for his twin.

"That's okay. If you have to fight, use them both, like a club. Now I don't cherish the idea of running through the swamp barefooted, but what do you think? Just get out of here?"

Before Jeremiah could answer, they heard vehicles pulling up near the house. They looked at one another. "Damn," he said. "We almost made it."

"Get in the bathroom," Isiah said. "If someone comes in here, we bust out that door, plow them over and dive through that window. Doing something is better than doing nothing."

They moved silently into the bathroom and closed the door most of the way. They heard heavy footsteps outside on the porch. They weren't Cowboy's.

"Maybe it's the cavalry?" Jeremiah whispered in Isiah's ear.

"Maybe. Maybe not."

He heard a woman's voice, then a man's. They were arguing. The boys held their breath and tried to listen to the words.

"Not doing that . . . the money . . . the boys . . ."

Isiah looked at Jeremiah. "A lady?" he mouthed. Jeremiah shrugged.

"Bitch . . . you get outta the way . . . kill them . . .."

"Earl, honey . . .." the words faded as the pair moved away from the cabin.

Their talking was just a buzz, and then there was silence. Jeremiah pushed open the door slowly. "We are out of here, right this minute."

Isiah nodded, and they bolted for the door. When they got onto the front porch, there was a shiny new F150 sitting not a hundred feet away.

They ran to the best thing they'd seen in two days. They were home free now. Isiah reached for the door handle and pulled, but it didn't open. He looked at Jeremiah. "Locked."

"Then we get out on foot. Can't be too far from civilization. I've heard church bells all day today." Jeremiah looked at the battered, overgrown trail worn down by the recent traffic to the cabin. "Let's stay off the trail but run alongside it. That way, we can hide when they start looking for us, but maybe we won't get lost."

"Sounds like a plan to me," Isiah said, taking the lead. "I wish I had my boots, though. I just know we're gonna find a snake."

"As long as you see 'em first, no problem," Jeremiah replied.

"Where do you think that guy went?"

Isiah shrugged. "No idea. And where's Cowboy? Sooner or later, they're gonna find us missing, and I want to be long gone. Man, Dad's going to be madder than you ever saw if Sherri had any part of this. I hope he doesn't kill her. He'd hate prison."

"Mom's not gonna be thrilled either," Jeremiah said. "Maybe it's one of Sherri's friends—I couldn't say it was Sherri. Let's just hope we can find our way outta here. It's a lot thicker than I thought it was."

The boys ran as fast as Isiah's pain and the overgrowth would allow. Then Isiah stopped and placed his hands on his knees. "Do you still see the trail?" he called to his brother.

Jeremiah stopped, looked over his shoulder, and began to walk back to Isiah. "Not really, but we gotta be okay. So dark in here, I can't see the sun for direction anymore, though."

"That's the timber," Isiah said, his breathing coming in gasps. He thumped Jeremiah on the shoulder. "We're making a ton of noise – let's stop and listen a minute. Do you still see the trail?" Isiah whispered, slowing his breathing.

"Not really."

They dropped to the ground and sat cross-legged. Isiah rubbed his face gently and willed the pain to ease up. Running hadn't helped any.

Jeremiah got to his feet and then reached down to help Isiah off the ground. They'd taken two steps when they heard the report of a gun. A big gun from the sound of it.

They hit the ground and froze. "That can't be a good thing, Ike," Jeremiah whispered.

Isiah shook his head. "Nope. Let's stay put. See if the truck comes back. If not, we get the hell out of here."

The gun report had silenced the nature around them except for whatever crawled up Jeremiah's pant leg. "Ugh..."

"Shhh."

They didn't move until the birds were singing and moving again. Jeremiah hopped to his feet and danced around, shaking his right leg. "Guess it's gone," he muttered.

Then they heard the big engine of the pickup truck come roaring along the rutted path. They were a lot further from the trail than they'd intended. They couldn't see it or who was driving it. But that meant whoever was driving hadn't seen them either.

"Wonder what that was all about . . ." Jeremiah mumbled.

"Don't care. I just want to go home. Let's get going. We'll be safer now that it's dark, I think."

Jeremiah laughed. "Unless we get lost and end up back at the cabin. But let's go. Standing around here won't get us anywhere. Do wish I had a horse, though."

"Me, too," Isiah said. "Or at least my boots."

They walked and ran for what seemed like hours, tired, silent, each one listening and looking for threats from any direction. Even the church bells would have been a welcome sound. Then Jeremiah held out his hand and stopped Isiah.

"I hear water, I think. At least we can get water. Take a rest. Somehow, we got turned around, big time."

They walked toward the sound and spotted a deer, drinking from the small stream. They stood still and waited until she had her fill and strolled away. Isiah dropped down onto a rock and cupped his hands, catching enough to get a drink. "It's good, J."

Energized from the water, they decided to follow the stream in hopes they'd find a road or homestead.

"Gads, it's dark in here," Isiah grumbled.

"I know. Be careful not to fall – we get hurt and we might never get out of here," Jeremiah said.

The boys walked on in silence, careful to keep the stream to their left. They were keeping up a reasonably good pace when Isiah tripped over something and fell flat on his face. He let out a yelp that was probably heard in Texas.

"Shh," Jeremiah hissed at him. "What did you trip over?"

Isiah's nose was bleeding like a faucet now that he'd hit it again. He got to his feet and nudged something with his foot. "I thought this was a log, but it's too soft. Take a look. I can't bend over with my nose bleedin' like this."

Jeremiah went to his knees and placed his hands on the dark mass, which was lying half in and half out of the creek.

"Oh, Lord in Heaven," Jeremiah cried. "It's a man. A dead man!"

"Quiet, J! You sure he's dead?"

"He's not moving. We need to go. Now."

"Let's get out of here," Isiah said.

"I'm right behind you, Ike. Keep moving!"

****

The sun was just brightening the eastern sky with gold, pink, and blues when Isiah and Jeremiah stepped foot on a paved road. Shaking with exhaustion and fear, they had no idea which direction to go to get back to Merciful but heading toward the sunrise seemed like a good idea.

They'd walked about a mile when an Alachua County Sheriff's car pulled up alongside them. He took one look and called them by name before he jammed the cruiser into Park and opened his door.

"Yes sir, we're Jeremiah and Isiah. And we're sure glad to see you!"

The deputy grinned. "Not nearly as glad as I am to see you." He looked them over from head to toe and motioned for them to sit by the car. He pulled out a pocketknife and motioned at the zip ties with the tip of the blade.

"Let me get those off, and we'll go from there."

He put on a pair of latex gloves, cut the ties, and carefully laid them on the seat of his cruiser. He looked at Isiah's black and blue face and winced. "Are you okay, son? You're a bloody mess. Need an ambulance?"

Isiah shook his head. "I'll live. But there's a guy back there in the woods that's dead. In the stream. Big guy. Maybe twenty minutes upstream–"

"Get in the car. I'll get you some water." The deputy radioed the dispatcher that he had the boys in his car, that they'd reported a dead man, and provided an approximate location. Dispatch promised K9 and other units to respond immediately.

"Do you need a medical response? Over?" the dispatcher asked. "It'll be more than an hour, though. Big accident on the interstate."

"Negative. I'll get the boys to the hospital as soon as another car gets on scene." He ended the call and turned to Isiah. "You need a medic, son."

"No, sir. We just want to go home," Isiah said. "Our folks are going to be going crazy."

The deputy smiled as he opened the trunk of his car and came around to Isiah with a first aid kit. He pulled out a stop-bleed compress and gave it to him. "Hold that on your face. It should stop the bleeding pretty fast."

Before rechecking Isiah's condition, he bagged the ties and marked them, put them in the trunk, then pulled out bottled water and two blankets. He looked carefully at Isiah's injuries and handed Jeremiah the water.

"I'm going to take you to the hospital in Gainesville. Your folks can meet us there. They already know we've got you. Just try to relax, and we'll get you settled, okay? Isiah, you keep your head back and drink that water."

"Yes, sir, and thank you."

The boys rested their heads against the back of the seat and listened to the conversation coming in and out on the radio.

"We made it, Ike. I never thought I'd be so happy to be in the back of a squad car."

Isiah put his hand on Jeremiah's wrist. "Me, either."

CHAPTER TEN

Thankful

Forty-five minutes later, the boys were being ushered by the deputy through the Emergency Room doors of UF-Gainesville hospital. A quarter of Merciful seemed to be camped in and around the waiting area when they arrived.

Jeremiah and Isiah rushed into Faith's open arms. "Mom!"

Faith thought her heart would burst with joy, and she sobbed and laughed at the same time. Thank you, Lord. Thank you for my boys coming home safe.

"Mom, don't cry. We're okay. Well, mostly okay. Isiah's nose is a mess, and he looks like a raccoon, but we're good."

Scott joined the trio and laughed. "Your mom has earned those tears, son. Those are pure tears of joy."

She untangled herself from her sons and looked them over. "Isiah, that's got to hurt. That must have been some fall you took. We'll get you some ice...." She spun around in her chair and looked at Jeremiah from the top of his head to his scratched and bloody feet.

"Oh, J, you're a mess, too. Those feet need fixing. I can't

believe you're both so beat up...."

She wheeled herself to the nurse's station. "Can they be seen now? We need ice and antiseptic pretty fast."

The nurse looked up; exhaustion etched clearly on her face. "I'm sorry – but that highway accident has made a mess of the triage area. We've got two fatalities and three other injuries. Hear that baby screaming? She's one of the ones injured. For a few minutes, the boys need to stay here. We'll get you ice and get them in as quickly as we can. Here's their paperwork," she added, handing Faith a clipboard and a pen before vanishing behind tall doors.

She moved back to where the boys now stood with their grandfather. Jeremiah reached for her, and she held him as tight as she dared. Then she felt him relax a bit and he straightened up.

His eyes filled with tears. "I'm so sorry, Mom. We shouldn't have gone with people we didn't know. We were so scared I can't even tell you. Is Dad okay?" He dropped his voice to a whisper. "What is Grandpa doing here?"

A deep voice answered. "With you back safe and sound, I'm doing better than okay, son," Beau said. "You were kidnapped for a ransom. Your grandfather flew here to help with the money."

He held the two boys in his arms. "You were in the woods. I can smell pine on you. Did they let you go, or did you figure your own way out?"

"We got out ourselves, but I think we had some help," said Isiah. "But one of the kidnappers is dead. Shot dead. Lying in the creek. We heard him get killed."

"What?" exclaimed Faith and Beau at the same time.

"Are you sure?" Faith asked with her heart lodged in her throat. Oh, my Lord, no.

Jeremiah nodded. "It wasn't the guy guarding us – he was smaller than the guy we fell over. Maybe he was the big guy driving the truck that picked us up at the church."

The deputy came forward from his post near the wall by the entry. He extended his hand. "I'm Deputy Abe Langston.

The boys told me about the body they discovered, and the crime scene is being processed right now. We'll need formal statements from the boys, but for now, we've got enough to get started on to look for the pickup they saw at the cabin. The boys need medical attention, so that's the priority."

Hope and Eddie joined the discussion, one standing on each side of Faith's wheelchair. "Will they have to go to the office to do that?" Hope asked Langston.

He shook his head. "No ma'am, the District Lieutenant and the Special Victims advocate will be out to the house in the morning. They'll do a full, recorded interview, and then it'll be transcribed. Signing the written report is a formality, but again, it can be done with a sworn officer at the house. After they get fixed up, the boys need to go home and get some rest." He smiled. "You all could use some rest, I'm sure." He looked around at all the faces in the room.

"Jeremiah said that their step-mother set them up—or it was someone using her phone. Is she here?"

Faith glanced in Beau's direction. "No, she's not. That's my ex-husband over there," she said, pointing at him. "He may know where she is."

At that moment, a doctor that didn't look to be too much older than the twins strode into the waiting room. He glanced around.

"Hey, Scott. How are you? Is this your family?" he asked.

Scott shrugged. "Maybe someday, but for now, they're really good friends. Take good care of them, Doc."

"That's my motto, buddy." He pointed at Isiah, then Jeremiah. "Where's Mom?" he asked.

They looked at Faith, who was still holding the clipboard in her lap.

"Mrs. Walker, you take care of that stuff, and we'll take care of the boys. I'll come to find you if I need to." He turned to the twins.

"Boys, let's get you in the back and give you a good going over. Are you thirsty?" the doctor asked as they disappeared into the treatment area.

When the doors closed behind the doctor's retreating back, the family gathered around Faith. Hope and Eddie sat on a small double-chair holding hands while Annie and Bill sat side by side in chairs against the outside wall, facing the television and glaring at Beau. The Reverend and several other friends occupied the rest of the chairs but kept an almost silent vigil there.

"Well," Faith said softly, "paperwork I can handle." She pulled her wallet out of the side pocket of the wheelchair and began filling in the information for the hospital. She hoped that the shaking would slow down so she could write legibly. Scott squeezed her shoulder and smiled at her.

"What happens now?" Beau asked Eddie.

"The law enforcement teams will probably interview the boys several times to get all of the story and facts. In the meantime, the sheriff's office is probably taking care of the body and working the crime scene to gather evidence. They have kidnappers to catch, but they also have a murderer now, too." He glanced at Faith, then at Hope. "The boys believe the two crimes are connected and they probably are, but it still has to be proven. There's lots of work to be done. This is far from over."

Beau glanced at Faith, who was listening to something his mother, Annie, was saying. Neither woman looked his way. He got to his feet, and Eddie looked up at him. "Where are you going?"

The big man shrugged. "Nothing I can do here. The boys are fine, so I'm going back to the hotel. I'll call the farm later. I'm sure the law will want to talk to me, too."

Eddie stood. "Faith knows you love them, Beau. See you soon."

"Sure," he said. He moved toward where Faith sat, then detoured for the door.

Faith watched Beau until her phone buzzed. She glanced at it and smiled. As soon as Lt. Weston and Sgt. Taylor had told her the boys were in a squad car, she'd texted her sister. She looked at Hope, then put the phone to her ear.

"Grace! The boys are okay! When are you coming home?"
****

With nine people milling around, the large farm kitchen felt almost claustrophobic to Faith. And she wouldn't trade it for anything in the world. Being smothered with the love of friends and family had never felt better.

They'd only been home ten minutes when Grace called the house, and the boys took turns assuring her that they were all right.

"Scouts honor, Aunt Grace," Jeremiah said at last. "We're going to shower, eat, and go to bed. Will we see you soon?"

He listened and then ended the call. "She said she could be home next week."

Faith winked at him. "Okay, boys, go get out of those hospital scrubs and into the shower. When you get done, we'll have something ready for you to eat."

"Mom?" Jeremiah said, "will we get our clothes and stuff back? I liked that belt a lot."

"No idea, son, but we'll ask in the morning, all right?"

"Where's Dad, do you know?" Jeremiah asked.

"He was pretty worn out. Said he was going to his hotel. He'll call later or tomorrow," she said.

J nodded and took off up the stairs behind Isiah.

Hope looked at Eddie and Scott. "Can you two stay another night?"

Scott looked at Faith. "You okay with that?"

"I am, but are you sure? The squad must be feeling your absence."

"I'm due back tomorrow night now that the kids are okay, so I'll pull out when the law pulls in, how about that?" he said with a tired smile. "Eddie can handle the legal stuff, right?"

She glanced at Eddie. "You will be here, right? I know these are witness statements, but I'd feel better if you were here."

"Sure, not a problem. However, I'll forego another sandwich and head for the bunkhouse if that's okay."

Hope took his hand in hers. "I'll tuck you in."

He kissed her on the top of her head. "You got a deal."

Scott followed suit and kissed Faith firmly on the lips. "I'll be on the back porch for a bit. I'm not ready to sleep just yet. Join me if you can."

****

At ten o'clock in the morning, Lieutenant Weston and Special Victims Sgt. Mary Seymour were seated at the dining room table with Isiah, Jeremiah, Faith, and Eddie. Faith had slept poorly, all the what-ifs running through her mind until totally exhausted, she'd fallen asleep around four.

Weston set a tape recorder on the table, and Sgt. Seymour had a pen and a yellow legal pad in front of her.

After stating the date, time, and the name and rank of both attending officers, Lt. Weston began the formal witness statement.

"I am Lieutenant Lawrence Weston of the Alachua County Sheriff's Office, conducting a criminal investigation. This interview is being conducted at the home of Isiah and Jeremiah Walker, Merciful, Florida, Alachua County."

He took a sip of his coffee and continued. "I am interviewing Isiah and Jeremiah Walker. Persons present at this interview are Faith Blessing Walker, Isiah Walker, Jeremiah Walker, and Eddie Highspring, Esquire.

"Before we get started, I'd like to confirm that this statement is a voluntary statement, that no one threatened you, coerced you, or induced you to give this statement, is that correct?"

He looked at both boys, who nodded in unison. He smiled. "You need to answer the question for the recording. Isiah, do you agree with what I just said?"

"Yes, sir."

"Jeremiah, do you agree with what I just said?"

"Yes, sir."

"Good. I'm going to place you both under oath. Do you know what that means, boys?"

"Yes, sir," they answered in unison.

Weston cleared his throat. "This will be a sworn recorded interview, taken by a law enforcement deputy pursuant to F.S. 117.10. Please raise your right hand. Do you swear that the statement you are about to give is the truth, the whole truth, and nothing but the truth? Isiah?"

"Yes, sir, I do."

The lieutenant looked at the other boy. "Jeremiah?"

"Yes, sir."

"Good, then let's get going. How did they take you?" Weston asked Jeremiah.

"They were waiting for us outside the community center, and said they were friends of Dad's, and that he sent them to pick us up and go meet him."

"I got a text message maybe ten minutes earlier supposedly from Sherri that said we'd all be meeting for dinner."

"Why in the world did you go with strangers? You know better than that," Faith said.

"Mrs. Walker, please don't interrupt the interview," said Sgt. Seymour quietly.

Eddie reached over and rested his hand on top of Faith's. She replied with a curt nod. Hadn't she done a better job at warning her sons about these things? Why didn't they remember those warnings she'd drilled into them for years?

Jerimiah looked at her. "Mom, they knew our names and knew a lot about Dad, and the ranch, and all of us. We thought the lady on the phone was Sherri." He bit down on his bottom lip. "They even knew about you and what happened to you. They knew everything. We just thought they were giving us a ride to meet Dad."

"What happened after that?" Weston asked.

The boys told the Lieutenant about the ride out of town, the drugged water, and their days in captivity. The tape player's red light kept blinking, and Faith kept fighting to keep the panic from taking over. How terrifying it all sounded. She could almost feel the hot, dark cabin all around her. Eddie patted her hand and pushed a glass of water her way. She picked it up and sipped. If she ever got her hands on those creeps, she'd–

"Were you set free, or did you escape?" Weston asked.

The twins glanced at each other. "Escaped," they said in unison.

"How did you do that? You said you were all tied up and drugged all the time."

The boys recounted the details of their escape and the conversation they'd overheard before they got out of the cabin.

"We never saw Cowboy after breakfast on Sunday, and he didn't tie us up as tight, either. And I don't think the water was drugged so much," Isiah said.

"Yeah, almost like he wanted us to make a getaway," Jeremiah said. "He even gave us coffee with breakfast. Anyway, we were hiding, ready to jump whoever came in the door when we heard some arguing outside. It was a man and a woman, but that was about all we could tell."

"Think hard, boys. Did you hear anything that would give you a clue about who they were?" He glanced down at his notes. "Could they have been the cabin owners, maybe?"

"Maybe," Jeremiah said slowly, "but the lady mentioned 'boys,' so we figured that meant us. We didn't look out the window, so we didn't see them," he finished.

"Wait!" said Isiah looking at Jeremiah. "Didn't the lady call the guy Earl?"

Jeremiah thought a long minute, then nodded slowly. "She did. That was just before they went off into the woods somewhere. And a little while before we heard the gunshot."

"Did the lady's voice sound familiar? Did it sound like the voice on the phone call?" Seymour asked.

The boys thought for a long time. "Jeremiah took the call at the teen center," Isiah said, "so I didn't hear that voice. And to be honest, the lady in the woods only said a couple of words I heard. It could be Sherri, but it could be anyone, I guess. I'm sorry."

"I feel the same way," Jeremiah said with a frown. "I mean, when I got that call, it was from Sherri's number, so I just figured it was her. I wasn't listening super close. And the lady in the woods–well, I was concentrating on getting out of there. It was just a lady's voice. Maybe it was Sherri – or not," Jeremiah said.

Lt. Weston continued. "That's okay. So, you took off after the voices went away. Go ahead and tell the rest."

"We wanted to hide from them, figuring somebody, maybe Cowboy, but maybe the lady and the guy Earl would be looking for us sooner or later. We didn't know where we were, and when it got dark, we got all turned around. When we found the creek, we just kept walking that way. Then Isiah tripped over something, and when we looked, we saw the body lying there, with his eyes opened, bled out."

"Did you boys touch anything on the body? See a gun?" Weston probed.

"No!" Isiah said, a shudder shaking his narrow shoulders. "Once we saw him layin' there, we ran until we hit the road and Deputy Abe found us."

"Okay. I had to ask," Weston said. After a few more minutes of questions and answers, he smiled at the boys. "At this time, we will conclude this interview." He stated the time and shut off the small recorder.

"We found the cabin last night. The crime scene team is still working there. We'll get your fingerprints. That way, we can identify what prints we find there."

"Officer?" Jeremiah said when Weston and Seymour were on their feet. "Do you know who the guy was in the creek?"

Weston shook his head. "Not yet, but we will. He was taken to the morgue this morning, and they'll run prints and all that."

Isiah looked at Faith, then at the Lieutenant. "Is everything okay with our dad? I mean, he isn't here this morning, and we thought he would be."

"Not to worry. We just asked him not to be here so we could get your statements, that's all. We have to go take his statement, too." He looked at Eddie and Faith.

"We do need their fingerprints and would like them to work

with a sketch artist to see what they can come up with on the men who picked them up. Especially the guy they call Cowboy."

Isiah looked up. "Cowboy was one of the men in the truck. We just called him that because we didn't know his name and he wore a big cowboy hat. But we didn't see his face. He wore a red and blue bandana." He looked at the floor, then lifted his gaze again. "He's the one that broke my nose."

"So you said," Weston replied with a smile. "But when you begin working with the artist, you may remember things you don't even know you noticed. I can ask the tech and artist to come by later this afternoon—if that's okay with all of you. The sooner, the better."

Faith looked at Eddie, who indicated it was the thing to do if they could.

"Boys? Are you up to this?" she asked, watching them closely.

"Yes, ma'am. We want these people to get caught. Do you think they'll try to come back for us?" Isiah asked.

Faith gasped, then covered her mouth with her fingertips. Lord, how she hated her sons being afraid. Damn it! When she saw Beau again, she was going to punch him in the eye, at least once.

Lt. Weston looked at them. "I can't tell you that's impossible, but I can tell you that's not how this usually works. Once people like this get run off, they don't usually come back – they concentrate on getting away. We'll have patrols in Merciful until we get a handle on this, though."

Sgt. Seymour tucked her pad back into her buttoned top pocket. "Thank you, boys. We know this has been a rough ordeal, and you've been extremely helpful. If you have any questions or any problems, please reach out to me. It's my honor to help you if I can." She handed a business card bearing the seal of the Alachua County Sheriff's Office to each of the boys, Faith, and Eddie.

When the officers left, the boys looked hard at Faith. "What do we do if they do come back?" Jeremiah asked.

CHAPTER ELEVEN

Wrong Answers

Beau looked up when the door opened. If he honestly thought he was free to go, he'd have walked out forty minutes ago, but sometimes an "invitation" from the police wasn't exactly something you could decline. *What the hell is going on around here?*

Detective Becker dropped a manila folder onto the table. "Can I get you a cup of coffee, Beau? Anything?"

"No, sir. I had some water. I'd like to get finished here and get back to my family. I thought I was done when the other detective was finished. What's going on?"

"Well, we got some information from our evidence team, and since you're here, I thought we'd go over some of it. You want to catch these people who hurt your sons, right?"

"Damned right, I do. What can I help with?"

"I'd like some clarification, okay? You and Faith Walker are divorced, is that right?"

Beau tilted his head a fraction, narrowed his eyes, and

raised his chin. "That's right. What's that got to do with anything?"

"We're just trying to get all the moving pieces into place, that's all. Your ex-wife sounds as though the marriage has been over a long time. You sound like it isn't over at all. Which is it?"

"It's over. We divorced almost five years ago. I'm remarried, but I spend a lot of time with my boys. Or I did until Faith got hurt, and they wanted to spend their summer here where they could visit her in the hospital."

"Where's the current Mrs. Walker, Beau?" Becker asked, making notes in the folder.

Oh, crap. If Sherri's part of this, I'll– Beau shrugged. "I'm not sure, to be honest. I think she's on her way out, too. When I left Texas, I tried for two days to reach her, but she never called me back. I'm not so good at this marriage thing, I guess."

Becker nodded. "Lot of that going around these days. Your father seemed surprised to learn that you'd just relocated to Florida last week. Did your wife know you were doing that?"

"If she'd called me back," Beau said, hating how he sounded, "I'd have told her. To be honest, Sherri's been spending us into the poorhouse, but I just learned how bad it was a few weeks back. As far as things go with my father, I just decided sort of last minute. I'd have filled him in if the boys hadn't gotten kidnapped before I could."

"I see. And why did you do that last-minute relocation, Beau? Running from someone? Your ex-wife seems to think that's possible. Heard you're a gambler."

Beau gritted his teeth. *Just screw up once, and people never forget.* "I was a gambler. When I was married to Faith, I gambled on everything and anything – including my marriage. When she left, I stopped. You can check that with anyone who knows me the last five years." His smile was bitter. "Including my father."

"Well, I still want to know what prompted you to ditch your new wife and take up residency in Florida."

Running his hands through his hair, Beau sighed heavily. "The boys told me that Faith had inherited an oil field. I came to see if she'd help me out with a loan."

"What do you need the money for?"

"Damn it, do I need an attorney? I mean, what's this got to do with my boys getting kidnapped?" *They think I did this....*

Becker put down his pen and looked Beau in the eye. "You can have an attorney any time you want one, but I'm wondering why you'd need one at this point. We're just talking here. I don't know what the kidnapping is about yet. I'm working on a murder. But if you ditched your life virtually overnight in hopes of a payday from the ex-wife, I have to wonder if you'd be part of a scheme to extort money in the form of a ransom."

"No!" shouted Beau, getting to his feet so fast the chair hit the wall.

"Sit, Mr. Walker. You asked me about my questions, and I told you why I'm asking them. I didn't say you had anything to do with the kidnapping."

Oh, hell, now I'm, Mr. Walker? That can't be good. "Look," Beau started, sitting in his chair again. He put his hands in his lap and intertwined his fingers. "In the past couple of days, I've taken a hard look at myself. The idea of my boys being hurt or killed or lost forever had me more scared than I've ever been in my life. I brought it on them – that's what the note said. Maybe I did. Going to be hard to forgive myself for that.

"They're the only thing I've done right in my whole adult life. Coming here was stupid and selfish, and I'm going to be honest with Faith for a change. But I didn't have anything to do with whoever took Jeremiah and Isiah. If Sherri weren't spending money like it was going out of style, I wouldn't need money, but no matter what, I couldn't be part of anything that would hurt my kids. Hell, if I knew who did this, I'd have taken care of it myself."

A knock sounded on the door, and a uniformed deputy came into the room with bottled water and two sodas. Becker thanked him and the deputy left without a word.

"Okay, let's move on, Beau. I want you to look at some pictures, okay? You need to tell me if you recognize the person in the photos—or anything else in the photos."

Beau reached for a soda, popped the top and took a sip. He had some pretty sad skeletons in his closet, for sure. One in particular he knew would cost him big time, someday. But it wasn't murder. He didn't kill people. He played them sometimes, sure, but set up his kids? How did he go from being a Goodtime Charlie to being suspected of murder? He sighed. Things were a real mess, this time.

"Okay. Go ahead."

Detective Becker opened the folder to a photo of a dead man lying face up. "Do you know this guy?"

Beau studied the photo. "He sort of looks like someone I knew years ago, but I don't think I know this man." He shook his head.

"Are you sure?" Detective shoved the photo closer to Beau. "Take your time."

Beau leaned onto the table to get a closer look. Then he picked up the picture and gazed at it. "No. I'm sorry, Detective Becker. I never saw this man before."

"We ran his prints, so we have a name. He's been arrested a couple of times, once for assault, once for fraud." The detective pulled out an older booking photo from the folder. "Do you recognize him now?'

Beau once again studied the image before him. "Wait a minute." Beau grabbed the photo. "He does look a little familiar."

"Where have you seen him if he looks familiar?"

"In Oklahoma." Beau continued to stare at the photo. "More than ten years ago, there was a bronc rider name of

EJ that took my ride after I got hurt. Hell, he beat me out of five grand, but I haven't seen him in all that time. Maybe this could be him. Looks different, though. Too old, I think."

"Well, people age in ten years. How did he beat you out of the money?"

Beau shrugged. "Stuff happens. He took my ride, never paid me my fee."

"And you didn't go looking for him? For five big ones? Really?"

"I was pretty busted up. In the hospital a while, then at home. He was long gone, and I was off the circuit for almost a year."

The detective nodded. "Okay, thanks. Do you own a gun, Beau?"

"Sure," Beau said with a nervous laugh. "Doesn't everyone?"

"Do you know where it is?"

"Yeah. It's in the bottom section of my truck console."

"When did you see it last?"

Beau shook his head. "I don't even know. That box locks, and I don't carry the gun around with me, so I don't know, maybe a month ago?" He thought a little longer. "Yep, was about a month ago. I was thinking of putting a laser sight on it. Had it looked at by a buddy who's a gunsmith."

Becker smiled, uncapped the bottle of water, and took a long swig. "This gun look anything like yours?" The next photo was a picture of a Smith and Wesson .38 revolver with an ivory handle.

Beau felt the color drain out of his face, and the contents of his stomach start to churn. The custom handgrip bore the initials BW.

"Yes, sir, that's my gun," Beau whispered. "It was my granddad's. Where did you find it?"

The detective pulled out one more photo. It was an image of a belt buckle. A very special belt buckle.

Beau's breath caught. *Damn it. What an idiot.*

Becker looked at him. "You recognize this?"

Beau shook his head as if to clear his vision. "Yes sir, that's a 2005 championship buckle. Was this yahoo wearing that buckle?" he hissed. *It should have been my buckle....*

Then he looked at Becker with surprise in his eyes. "Is that the guy my boys found in the woods?"

Becker gathered the photos from the table and tucked them back inside the folder without saying a word.

"Mr. Walker, you asked me about an attorney a little while ago, and I think that now would be a good time for you to consider getting yourself one."

Beau sat in the chair, clutching the soda can. He looked up at Becker. "You've got this all wrong."

Becker motioned for Beau to stand. "Place your hands behind your back."

Beau placed his hands behind his back and shuddered as the cuffs closed around his wrists.

"You are being detained concerning the murder of Earl Foster Jr. You have the right to remain silent. Anything you say right now can be held against you in a court of law. You have a right to an attorney. If you do not have the means for an attorney, the court will appoint one...."

****

Faith busied herself in the kitchen with Margaret Ann to make an early dinner for the family. She'd spent so much time in the wheelchair the past few days that she was getting blisters. And the Lord knew she needed the distraction. Margaret Ann shaped a large bowl of ground beef into burgers while Faith sat at the counter on a tall stool and peeled potatoes.

She wondered where in the world Beau had gotten to but was relieved that the boys had finally gone into the den with their grandparents to watch a rodeo on ESPN. She'd just dropped the last potato into the pot of water beside her when the phone rang.

She reached across the counter and picked up the receiver. "Blessing Farm."

She listened and glanced at Margaret Ann, who was looking at her, burgers forgotten. Her cop radar must have been on full alert.

"Yes, I'll accept the charges. Thank you." She frowned. A collect call from the Alachua County Jail? She'd bet this wasn't good news.

"Beau? What's the matter? Where are you?"

Again, she listened, but she couldn't believe what she was hearing. "Slow down, Beau. I don't understand." *Will this nightmare never end?*

"What do you...arrested? Good Lord, Beau, you may be guilty of some foolish things, but I know you didn't murder anyone."

She grabbed the pad and pen kept near the phone and jotted the information down. "I promise we'll get you help as soon as we can. Bye."

She reached over and hit the trucking company line and called the office on the intercom. "Hope, where can I find Eddie? Or do you have Jack's number handy?" She looked over her shoulder to be sure the boys weren't within earshot of her conversation.

"Beau's been arrested for the murder of the man the boys found in the woods."

She listened a moment, then nodded. "Just ask someone to get to the Alachua County Jail and see what they can do, okay? I'll do what damage control I can here."

****

The stocky man held out his hand and shook Beau's. He laid his briefcase on the table along with a paper sack that smelled like grilled onions. He pulled out his business card and put it on the table.

"Since Eddie doesn't do criminal law, he sent me to find

out what's going on here. My name is Jack Edwards. Let's see what we can do about these charges. You eat and try to relax, and I'll see if Detective Becker will join us."

The steak sandwich was finished when Jack and Becker returned. "The detective has a couple more questions for you. If I don't object, you can answer. If I do, you stay quiet. Is that understood?" Jack asked Beau.

"Sure is," Beau answered. *Okay. Maybe I'll get out of here, yet.*

Detective Becker asked about the gun again. "So, Beau. What's your explanation?"

Jack inclined his head, and Beau answered. "I don't know what to say." He fanned out his hands. "That is my gun. How it got there by the creek with EJ, I don't know. I have no explanation for any of this, but I sure feel like I'm being set up."

"Your prints are smudged some, but they're all over this gun." The detective pointed to the photo. "Where were you last night after you left the Command Center?"

Again, Jack nodded.

"Frantically looking for my boys."

"Anyone with you?" Becker asked.

Beau looked at Jack, who indicated it was all right to answer.

"No. After we lost the call, I needed to do something. Anything. I drove toward the highway, headed for the truck stop where the first calls came from. I bought a cup of coffee, then sat in my truck and watched the payphones. When Faith called me and let me know the boys were headed to the hospital, I went straight there."

"It's the time before you arrived at the hospital that concerns me." Detective Becker drummed his fingers on the desk.

Beau looked at him. "I've told you the truth. Next question."

Becker shrugged. "You were arrested in a bar-room brawl

in Texas six months ago. You want to tell me about that?"

Jack looked at Beau. "You don't need to answer this. It isn't relevant to these charges."

Beau shook his head. "It's all right. My new wife, Sherri, was an exotic dancer in a club, and a guy was talkin' bad about her. I defended her, and it went on from there. I paid for the damages to the bar. Look, Detective Becker, I have had my share of brawls, scrapes, whatever you want to call them. For sure, I'm no saint – I'm on the rodeo circuit. Sometimes things get a little rough."

"Well, Beau, things might get a little rough for you right now, too. You're going to be arraigned for murder." Becker turned to Jack. "You know the drill, Counselor. He'll go before the judge later this week, and you can discuss bail at that time. Until then, he stays here with us, a guest of the Alachua County taxpayers."

"Detective, this man doesn't know this county or the woods the boys were in. To think he killed that man is quite a reach."

"Tell it to the judge, Jack."

Beau thought he'd choke on the panic that rushed up through his chest and settled in his throat, but he'd be damned if he'd let Becker know he was worried. He looked at Jack.

"Guess I'll see you then, right? Tell my kids – and my dad – that I didn't do this and not to worry."

Jack stood and collected his case. "I will. You take care of yourself and don't get into any trouble. You've got enough already. Want me to bring you anything when I come back?"

"No, sir. But you get someone looking for Sherri. The missing money from the ranch, she's not taking my calls, that belt buckle showing up on this guy – the only way Earl could be wearing my belt buckle is if she gave it to him because I sure as hell didn't. And she'd have access to my gun, too. She has a set of keys to my truck, including the gun box lock. She's the only other person with a set of those keys."

Jack looked at Becker. "You heard him. Will you be looking

for Sherri Walker, detective?"

Becker glanced at Jack, then at Beau. "Oh, yes, indeed. We're extremely interested in finding the other half of this Bonnie and Clyde team."

CHAPTER TWELVE

Letting Go

"Nice to see you, Reverend," Faith said to Shawn Jackson when he knocked on the door to the back porch. "Come on in and sit awhile."

He pulled open the screen door and made sure it closed silently behind him. Then he settled himself on the bench to the picnic table.

"I won't stay long, but I wanted you to know that we'll be keeping watch on the place all night for you. We don't want you all worrying about these people coming back here."

Faith smiled and reached her hand out to him. "Thank you very much. With Scott back on duty, Eddie was insisting on sitting out on the front porch all night just so the boys would feel safer. I think the sergeant was right, though. These guys are probably long gone."

The reverend's shoulders lifted. "Maybe yes, maybe no. But Eddie, Margaret Ann, me and a couple of other folks will be keeping watch. Blessing Farm will be the safest place in the county." He patted her hand. "Is there anything else I can do for you, Faith? I know you're exhausted from all this, but something else on your mind?"

Good gracious, what isn't on my mind? She missed her sister Grace more than she thought possible, Beau was in jail for murder, and she hadn't even told the boys yet, and the police didn't know who the woman at the cabin was or if they'd ever find the other kidnapper. But maybe it was all just fatigue getting the best of her. She started to shake her head, but when she looked Shawn in the eye, she couldn't lie and tell him everything was all right. Nothing felt right, and she didn't like that feeling—like she'd been disconnected somehow from every bit of peace and sanity she'd won in the years since she'd left Beau.

"Reverend, I'm so mad at my ex that I almost can't think straight. I've got rage in my gut that almost hurts when I think of what he's brought on our sons. They'll never be the same. And I don't think I can forgive him for that."

Shawn didn't reply for a long moment. He got to his feet and turned away, looking out into the pitch dark of the pastures.

"Well, you know about what unforgiveness can do." He settled his hands in the front pockets of his slacks, still speaking into the darkness. "Betty Jo's unforgiveness and anger toward your sister almost cost Hope her life, you your life, and me, my life. I may not have killed her intentionally, but I did kill her. More than my life, it could have cost me my soul. And because I had secrets to keep hidden, I did stupid things that led up to that showdown at the lake."

He cleared his throat, then turned to face Faith. "I suspect that Beau has secrets, too. And so, he keeps doing foolish things that get him into trouble. You can't control all of that, but you can pray to the Lord for His grace to work on your ex-husband. And ask the Spirit to help you with your anger – to take it out of your heart and set you free from it. It will only hurt you and your sons, Faith. This isn't easy stuff, but it will take away that abandoned feeling you're struggling with."

Faith felt the tears leak from the corner of her eyes as he spoke. She wasn't sure she was strong enough to do what was needed, even though her heart told her that he was right. She couldn't speak around the lump in her throat.

Shawn sat down again, facing Faith, their knees nearly touching. He opened his large hands and waited for her to place her hands in his. When she did, he gently squeezed them with his fingers.

"Dear Lord, you are such a gracious and wonderful God. We thank you for today and for the safe return of Isiah and Jeremiah. We ask you to continue to look out for them and all those protecting them. We ask you to help their father with his current trouble and to ensure that justice is done, Lord. Please protect the law officers from harm and show them how to apprehend the people who did this thing. We also ask you to help Sister Faith with her troubled spirit, knowing that you will always help us when we cry out to you. Take away her pain, her disappointment, and her anger, Lord, that she might be the mother and woman you designed her to be, with joy in her life. And we ask you to help her to continue to get stronger and to walk again soon. We ask these things, Heavenly Father, in the name of your Son, Amen."

He released Faith's hands and got to his feet. "You go get some sleep, and we'll see you in the morning, okay? Margaret Ann took the early morning shift, so she'd be here to help with breakfast. I don't think anyone makes biscuits like that woman. Must have gotten the recipe from an angel."

Faith smiled and it felt good. Maybe the weight was lifting already. Could she believe that was so?

****

Hope and Eddie sat side by side in wooden rockers on the front porch of the farmhouse. They held hands as they gently rocked in the damp night air. In the distance, a whippoorwill called in the darkness.

"Penny for your thoughts," Eddie said after some time.

She chuckled. Just like him to leave himself open like that. But then she knew he wouldn't have asked if he didn't want to know what was on her mind.

"Actually, I'm not thinking much of anything. Just thankful the boys are home safe, and I'm enjoying the night sounds." She sighed. "Grace will be home next week, and I'm excited about that, but I'm wondering what her plans are, too."

It was Eddie's turn to chuckle. "Still the mother hen, Hope. Maybe she doesn't have any plans yet. She's been in the service for over thirty years – I'll bet there will be some adjustment time needed."

"Just for that reason, she'll have a plan. Grace doesn't like leaving things to chance or to waste a moment in indecision. She said she had a surprise for us when she gets back, so I guess I'll have to wait and see, but I'm sure curious."

"I like Scott," Eddie said. "I think he's good for Faith. What do you think about that?"

"I think she's old enough to make up her mind about the men in her life, but I like Scott, too. He's crazy about her, and I think the feeling is mutual – she's simply scared to get involved again, I suspect." Hope sighed. She'd worried about her sisters being heartbroken back in high school. It seemed she still worried about them, four decades later. Mother hen, indeed.

"I'm more concerned with how she's going to be with all this new trauma. Being nearly knifed to death by a madman is more than enough trauma for someone, then to almost lose your children? What is the Lord thinking?"

"Hey, you're the Bible study teacher, not me, honey. Isn't there stuff written about strength through testing or fire, or something?"

Hope's laughter echoed in the darkness. "Yes, that's right. Lordy, you need to get back to your Bible, counselor."

The chairs made a clickety-bump sound as they rocked without speaking for several minutes.

"What about you?" Eddie asked softly, rubbing the back of Hope's knuckles with his thumb. "Are you still afraid I'll hurt you again?"

Hope stopped rocking and looked at him for a long time. The million-dollar question. *Am I?* When she finally answered, she resumed rocking. "I don't think so. The anger's gone. The fear's gone, too — at least the fear of you hurting me."

"Then what are you afraid of?"

"I'm not sure, Eddie. Maybe I'm afraid that I don't know how to love you the way I once did."

This time he stopped rocking and looked at her. "Well, that's good, I think. I don't want you to love me like you did when we were kids. Now we're adults. It should be a different kind of love, don't you think?"

"I guess it probably is. And I guess it's getting to the time to talk about where we're going, then, Mr. Highspring."

He was quiet a moment, but his hand squeezed hers. "I love you. I have loved you for a lifetime already. We'll go wherever you want to go. Have you decided?"

She squeezed his hand back. "I'm getting there, Counselor.

I'm getting there."

They resumed rocking, and Hope smiled in the dark. Her mother and father rocked in these same chairs all those many years ago. She could remember hearing the murmuring of their voices on the porch below the open window in her room. The room where Isiah and Jeremiah now slept. Another generation at the Blessing Farm – a fact that made her feel warm in her heart.

Precious Father God, please help me to do the right thing with this man. And protect us all from bad decisions, wrong turns, and evildoers.

"You know," murmured Eddie beside her, "when all this chaos settles down, we should take a short cruise. Maybe when Grace gets back. A change of scenery might do Faith a world of good."

Hope sighed. "I just want it to end now. Find the kidnappers. Get Beau off the hook for a murder we all know he didn't commit. But I don't know. It could be a long while before things are calm enough around here to go anywhere."

****

In the guest house, Bill and Anne laid together in the dark, the large paddle fan above them moving the cooler night air over their bed.

"When are you going to see Beau?" she asked him.

He'd dreaded this conversation all day. He was fed up with his son's carelessness and trouble. But he wouldn't turn his back on him. He just needed to cool off first.

"I'm not sure. I think it may be a good thing for him to stew a bit, this time. We'll help by paying this attorney, but I think we've rescued him too often for his own good. My heart hurts thinking about the suffering he's brought on this family. He's fifty-five years old. He needs to grow up."

She cleared her throat. "I understand, but you know he didn't do this, right? He didn't murder that man."

"I do know that."

"Is this attorney a good one? Innocent people go to prison all the time. I can't bear that idea for our son, Bill. Not if he's innocent. And I know he is."

Bill wrapped his arm around her slender shoulders, and she settled her head into the crook of his arm. "Jack is the one that got Hope out of the mess she was in when she was suspected of murdering the bank lady. Eddie says Jack is one of the best he knows."

"Okay, then. I will just keep faith that Eddie isn't wrong," she said. "The boys want to visit Beau in jail. I don't think they should go there — they've had upset enough for now, don't you think?"

Bill patted his wife's arm. "They can go with me if they want to visit for a few minutes. It will lift Beau's spirits, and maybe the boys should see how bad decisions turn out. But it's up to Faith — if she allows them, I'll take them. It will be all right, don't worry, Annie. It's not great for your blood pressure."

She rested her left hand on his arm. "Will you go tomorrow, Bill?"

"If not tomorrow, the next day for sure. I have to make an appointment, so why don't we see what tomorrow brings our way and then decide."

They said their goodnights, kissed, and Annie turned on her side. Bill stayed on his back, staring at the ceiling he couldn't see and listened to her breathing. She was the strength of their marriage, and he knew her heart was failing though she kept telling him she was okay.

She didn't know that he knew about the valve that needed replacing, just like Beau didn't know that he knew the truth about that prize buckle.

No matter, he wouldn't give up on his son, any more than the father of the prodigal son had, but it was sure hard not to want to beat the tar out of him.

He rolled on his side and wrapped an arm around his sleeping wife. *What boiling oil will the good Lord heap on us tomorrow?*

CHAPTER THIRTEEN

Growing Up

"Boys," called Faith from the foot of the stairs. "Breakfast is ready."

She swung her walker around to navigate back to the kitchen with slow, but less unsure steps than the day before. She could hear Isiah urging Jeremiah to get moving. She smiled as she listened to their heavy footsteps overhead.

Before Hope had the bacon on the table and Margaret Ann had her biscuits out of the oven, Isiah and Jeremiah blew into the kitchen like dirt devils on a hot Texas evening.

"Hey, Mom," Isiah said as he reached for a plate. "How are the legs today?"

She laughed. "They are working better than yesterday. Thank you for asking."

Isiah kissed her on her left cheek as he paused beside her. "You're doing great. Pretty soon, we'll be retiring that old wheelchair for good. Maybe we can put an engine on it and make a cool cart out of it."

Hope turned around and handed him the plate of bacon and turned him toward the dining room. "Please," she said. "I thought maybe we'd turn it into a planter out by the barn."

"Please don't go chopping it up just yet. Around the house, the walker is working great, but I'd hate to have to go too far on this thing."

In less than fifteen minutes, everyone had assembled in the dining room. Shawn Jackson offered to say the blessing once Eddie, Bill, and Annie had joined them.

"Lord, we thank you for a safe and uneventful night, for Faith's healing and for your guidance and protection throughout the day. In His name, Amen."

Everyone added an "amen," grabbed a plate and silverware. The boys loaded up on eggs, bacon, and biscuits and headed for the kitchen to sit at the counter.

Faith breathed a prayer of thanks, too. Thanks for her boys, thanks for a safe night. Thanks for another day. She heard Jeremiah and Isiah murmuring in the kitchen.

"Wonder what Dad's eating for breakfast," Jeremiah said.

"Probably what we're eating but not nearly as good. I heard they use powdered eggs in jail, like in the Army and stuff."

"Ick," Jeremiah replied. He sounded like he had food in his mouth.

Faith picked up her juice and struggled to take a sip. The boys loved Beau, especially Jeremiah, who worshiped him. Her heart hurt for them. There was nothing she could do to ease their minds until he was freed.

Everyone around her sat at the dining room table, and for ten minutes or so, no one said a word. But once the first cup of coffee and at least one biscuit were consumed, conversation began.

"So, what's the plan for today?" asked Eddie.

Hope swallowed and glanced at Faith. "We'll drop the boys off at school, then we've got some loads to get on the road. I'm going to ask the boys to work the horses this afternoon for a while. I'm not going to have time, and it's been a few days. They'll be busy and safe here."

Faith looked at Bill. "Are you going to go visit Beau?"

"I called to get the visiting schedule and made an appointment for tomorrow at eleven."

Eddie poured another cup of coffee and offered to do the same for Hope, who nodded. "Beau can see Jack anytime during the day except for mealtime. Attorneys tend to get there around seven-thirty and get out before court. But the family can visit him for a half-hour or so up to twice a week. Since the boys are still minors, they can go in with an adult – or up to three adults, but that appointment is important. If you decide not to go, call and cancel it."

Before Bill could say anything else, his daughter Mary Lou joined them. "I'm going this afternoon, Dad. Figured I'd take him a couple of magazines and see how he's doing."

Faith swallowed her tasteless eggs. Beau was far more fortunate than he deserved to be. His family would not turn their back on him no matter what he did or what he got into. Like hers.

She could barely swallow past the lump in her throat, but she was spared from commenting when her former sister-in-law enveloped her in a long, tight hug. Faith clasped Mary Lou's arms. She was lucky they were still in her life, too.

"I will kick him in the butt for you," Mary Lou said as she squeezed in between Faith and Shawn. Faith smiled and put more eggs in her mouth. If she had food in her mouth, she'd be less likely to put her foot in it.

Annie pointed her fork at her daughter. "You never mind. He'll be glad to see you, and you know that. But he doesn't need any grief from his sister, so take it easy."

"Mom, it's about time he learns life isn't all about him. He's in serious trouble. If he wasn't always so busy trying to look good, he might not be where he is right now."

Her mother shook her head. "It's the rodeo life, Lou. It's all about winning. All about looking good. It's a world of smoke and mirrors." She looked at Bill, who didn't avoid her gaze. "I've seen your father with his fingers nearly severed because they got caught in a bull rope, and he just smiled like nothing at all was wrong. Of course, when he got in the ambulance, he cried like a motherless calf, but he wouldn't let on."

Bill nodded. "Your mother's right. The whole rodeo world is easy to get caught up in. And Beau's always been competitive. Maybe I contributed to it by pushing him so hard when he was a kid, but I just wanted him always to do his best."

"He always wanted you to be proud of him, Bill. You were a good father. You weren't overly hard on him. He's just always needed more . . . something," Annie said, her sorrow evident.

Faith knew what Annie meant, but she'd always taken it personally as though maybe she hadn't been enough to keep Beau happy in their marriage. Especially after the twins were born. She'd been so exhausted, then sorrowful, then angry. Angry enough to not even care if he ever grew up at all. Now she felt something else, though she couldn't label it. She looked toward Reverend Jackson, who caught her gaze and smiled.

"Sometimes, people have an emptiness inside, which isn't from their parents. The Lord gives us all a special place inside that's just for Him. And then some event happens, and we think we aren't good enough to be with the Lord, so that special place gets shuttered, but of course, it doesn't go away. So, we work harder, try to make more money, buy a fancier truck, whatever. God never goes away. And He'll wait until we invite him back."

Jeremiah and Isiah came into the dining room. Jeremiah looked at Faith. "Mom, I want to go see Dad."

She sighed. "I'm sure you do. Your grandfather made an appointment for tomorrow. You go to school today and get your work for tomorrow. Okay?" She watched him set his jaw the way his father would.

"I want to go today and make sure he's okay."

Isiah grabbed Jeremiah's shirtsleeve. "He's fine. We'll go

tomorrow. Come on, let's get the horses fed."

Jeremiah shook his arm free. "You don't even want to go, you said. And you don't have to—but I do."

"Boys," Faith said sternly. "Neither of you must go, but if you want to go, it has to be tomorrow. The jail insists on appointments. It's out of our hands. But your Aunt Lou is going this afternoon, and she'll let him know you're worried about him. Get the horses fed and then get yourselves ready for school."

She held Jeremiah's gaze for a long time, then he turned on his heel and marched out through the kitchen doorway. Isiah rolled his eyes and followed him.

Shawn Jackson reached over and rested his hand on the back of Faith's. "Jeremiah is angry, but not at you. It's just safe to vent it with you."

She shook her head, needing a minute to fight back her tears. "He's been angry a long time about the divorce. In his mind, I should have stayed and made it work."

Bill pushed his plate aside a few inches. "The reverend is right. They don't understand everything. Not even enough to know why staying wasn't an option."

Mary Lou put her hand on Faith's shoulder. "Maybe you should have told them the facts. They'll need to know someday. J doesn't need that chip on his shoulder, and you don't need to bear the brunt of it."

"They're only fifteen, Lou. Their father loves them, and I love them, and that should be enough. Sometimes marriage just doesn't work out."

Annie looked pained. "And sometimes there are good reasons for marriages not working. I know my son wasn't a good husband, and that falls on me. I didn't teach him how to be a good husband. I spoiled him, I guess. But he was different after the divorce. He did learn a valuable lesson. He stopped running around, and he stopped gambling, too."

Faith looked at Annie. "I'm glad that Beau changed. I changed, too, though I don't know if my changes were as positive as his were. Maybe they were. I got stronger, more self-reliant. But less trusting, too. However, I have no desire to tell the boys the dirty laundry of our marriage."

Eddie glanced at Hope, then captured Faith's gaze. "I can tell you from personal experience that some of our mistakes are tough to own. Even tougher to try and make things right, but the one thing I am sure of is that honesty is a super important ingredient."

"The truth shall set you free," whispered Mary Lou.

Annie got to her feet. "This is Faith's decision, not ours. No one is going to tell the boys anything except their parents. Agreed?"

Everyone nodded except Bill. "Bill Walker?" she said.

He looked at her and got to her feet. "I won't bring it up, but I won't lie to those boys. I won't make the same mistakes with them that I made with their father."

Faith struggled to take a deep breath. The beautiful breakfast was over, and life had sucked all the air out of the room. "No, nobody needs to be lying about anything. Not to the boys or anyone else."

The wooden door to the back porch slammed, and the sound broke the tension as her young men bounding through the kitchen.

"Mom, look what we found out by the barn," said Jeremiah with his hand outstretched. Isiah was white as a sheet.

Faith fought to keep her heart from jumping out of her chest. In Jeremiah's hand were three bullets.

****

Sherri tugged the ball cap down and kept an eye on the door, but she had to keep her head. Panic wasn't going to help anything, but the situation wasn't right. A trucker at the lunch counter slapped another on the back, and they both laughed loudly, but they paid her no attention. She exhaled.

The waitress came by with a pot of coffee to refill her half-empty cup. "Your lunch will be out in a few minutes. We're a little short-handed today."

Sherri forced a smile. "It's okay. I'm going to be here a little while anyway."

The waitress dashed off to the counter, and Sherri pulled a cell phone out of her pocket and punched in a number. She lowered her voice and kept scanning the diner for trouble.

"Denny, call me back, please. Where are you? I'm leaving in a few hours, but I want to know you're okay." She closed the phone and stuffed it back in her shirt pocket. She watched her waitress head toward her table with lunch. Had Earl killed Denny as he'd threatened?

The waitress laid the meal ticket on the table after placing the burger and pie down. "Anything else, honey?" she asked.

Sherri shook her head. With less than a hundred bucks to her name, she needed to be careful. Going back to Texas was out of the question, but so was Buenos Aires. She almost laughed aloud. Damn you, Earl.

The truck rental was paid for another couple of days. She could be in Mexico by that time if she kept moving. Maybe that would work. They had cowboys, too. Cowboys who loved blue-eyed women. She hoped, anyway.

Beau would get some R&R at the expense of the Florida taxpayers, his boys were safe with their mother, and she was finally off that dusty, smelly ranch.

She left two dollars on the table, swiped the ticket off the table, grabbed her jacket, and headed for the register. She'd get a couple of maps before leaving the rest stop and then figure it out on the highway.

She was almost to the pickup when she spotted them. Two trucks parked side by side with the Amazing Grace Trucking Company logos on the doors. Suddenly there was no air to be had. Where were the drivers? In the diner? In the showers?

She looked around but didn't see anyone. It's okay, she thought. They don't know me from the Princess of Wales. She walked fast to the pickup, climbed inside, and locked the doors.

She took a deep breath. Time to get out of Florida and stay out. But no matter which direction she drove, she had a long way to go.

Curse you, Beau Walker, and your broken promises. And you too, Earl Foster. And where was Denny and his stupid cowboy hat?

CHAPTER FOURTEEN

No Hiding

"How are you feeling this morning, Beau? Getting any sleep?" Jack asked him.

How was he feeling? Like he'd entered the wrong haunted house, and there was no exit door. "Been better, I guess, but not too bad. I had a shower and shave, so at least I feel human. Sleep is out of the question except for a half-hour at a time. I just want to get out of here."

Jack nodded but didn't reply.

"How are the boys doing? Are they calmed down? Any word on Sherri?"

"The boys are doing okay, according to Faith. I talked to her this morning. That's why I'm here. Jeremiah's asking to see you. How do you feel about that?"

"I don't want the boys here. It's no place for them."

"They aren't children, Beau. They're young men. Soon to be driving and making decisions. Visiting you might reinforce them making good decisions. You think about it, but I suspect if they decide they're coming to see you, they won't be stopped."

Beau hung his head, then shook it slowly. No truer words had ever been said. Those boys were as stubborn as their mother. Jeremiah was determined to follow in his father's footsteps; Isiah was committed not to. He felt a smile tug at his face. Yes, indeed, they were no longer little boys.

"I suppose you're right. Is Faith coming with them?"

"She may," Jack said, pulling out a notebook as he talked. "Sounded like your father wanted to visit, too. I don't know if they settled it. They just asked me to warn you."

"I'm surprised my father is willing to come. He doesn't think much of me these days."

"Why's that, Beau?"

He shrugged but couldn't look Jack in the eye. "I'm a large disappointment to him, that's all. I'm a much better rodeo rider than I am a son, that's all."

Jack looked up from his notebook. "You know, sometimes I've thought I was dead right about something only to find out I wasn't. Worried myself sick over terrible things – at least in my mind and memory. Then I found out that the terrible thing wasn't so terrible at all."

Beau looked at his attorney. "Well, no matter. My dad has good reason to be disappointed in me, and it doesn't have anything to do with this mess."

They looked at each other for a long minute, then Jack closed the notebook and got to his feet. "I've been reading people for a long time. They say as much with what they won't say as they do when they finally open up. I'm not so sure your father doesn't figure in here somewhere."

****

Faith and Hope met on the back porch shortly after two. "Manny and Pat think they spotted Sherri this morning at the rest stop where those calls were made. Thank the Lord it was after their delivery because they've spent the whole rest of the morning with deputies."

Faith inhaled. Could this nightmare finally be nearing the end? "Did they catch her by any chance?" she asked.

"No, when they got out of the diner, they lost track of her. But Highway Patrol is treating it like she's still here in the state, so maybe they'll find her." Hope took a sip of sweet tea and swallowed. "The boys gave the F150 description, so even without a plate number, the law has something to work with."

****

Faith sat beside Hope as they drove toward the high school to pick the boys up from school. "How are the boys handling being chauffeured to and from school?" Hope asked.

Faith looked out the side window at their neighbor's draft horses. She forced herself to unclench her jaw. She needed to remember that the Lord had brought her sons home safe to her. Even though the boys were still frightened and angry about all the security, everyone had much to be grateful for.

"Jeremiah is exceptionally quiet, which means he's trying to keep a lid on his anger. And that's not good. Isiah is embarrassed by all the attention. I'm just trying to listen to them and reassure them things will calm down as soon as the law gets the other two kidnappers into custody."

"And it will, Faith. The cops are closing in on the woman, at least. Doesn't seem to be much info on the one the kids called Cowboy."

Faith shook her head. "The boys think he helped them to get away, so I don't even care if they catch him or not."

Hope nodded with a wry smile. "I hear you." She made the turn into the high school driveway and parked behind the other cars waiting for student dismissal.

"I only have another week at rehab, so it's time to get our lives back. I'll be happy as a clam when I can leave the walker behind - but the walker is a heck of a lot better than the wheelchair."

The doors burst open, and a million young hormonally-charged human beings dashed down the sidewalk toward waiting cars and busses.

"Good grief," muttered Hope. "They're more revved up than usual."

Faith laughed, something she hadn't felt like doing in a week. "Maybe normal is regaining a footing." She stared out the window, anxious to spot Isiah and Jeremiah. Would the residual terror of their abduction ever fade for her, too? She'd add that to her prayer list today - how would her boys mend if she didn't?

It was another five minutes before she spotted their lanky frames jogging along the sidewalk toward the truck. The doors opened, and the boys folded long legs and heavy backpacks into the pickup's extended cab.

"How was your day?" Faith asked them when they were seatbelted, and Hope pulled out into the line of traffic to leave the school.

She was almost afraid of the answer, but there was no way she was going to risk disconnecting with them now. They'd soon be driving, and then her opportunities to stay close would be severely limited. She was determined not to lose them over this intrusion in their lives. She shifted a bit to look at Isiah through the split in the front seat.

"It was okay," Isiah replied. "Same old stuff. I have a science project due next week, so I'll need to work with my team to get it done."

"Okay, ask them to come to the house - you can work together in the library. Or maybe you can work at the teen center with Reverend Jackson."

"We're sick and tired of being watched, Mom," Jeremiah snapped. "There's a guard at the classroom doors, we have to be dropped off and picked up every day like we're in kindergarten, and now we can't even go to our friends' houses. The bad guys run around free and we're trapped."

Faith wondered how to reply. What could she say to that argument? He was entirely right.

"One of those bad guys is dead, J. We don't want the same result for either of you," Hope said evenly.

Isiah cleared his throat. "It is nerve-wracking, Mom. We just want to be normal again. Our friends understand, but other students don't. And nobody's parents understand. We might as well have some deadly contagious disease. The teacher suggested that I provide my input by phone."

"I get it, boys, I really do. This whole thing is a mess with your father in jail for a murder he didn't commit, and you need to be kept under lock and key. No one is sorrier for all this than I am, but until we're sure the kidnappers don't still have designs on you, we can't afford to be careless. My life would be over if anything happened to either of you."

"We're not helpless, Mom," Jeremiah said. "We got ourselves out of the cabin, right? We'll be extra careful, I promise."

They made the turn onto Main Street and headed for the farm. "Can we go to the church center today?" Isiah asked. "I want to see the finished project."

Faith glanced at Hope, who shrugged. "Why not?"

Hope made the right onto Church Road, and they drove in silence past the Chapel, then turned toward the creek to the new Merciful Community Center.

"Well, let's see if anyone's here," said Hope, parking in the dirt lot beside the building.

Faith undid her seatbelt and turned to look at the boys. "If Reverend Jackson can bring you home, you're welcome to stay. Will that help you feel less trapped?"

"Yes," they answered in unison.

Before they got to the door, it opened, and the Reverend stepped out to hold it open for his visitors.

"How great to see you all," he said, reaching out to steady Faith, who was now walking with her walker.

"The boys are feeling like prisoners. Can they hang out here with you for a few hours?" she asked him when they were inside.

"They certainly can, and I'll even bring them home in time to feed the horses. How about that?"

Jeremiah groaned, and Hope laughed. "You're invited for dinner, then," Faith said. "Margaret Ann dropped off two apple pies this morning, so we even have dessert."

"Apple pie?" Jeremiah asked with a grin. "This day just improved, for sure," he muttered. Faith looked around the large room with the floor to ceiling windows, round dining tables, and two ping pong tables. "The place looks wonderful, Shawn. Is it getting used a lot?"

He grinned. "The ladies are starting up a Bingo night. The Cub Scouts are here on Monday nights, and 4-H is here with their Tech Wizards on Thursdays after school. We're off to a good start." He looked at the boys. "Are you giving your mother a hard time?"

"No, sir," said Jeremiah.

"I hope not," the reverend said. "How about helping me set up for the scouts and then have a game of ping pong yourselves?" he asked. "Once they get here and settled, I'll take you home for dinner."

"That's cool," Isiah said.

Faith and Hope said their goodbyes and left the boys in

the care of Shawn. "Lord, please keep my boys safe," Faith prayed as Hope turned the truck toward the farm.

"Try not to worry," Hope assured her sister.

Faith wondered. Will I ever regain that sense that they're safe?

****

Faith passed the mashed potatoes to Reverend Jackson, who sat to the left of Jeremiah and across from Hope. For the first time in days, Scott was able to join them, and he sat between Isiah and Faith. Bill, Annie, and Mary Lou were scattered around the table, too. Faith looked around the room, thankful to have her family safe and sound.

After grace was said, Faith noticed Jeremiah wasn't eating with much enthusiasm. She addressed a question to Shawn Jackson.

"Is the scouting program growing?" she asked. "I hear we've got a few new families in town, so I'm hoping that means more kids involved in good things."

He nodded. "We have a few new families in the church too. The 4-H group gets the most attendance, though. Those kids have a lot of fun making their robots and learning about circuits and computer intelligence." He sipped his sweet tea and reached for a biscuit. "We're planning a home-schooled program at the church, and I hope all of you might help me get it figured out."

"Can we do that, Mom?" Jeremiah asked. "Do homeschooling? You know you can attend school on the computer now. We only have another year or so. Then we could help around here if we aren't going back to Texas."

Faith picked up her tea and took a long sip. Was it a bad idea? Maybe the better question would be, is it a good idea?

"I don't know, J. There are things you learn in school beyond the academics, like how to interact with people and how to manage conflicts, and then there are the sports opportunities, friends, things like that."

His scowl communicated his feelings loud and clear, but Faith decided to tackle what she thought was the crux of his issue.

"Do you want to go back to Texas? I know you miss your friends there, and I appreciate that sacrifice to be with me, but I thought you were happy enough to finish school here."

He shrugged but didn't look at her. "Well, I'd only want to go back to Texas if Dad gets to go home. And we don't know if that's going to happen."

"Of course, he's going to go home," Faith said. "We all know that he didn't kill anyone, J. The truth will be proven, and he'll be out soon, I'm sure."

Bill cleared his throat and pushed his plate forward. "You're both always welcome to come stay with your grandma and me. Your mom, too. But your mother's right, your father will be out of there real soon."

"Well, I'm not so sure," spat Jeremiah. "That's what Isiah keeps saying, but it might not happen. All of this is so unfair," he said to Faith before turning toward Bill. "But you don't even like Dad, G'daddy. You think he's a bad man and he's not."

Annie placed her hand on Bill's wrist to quiet him. Bill sat back in his chair, but he didn't take his gaze off his grandson.

"Boys, things are not always what they seem," Annie said. "Your father is a good man, and both your grandfather, and I know it, but he has not always made good decisions. Nonetheless, this whole incident has changed everyone in and around this family forever, not just you, so try to remember that."

Bill leaned forward and rested his elbows on the table

edge. "Faith, is it still all right to take the boys to see Beau, tomorrow?"

She glanced at Isiah, who almost looked like he wanted to cry. "Obviously, Jeremiah wants to go, so that's fine if they want to go with you. I'll let the school know they're going to be out of class tomorrow."

Isiah spoke up. "I don't want to go. I've got a school project I don't want to miss."

Jeremiah was speechless, and Faith understood. They were finding their paths in life, no longer attached psychologically. She'd experienced it at nineteen when her sister Grace had announced she was joining the Army. Faith remembered the secret tears she'd shed for weeks. She felt betrayed even though she'd been excited for her twin.

"That's fine. You don't have to go. Or you can go with Mary Lou and me on Saturday morning if he's still there. Jeremiah, you be ready to go with G'daddy tomorrow, and I'll go graduate from physical therapy."

Scott rested his arm across the back of Faith's chair. "We'll go to lunch to celebrate if you want," he said.

Jeremiah shoved back his chair and got to his feet. "Sure, you two just celebrate life while my father's rotting in jail. Have a great time." His sarcasm lingered in the air long after he stormed out of the room, and the porch door slammed.

"I'm sorry," Faith whispered to Scott, who had withdrawn his arm but hadn't moved away from her.

"No problem. He's upset. You're all upset. I understand that. You've worked hard to get back on your feet, so I think that deserves a nice lunch, but it can wait if it's a problem."

Beau's sister Mary Lou got to her feet and began reaching for plates to clear the table. "You two go have your lunch. I'll be here tomorrow and so will Hope. If the boys need something, we'll handle it. You deserve a break, too."

Faith wasn't sure. Maybe seeing Scott wasn't going to work for her sons, and she couldn't do anything to add to their uncertainties. But if that was her final decision, she'd tell him face to face. She nodded as Isiah came up behind her and wrapped his arms around her shoulders.

"J will be okay, Mom."

She patted his forearms and pushed back her chair. She appreciated his support, but she wasn't all that sure he was right. Could she find a way to reach Jeremiah before it was too late?

CHAPTER FIFTEEN

Hard Truth

The farmlands, woods, and lakes flashed by outside Jeremiah's window, but he didn't pay much attention to the view as his grandfather drove toward the Alachua County Jail. *Where my Dad is.* Everything looked different though he'd been to Gainesville lots of times with his Aunt Hope.

He'd pushed his mother hard to let him visit the jail, but now he almost wished he hadn't. He hoped he wouldn't throw up in his grandfather's truck. He'd skipped breakfast because his stomach was full of butterflies when he woke up, but he still felt awful.

Just as the Alachua County Sheriff's Office sign appeared, his grandfather cleared his throat. "You doing okay, son?"

Jeremiah shook his head. "No, sir. I'm feeling pretty queasy."

G'daddy kept his eyes on the road. "Need me to stop? We could get a soda or something first."

"No, sir, I just want this to be over. All of it. It's been eight days since we got free, and it don't feel like we're getting anywhere. I want to go home. I want Dad to go home."

"Doesn't," corrected his grandfather.

"Huh?" Jeremiah said with a frown.

"It doesn't feel like we're getting anywhere. You know how to speak English properly, and I'm here to tell you there's no excuse not to. People judge you on how you speak, how you dress, how you behave and don't be fooled into thinking it doesn't matter. It's not about looking good. It's about being and doing your best always because that's what the Lord wants from us. You're not a little boy. You're a young man now. Okay?"

"Yes, sir. But the Lord doesn't seem to care about what we want. Is He angry with Isiah and me or with Dad?"

G'daddy chuckled as he glanced at him. "It's not about God being angry with anyone, J. God has a plan for us all, and while we're learning that and learning that God has his own timing, our job is to be better people today than we were yesterday. He lets us fall and take our lumps, so we learn important lessons. Your daddy, and all of us, have mistakes to make and lessons to learn. Just part of life." He cleared his throat. "I'm sure that you two had some divine intervention in getting away without serious harm to you."

Jeremiah was quiet a mile or two. "Maybe. Maybe Cowboy is really an angel." He frowned. "Is God going to let Dad take the fall for this murder? Because he didn't do it. You know that."

They waited behind an SUV at the light on NE 39th, and G'daddy looked over at him. "I can't tell you what the Lord has planned. I do know that you're right, your father didn't do it. We'll do everything we can to make sure the truth comes out. But that may be the whole point. The Lord wants us to be truthful, first to ourselves, and then always to others. Your father has had some issues with the truth. Maybe God's trying to teach him – all of us - how important the truth is."

They were ten minutes early when his grandfather parked the truck. "Do you need a minute, son? We have to get registered for the visit, but we have a few minutes if you want to take a walk or sit here or even say a prayer."

Jeremiah squared his shoulders and raised his chin. G'daddy was right. He wasn't a baby–he was a man. He was nearly old enough to drive – he could certainly handle a visit with his father, even if it was in jail.

"I'll be fine, G'daddy. I'm pretty mad at God right now, so you pray if you want, but not me. Let's go hug Dad and make sure he knows this is going to come out okay."

"I'm with you, young man. Let's get this show on the road, as they say."

****

The jail Lobby Clerk handed back their identification. Then he handed them visitor badges and instructed them to wear them during the entire visit. She nodded to the escort in the lobby and wished them a good visit.

Jeremiah kept swallowing the sour taste in his mouth. They'd been scanned and ordered from one place to another. He could hear men talking loudly in the distance. Then low laughter.

His grandfather squeezed his shoulder. "Going to be okay, son," he said softly. Jeremiah swallowed again.

They followed the corrections officer down the hallway and into an open area where inmates sat together at tables or sat in chairs reading magazines and books. Then the officer opened the door to a small booth and told them to take a seat.

The door closed behind them and they waited. The air was cool, but it smelled like the combination of a hospital and a gymnasium. Jeremiah focused on an old discoloration on the table.

****

Beau opened the door on the other side of the booth and stepped into the space, then took a seat on the bench. *Crap, this is hard.* He forced a smile. His son didn't need to know how scared his father was.

"Hey, Dad."

"You didn't have to come here, son."

Jeremiah blinked furiously. "Sure, I did, Dad. I had to see

for myself that you were okay. We'll get you out of this, don't you worry."

Beau nodded and knew he looked like a fool. His precious rodeo-loving son would have this memory forever burned into his mind. His hero in jail for murdering a loser.

"I didn't kill that man or anyone, ever. I swear that's the truth, J. How is your brother? Your mom?"

"Everyone is okay. Isiah has a big school project, so he didn't come today, but he misses you, too. None of us think you did this, and we know you'll be out of here soon."

"That's good. And you're right. But I'm sorry about all this, J. The kidnapping, the terrifying experiences, all of it. I wish I could undo it for you."

Jeremiah shrugged. "I know, Dad, but you didn't have anything to do with it. And if Mom hadn't left you, you wouldn't be here, either. None of us belong here – we all need to go home to Texas and put our family back together."

Beau shook his head. "Your mother isn't to blame. I chose to be with Sherri. Your mother didn't make me do that."

"She could have fixed things. If she'd stayed in Texas, she wouldn't have been stabbed and nearly killed, and we wouldn't be here. I'm just saying."

His father pointed at him. "Stop, J. She came here to help the family, and that's what family does. We can only move forward, not back. You need to respect your mother. Do you understand?"

Jeremiah looked at the table. "Well, maybe now that Sherri's gone, you and Mom can work things out."

"Don't worry about Sherri. And your mother isn't going to marry me again. I deserve all of that. Have you seen Sherri anywhere since the kidnapping? Has she called you again?"

Jeremiah shook his head. "No, sir. Haven't seen her since Texas."

"Okay," Beau said. "If you do, you tell your mother or G'daddy or someone right away. That's really important. And you don't go near her, okay?"

"Sure, Dad, but why did she set us up to be kidnapped, anyway? You don't have any money."

"It's more complicated than the money, J. Or, maybe it's not, but you're safe if you stay close to your mom and the ranch, okay? Promise me you'll listen to your mother and stay close to home."

Jeremiah looked around the little room for a moment, then nodded. "Okay. I thought it was like being a prisoner at home, but now I see it isn't the same. I'll try to lighten up on Mom."

Beau let out a long breath. His heart felt a little lighter. Faith deserved their support, not a hard time on his account. And his boys deserved to be happy and safe. He forced a smile.

"You give everyone a hug for me when you get home, okay? Now I need to talk to your grandfather alone for a few minutes. You wait in the lobby for him, and I'll be back in a few days, you'll see. I've got a good attorney."

Beau knocked on the door of the booth and let the officer know Jeremiah was to leave. His heart felt like it was in a vice as he watched his son step out into the hallway, shoulders stooped with more hurt than any fifteen-year-old should have.

If only he could have hugged him, but visits didn't include any physical contact, possibly the worst aspect of the whole damned situation.

When the boy was on his way back up the corridor with another officer, Beau turned to his father. "Have you lost your mind? You didn't have to bring him here. He didn't need to see all this, Dad."

Bill clenched his jaw. "I disagree. It won't hurt him to understand that there are consequences for all the things that we do, as well as the things that we don't. Besides, he couldn't rest until he saw you with his own eyes."

"You haven't lived a perfect life either, Dad."

"Truer words were never spoken, Beau. I'm sorry to sound like a tent preacher, but I'm running out of time to teach you or the boys anything, and there are important things for you to learn. Before it's too late."

Beau felt a chill run up and down his spine. His father was

getting up in years, sure, but certainly, he had a good number of them left, didn't he?

"Are you okay, Dad? Are you sick?"

Bill shook his head. "I'm fine as far as I know, but I'm not getting younger. I'm closer to eighty than seventy now. The body's bound to wear out. I think this episode has taken years off your mother's life as well as mine."

Beau stared at his hands, which were clasped in his lap, where his arms rested on his knees. "So, are you and Mom going to bail me out of here?" Like I don't know the answer to that one already.

Bill looked steadily at his son. "We've discussed it . . . and probably not. We'll support you by paying Jack's fees, but no bail this time, son."

"I see," said Beau, feeling as though the Rocky Mountains had just collapsed on his back. "Anything I can say to change your mind?"

Bill continued to look at him. "Let's start with the beginning. What in the world started this fiasco? How did Earl get your belt buckle? Why would Sherri set up your sons to be kidnapped by that maniac?"

"I don't know what she was thinking or why she'd give him my buckle. She was obviously pissed about something." Or a whole lot of somethings—

"Sherri didn't give that buckle to him, Beau. You didn't ever own that buckle."

Beau looked at him and laughed, but even to his own ears, it sounded like a coyote bark. "You just can't stand the fact that I won the buckle you could never win, can you? That I'm a better rider than you ever were?"

Bill sat still and said nothing. The silence stretched on.

"I don't know who your sources are or what they told you, but that isn't the truth," Beau said.

"Don't insult me by thinking I'm a doddering old fool. This whole mess is built upon a lie, and if you don't clean up the first lie, we'll never get through all the others. You wouldn't be the first innocent man to do time for a crime he didn't commit." He cleared his throat. "We've only got another few minutes. What happened at that rodeo?"

How can I tell the truth after all this time? He'll hate me until I die. Maybe going to jail is a better option. He recalled Jack's confession about fear being worse than reality. His father waited. And waited. The guard tapped on the window and signaled they had only five minutes left.

Beau hung his head, convincing himself not to storm out of the booth. His heart raced like he'd been running a four-minute mile, but he knew his father was right. Time for the truth if he wanted good things for his sons. And he did. He never again wanted to see the pain he'd just seen in Jeremiah's eyes. He blew out a breath through pursed lips.

He looked at his hands again, not his father. His words were quiet, but he knew in these precious few minutes he'd at least have the truth between them if nothing else.

"You know, since I was a kid, I wanted that buckle. The one you never got. The great William Russell Walker, Champion Bull Rider. The one so many never win. And then, finally, I was there. I'd won my way into the elimination rounds, and I was going to get my chance at big money. The big show."

Beau swallowed hard, then cleared his throat.

"I got into a friendly game of craps after the first round, and before the sun came up, I was short nearly ten-thousand dollars. The dudes that ran that hustle busted me up pretty bad, so I'd remember that I owed them, and I had the rest of the week to pay them in full. I got the ribs taped up and a shot of cortisone and got to registration in time to pull my straw for the bull that would make or break my chances at the win. I still thought I could pull it out.

"Anyway, the morning of the big event, I was number three on the board. I was in the trailer when some guys came on in and made me a deal – one that would cost me the buckle but would pay the debt." He shook his head as the memory of that day came back.

Talk about selling your soul to the devil . . . .

"What did you have to do for that kind of money?" Bill asked.

God forgive me even if my father can't. "I had to disable Loco, your prize bull."

"I see," his father said.

Beau swiped his hand across his eyes, then down his face. "No, you don't, Dad. I didn't mean to kill him. They gave me the syringe which was supposed to make him sick – too sick to compete – but they never said anything about killing him."

"Liars never reveal how bad things will get. Go on."

"Because I'm your son, they knew no one would question why I was visiting Loco before the event. But when the announcer told us over the loudspeaker that night that Loco was dead of an apparent heart attack, I almost had one. He was supposed to have colic, not die, I swear," Beau moaned. He swiped at his tear-filled eyes with his arm.

"I'm so sorry, Dad. I know how much you loved him and how much you lost when he died." When he looked up, he saw tears in his father's eyes, too.

"And so, the sharks owned you from that day forward, didn't they? Was Earl one of them?"

Beau shook his head. "I don't think so, but he set up the games. The bull I rode instead of Loco was a loser bull, and I couldn't make the points I needed to win. Earl's bull was from the Conrad farm, and you know those bulls, Dad. Almost as good as yours. Anyway, he was the winner that night."

"So, you pretended to win that buckle just to try and humiliate me?"

Beau bit the corner of his bottom lip to keep it from trembling. "I don't even know, Dad. I was obsessed with that whole status symbol, I guess. I don't understand it today. I really don't. It's not like I could wear a fake prize anywhere that mattered. But you remember – they posted me as the winner that night. Sure, I knew it was a mistake, but they didn't advertise the mistake or the correction until weeks later, so I figured it didn't matter. I can't believe that the kidnapping or Earl's murder has anything to do with that stuff, though. It's ancient history."

Bill nodded. "I don't know if it's related, either, but you and Earl are the common denominators. The fact that it makes no sense to you is a good sign. Maybe you've grown up some." He took a deep breath. "Don't be too sure there isn't some connection with all this, though." He paused. "That bull meant a lot to me, but he could never mean more to me than you. Can you believe that?" He looked away for a moment.

"What hurt most was knowing you lied and continued to spin the lies instead of coming to me. We could have stopped those crooks, then. Now, there's too much water under that bridge. Have they blackmailed you ever since then?"

Beau shook his head. "You might remember, I stopped riding the big circuit after Loco died. The necropsy showed the overdose, and I was terrified I'd be convicted of killing him. Then you lost the insurance money, and the rumors circulated that you had something to do with it. I couldn't fess up at that point – it seemed like too much to be forgiven for. And I'd have gone to jail as well as been banned from the circuit. When I started riding the charity circuit, there wasn't much reason for them to bother me. I was washed up."

Bill got to his feet and shook his head. "I hope you'll learn this: the truth is always the best option. I'm saddened by your judgment and sorely hurt by your lies and what they've done to this family. But I love you more than all of that. Now, you need to tell Jeremiah the truth about you and his mother. She doesn't deserve his anger, and he doesn't deserve to grow up believing lies."

The guard opened the door as Beau got to his feet. "I don't know, Dad. His opinion of me means more to me than yours does. He won't think much of me if I tell him I cheated on Faith because she gave my sons too much attention."

****

Denny saw the overhead signs for Atlanta, Georgia, and knew

he'd missed the exit that would take him back home to Chattanooga. It had been nearly five years since he'd made the trip, but with all the family buried around Morgan, Scott, and Cumberland counties, there hadn't seemed much reason to make the trip. Truth be told, though, he missed the peace of the Appalachian Valley.

He was tired. A different kind of tired than he'd ever known before. He'd heard on the radio that the boys had been found and he was glad to hear that. He was an only child, but if he'd had a sibling, he'd have wanted a twin. Sherri's stepsons were good boys and would grow up to be fine men. He knew it. He was sorry he'd gotten tangled up in Earl's scheme, but then again, Earl could put a hurtin' on a man who didn't do what he was told. He'd learned that the hard way over the years of traveling the circuit. And, he was looking out for Sherri, too. She was a nice lady. Lousy taste in men, but then being raised in foster homes probably didn't help much.

He'd tossed both of his phones in different trash bins along the way between Gainesville and Macon. He didn't want to be part of the whole mess anymore. There wouldn't be any big payday, only a boatload of trouble and jail time, he was sure. Getting lost in the mountains seemed like a good idea.

The news reports hadn't said anything about Sherri, so he hoped she'd gotten away, too. And the dead kidnapper had to be Earl, so the unpleasant question in his mind for over eighty miles was, who killed him—or did he shoot himself?

Earl had cleaned guns while drunk a million times, so it probably wasn't an accident. The news wasn't giving out any information at all.

He spotted a highway sign telling weary travelers that just up ahead, there was a Motel 8, a clean room, and an all-night diner. He'd get some chow, a shower, and rest, then make an early start in the morning. He had some backtracking to do, but it wouldn't be too bad.

Besides, he didn't have any particular schedule to keep. He just knew, somehow, that it was time to get back home.

CHAPTER SIXTEEN

Moving Ahead

"Miss Faith, you're doing beautifully. I think you're ready to retire this walker any day now. We're sure going to miss you, but you need to continue your exercises at home," her occupational therapist said after putting Faith through an intense session.

Faith couldn't help but grin like a five-year-old on Christmas morning. "You have all been wonderful to me, but I will not miss you . . . Well, I will miss you but not this place. I couldn't be happier to hear those words."

Her therapist laughed. "We're all so relieved to hear that your sons are okay. Let's get you checked out, and you'll be on your way with your hunky beau."

Faith glanced at Scott and felt her face get hot when he winked at her. She made the final appointment with the hospital to see her neurosurgeon for release and tucked the card into the tiny cross-carry purse slung across her chest.

With confidence, she shuttled the walker along, knowing she'd now be able to make the stop at the woodworking shop outside of town to select a cane. Scott had wanted to buy one for her weeks ago, but then, just out of the hospital, she wasn't sure she'd ever get to this point.

She stood on her own two feet while Scott folded and tucked the walker in the back seat of his Explorer and then opened her door.

"How do you feel about lunch?"

She looked at him, and her heart skipped a beat. His quiet confidence was calming, his gray eyes like the beacon of a peaceful harbor. *I've fallen for this guy big time.*

"Sure! I'm starving," she said, hoping that the lump growing in her throat would let her eat. He was such a good man, and at the very least, he deserved her to be honest with him. She'd tossed and turned most of the night thinking about him. "My treat, too," she said as she buckled her seatbelt.

He laughed. "I don't think so. We are celebrating your progress, lady. Now, what do you feel like eating? Barbecue? Seafood? Steak?"

"How about we eat at Adam's Rib on Thirteenth Ave? Food's always good, there."

"As my lady wishes," Scott said with a smile. He pulled into the late morning traffic. "My folks are driving in from Asheville next week. I'd like you and the boys to meet them. They're nice people, as parents go, at least."

Faith stifled a sigh and looked out her open window. His parents? Yikes! "I'd love to meet them, but I'm pretty concerned about Jeremiah's attitude these days. Maybe we can introduce the boys later – I have no idea what to do about J. I don't want to stress him out any more than he already is, but I don't want to lose us, either."

Scott drove two blocks and stopped at another red light. "I see. Well, you won't lose me over your kids. I'll never ask you to choose, I promise. But I understand your concerns. You sound a lot like most other parents with teenagers I've heard."

"I hate that I don't know what to do – would you have any

ideas, maybe? Did you rebel when you were his age? Maybe when we're not under such security, and he isn't feeling so victimized, he'll be less antagonistic. Maybe all this will go away by itself."

Scott smiled. "Maybe it will. I don't know."

She sighed. "I'm terrified I'll do the wrong thing. Well, actually, everything terrifies me some days. I used to think I could handle anything and most days, I don't feel like I can handle anything past brushing my teeth. Pull the covers up and just pray to feel better."

Scott reached over and brushed her wrist with his fingers. "Listen, someone nearly killing you with a bowie knife would be more than a lifetime's worth of trauma. You only lived by the grace of God, in my opinion. Then someone kidnaps your kids? You've got unreasonably high expectations for yourself, babe. Naps are highly underrated in my opinion."

They drove the next four blocks without a red light, and Faith pointed out the green and red UF truck. Scott turned in and parked. "I don't know about that, but your sons aren't the first or only ones to survive a divorce. And it may not go away until Jeremiah is in his twenties – then you'll be the smarter one again." He smiled at her, then winked. "We'll figure it out. I'm not willing to give up on Jeremiah or us."

When Scott opened the back door to remove the walker, Faith turned to him. "Leave it. I'll just lean on you. It will be nice to be free of that thing just for a little while."

He closed the door and held hers so she could get out, then put out his elbow so she could loop her arm through his. "You can lean on me all you like. Please don't worry yourself sick, Faith. It won't help your healing, and it won't help your sons."

She looked up at him, and her breath caught in her chest. For a long moment, their gaze locked, and for Faith, the world stood still. There was hunger, love, promises she didn't dare jump into right now. But maybe it would be all right to stay in Neverland for just another couple of hours. Then she'd be a grownup again.

She broke the trance and turned him toward the door. "Let's go celebrate the morning, how about that? Hope would tell me to let tomorrow take care of itself."

"Smart woman, your sister."

Once seated and their orders placed, Scott settled his elbows on the table and steepled his long fingers. "So, catch me up on things. I've been working so much I feel like we haven't talked in forever. What's the progress on the kidnappers? Anything solid yet?"

Faith sighed. "Alachua County and the FDLE are working on it – I hear from the sheriff's office every other day. They're looking for Beau's wife as a person of interest since she placed the bait call to the boys and can't be accounted for in over a week. It looks like she left Texas about the same time Beau did. Did he know about it? I think probably not, but the investigators don't know. They think Beau killed Earl because of the boys, but I know Beau didn't kill anyone. I don't think he has it in him. I really don't. He might have beat the guy bloody – something I'd have done if I had the chance – but he didn't shoot anyone. He carried that gun for snakes, mostly."

The waitress brought their sweet teas, silverware, and a fresh roll of paper towels for the table, then vanished again.

"Wasn't there another man, too? Any more information on him?" Scott asked.

"Yeah, the boys call him Cowboy. The guy wore a big hat with a bandanna over his face. Bowlegged as they come, I guess, so the boys gave him that nickname. He's the one that punched Isiah in the nose and broke it, so he's a strange character to almost knock out a kid and then loosen his bindings later. I'm not complaining, mind you. It's just strange."

Scott took a long sip of tea before replying. "Maybe he punched Isiah to save him – or save himself. They were in the truck with Earl when that happened, so maybe it was an act, something Earl expected Cowboy to do. Or maybe he thought if Isiah kept making a scene, Earl might kill him then and there."

Faith shuttered. "I guess that's possible. The lawmen are almost one-hundred-percent sure that these guys are not professionals at this and that it was a personal vendetta against Beau, so that's why they're still pursuing the angle that Beau killed Earl."

"What's Beau say in all of this? Have you gone to see him?"

She shook her head. "His sister visited yesterday, and his father took Jeremiah today. I don't see anything useful coming out of my visiting him, though I'd have brought the boys out if Bill couldn't do it." She took a drink, then continued. "Beau told Mary Lou that he knew Earl from the rodeo circuit, but they didn't have any history. She didn't buy it, but she didn't press it, either. Bill's been pretty quiet at the table, but I'm sure his heart is breaking for his family."

Scott nodded. "Gotta be hard. For you all. Please remember I'm only a phone call away if you want to talk. I'll stay away for a few weeks if you think that will help ease Jeremiah's concerns, but I'm not kidding about not giving up. I think we can work this out – all of us – once this investigation is over."

Their food arrived, and Scott thanked the waitress. Faith looked at him a long time before nodding. She wasn't sure she deserved such a good man, but she wasn't going to run him off. "Why don't you say the blessing and we'll eat. I want to be home when Bill and Jeremiah get back. I suspect J is going to want to talk to me, and it's time we had that difficult conversation."

Scott took her hands in his. "Amen to that, babe."

****

"How are you doing, son?" his Grandfather asked when he had the truck heading south on 301 towards home. "You're pretty quiet."

"I'm okay, G'daddy. I feel better now. I'm worried about Dad, that's all. He shouldn't be in there. And Sherri shouldn't have done this to us, either." He looked out the window. "Are we going to make things worse by giving the deputy those bullets we found?"

His grandfather shook his head. "They probably fell out of his truck when he first arrived and went to talk to your mother. I'm not entirely sure they have anything to do with this case, so maybe we don't need to turn them in. Everyone knows it was your dad's gun and ammo that killed Earl, the important question is who fired that gun?"

Jeremiah looked at him. "But you said we have to tell the truth. Maybe they can find something on them that will help Dad."

They drove in silence for a few minutes before his grandfather smiled a little bit. "You're absolutely right. I'm not thinking straight. We'll give them to the deputy tomorrow and pray that they help your father." He focused on the road and the building rush hour traffic.

Jeremiah stared out the window. Would those bullets help convince authorities that his Dad was innocent or give them more evidence to prove he wasn't? *Man, nothing is easy these days.*

When they pulled into the long drive at Blessing Farm, Scott's truck was parked down at the trucking company office.

Great. "Looks like Mom is back. Can you leave me here?" Jeremiah asked.

His grandfather stopped near the house. "I'll be back in a few minutes. Why don't you pour us some sweet tea?"

"Sure. Thanks." Jeremiah undid his seatbelt and opened the door. "I hope that Scott guy isn't staying. My mother's getting pretty attached to him."

Before he could get out, Bill stopped him. "Son, your mom is smart, attractive, and has been through a lot, especially this past year. Maybe Scott is who she wants to move on with. She and your father will never get back together. They aren't even good for each other – too different, I suspect. You should give Scott a chance – you might like him if you retire that chip on your shoulder."

Jeremiah answered with a snort. "They won't get back together if she's involved with a hero, that's for sure." He started the close the door, then pulled it open again. "Thanks for taking me, G'daddy. I hope we don't have to go back."

****

Beau met Jack in the booth a little after eight o'clock. *Now what? He doesn't look like he's got good news.* "Counselor! What brings you out this late at night?"

Jack dropped his heavy, worn leather case on the chair and shook Beau's hand. "I might have some good news, so I thought I'd stop on my way home."

It's about time. "You lawyers work more hours than a rancher does. So, what is it? I'd love some good news, especially after seeing Jeremiah today."

"How'd that go? Was he okay?"

No, he was not okay. He was visiting his father in jail instead of being in school. Beau took a deep breath and sighed.

"He shouldn't have come—and I don't want him coming back. My father thinks he's doing the right thing, but he put a load of pain on that boy."

Jack cleared his throat. "Life has got pain, Beau. Faith tells me the boys will be driving shortly. You're going to authorize them to get behind the wheel of a three-ton killing machine, so they'd better not be children because children have no business driving. Your son experienced something that might prove to be a life-changing day for him."

"He's had too many of those lately if you ask me. Okay, enough with the lecture. I'm worn out. What's the good news?"

"The Amazing Grace truckers spotted your wife at an area truck stop this afternoon. There's an official all-points bulletin out for her truck. They located the car rental company where Earl got the truck. Looks like he rented a Jeep, too, from another agency. Neither is back in yet, but they aren't due back until tomorrow."

Beau could not wipe the smile off his face. "This is the best news I've heard since the boys returned." He got to his feet. "Thanks, Jack. I appreciate you letting me know. Do you know when I go for the arraignment hearing?"

"Three days. Even if they pick up Sherri, that isn't a guarantee you'll walk, you know. But I think we can get bail with so much circumstantial evidence. It's going to be hefty, though. Are you going to be able to raise that much? It'll be cash, not bond—I'm almost sure of that."

"No. And Dad and Mom will pay your legal bill, but they aren't going to pay my bail. They think I'm better off in here – or at least that's what my father said today."

Jack got to his feet and picked up his case. "Well, we have a few days to figure it out. Get some rest and stay out of trouble."

As Beau walked along the concrete corridor back to his bunk, he forced his chin up, shoulders back. He sure as hell wasn't going to let anyone know how much he felt like crying. Three more days.

What if they don't catch Sherri? What if they do and she didn't do this?

CHAPTER SEVENTEEN

End and Beginnings

The Georgia State Patrol officer was out of Troop C and was four hours into his twelve when dispatch sent him to the Motel 8 just off the Interstate. An older property, it was clean and well-kept, the parking lot nearly full when he pulled up and parked in front of the motel office.

Inside, a woman rocked back and forth on a faded red armchair, sobbing for all she was worth. A harried desk clerk pushing eighty years old with dark circles below his rheumy blue eyes stood behind the polished reservation desk. The trooper strode to the counter, keeping tabs on the woman from the corner of his eye.

"Sir? Can you tell me what's going on?"

The older gentleman nodded, then pointed to the woman in the chair. "Tina went over to clean room twenty-four. He was supposed to check out this morning, but it's not uncommon for people to leave their keys on the bureau when they leave, so we didn't know if he'd gone or not. When the man didn't answer her knock, she went in. He was dead on the bed, just like he is now."

"What time was that, sir?"

"About an hour ago. Little before ten."

"I need to speak with Tina, but I need to see the room first."

They marched the five-hundred feet or so and stopped in front of the door sporting the number twenty-four.

"What's been touched, do you know?"

The clerk shook his head. "Tina said she didn't touch the body. She said she could just tell he wasn't breathing anymore. So, she touched the lock, doorknob, maybe the doorjamb, but that's it. She came running into the office so fast she wasn't breathing too good herself."

"Thank you. I'll meet you in the office. Let me call the medical examiner's office and some backup. Someone will come to get your statements and make arrangements for your fingerprints."

Fifteen minutes later, another GSP car pulled up, quickly followed by a car from Atlanta PD.

The Atlanta officer listened, then nodded. "The ME is on his way. If you'd get the statements and contact information of the two in the office, that would be a help."

"Want me to give you a handwritten report or send it to the system?" the trooper asked.

"File it in the system. I can access it there. Thanks."

The trooper nodded, handed Atlanta his card, then left the room and walked back to the office. He spoke with the clerk first.

"How did John Doe register and when?"

The clerk pulled up the record on his computer. "He came in last night around ten o'clock. Paid cash for one night. The name he gave was Dennis Carson." He showed the trooper the entry.

"Did you take his license by any chance? Get his vehicle information?"

The clerk shook his head. "If he'd paid with a card I would have, but since he paid cash and it was late, I gave him a key, a bottle of water, and wished him good night."

Tina told pretty much the same story that the clerk had told. The trooper collected and confirmed the contact information for both, thanked them, and closed his tablet.

The clerk called a cab to take Tina home to her husband, and the trooper returned to his car to file the requested information. In forty minutes he notified dispatch he was available for another call.

Mr. Dennis Carson, age undetermined, had probably died of natural causes. The ME would find the man's identification, give it to Atlanta PD, and they'd notify next of kin. The trooper got orders to move to I75 to assist with a multi-vehicle accident.

He hoped there was no fatality involved.

****

Sherri crossed into Mississippi well after dark with a long day on the road behind her. She speed-dialed Denny's number for the hundredth time, sighed, then tossed her cell phone over her shoulder into the back seat. The truth was glaring.

"Obviously, you've dumped your phone somewhere," she said to the darkness. "Left me on my own." She sighed. "I hope you're safe. I wish I was safe."

She was truly alone, just like when she was a kid. The memory made her sad. The other kids had laughed at her, stolen her clothes, taunted her about being a throw-away. But once she was sixteen and on her own, she'd decided she'd do the throwing away from then on – and that's precisely what she'd done. So, why was she so damned lonely? Why did it even matter?

And why Earl had gotten so stupid and selfish at the worst possible time, she had no idea. But if she had to do what she'd done again, she would. Killing those boys was not going to happen if she could help it.

Tonight, she was too tired and hungry to care much about anything. A glance in the mirror made her gasp. She looked pretty ragged with dark bags under her eyes and her hair going in every direction.

She spotted the highway signs for a rest area and mentally prepared for spending the night in the back seat. She'd stop for a takeout breakfast first thing, and when she got into Texas tomorrow, she'd dump the truck at the airport, get a room and rest a day. Then, off to Mexico.

She glanced at the locked glove box where her new identity was tucked safely inside a brand-new passport.

She parked at the bathroom building, grabbed her Dollar Store bag of essentials, and locked herself in the handicapped stall. Hair and teeth brushed, and as washed up as she could manage, she returned to the Ford and moved it, so she was parked between two big rigs. The truck wouldn't get spotted back there, even if anyone was looking for her. No sense getting careless but no sense being paranoid, either.

She locked the door, climbed into the back seat, and pulled Earl's ranch coat over her. His High Country cologne enveloped her, and she swallowed around the lump in her throat. She wondered how Beau was doing. Was he home with his sons or still in jail wishing her all sorts of bad things? In hindsight, maybe Beau wasn't all that bad a guy.

She sniffed. At least she had money on her now. Her engagement and wedding rings hadn't brought much, but pawn shops were like that. *Seven-hundred dollars ain't going that far.*

She felt some of the exhaustion leave her shoulders. "That's a dollar a mile," she whispered.

****

The ME pulled a wallet out of the back pocket of Denny's jeans and handed it to the Atlanta police officer on scene. "He passed early this morning, around midnight, I'm thinking. Get a better time with the autopsy. Maybe you can find his next of kin from something in there. Do you know which car is his? Might be something in there to help, too."

The officer shook his head. "Clerk didn't take that information, but we'll know soon – after we get the other vehicle owners identified. The clerk said there were only a half-dozen rooms booked for more than one night."

The ME nodded. "Well, let me get him ready for transport, and we'll get out of here. Good luck, Lieutenant."

"Thanks. I think I'm probably going to need it. Be sure to copy all the agencies when you get your report done, okay?"

The Lieutenant stepped outside the room and pulled the door shut behind him. Was there someone waiting at home for Dennis to return? If so, they'd be calling around later in the day looking for him and hoping that the police and hospitals hadn't seen him.

How often had they gotten these cases closed over the years with some stroke of dumb luck? He hoped for any kind of luck– dumb or otherwise. He planned to wait another few minutes, see what vehicles remained in the lot, and then clear those with the clerk's records.

He'd just settled into the driver's seat of his patrol car when dispatched called. "Go ahead. This is one-oh-nine," he replied.

"Are you still at the motel with the John Doe?"

"Affirmative. Ready to roll out in maybe twenty minutes. The ME has it from here. And we've got an ID."

"We just received an interstate APB. Any chance there might be a forest green 2007 Jeep Wrangler rental in that parking lot somewhere? It's a hardtop, has Maryland plates on it."

He felt the adrenaline kick in. "I don't know, but I'll take a look. Any word on why we're looking for it?"

"Standby, 109." The interior of the car was silent except for his breathing. Then the radio squelched again. "Abduction of two boys in Alachua County. Boys recovered, two perps at large. Four days ago."

The lieutenant shook his head. "I'll look, but chances are they're a lot further away than Georgia by now." He signed off, started the engine, and rolled down his window. The morning was warming up some.

He drove slowly past room twenty-four. A Jeep Wrangler

was easy enough to spot or should be, but everyone seemed to be driving mini-vans, pickup trucks, and SUVs, so he had to look carefully. As he rounded the back of the motel, he spotted it.

He approached it as he clicked the mike on his shoulder and called it in. It was the only Jeep Wrangler hardtop in the lot with Maryland tags, and the rental bar code on the window made it easy to confirm.

He parked his car and got out to take a closer look. He glanced inside the windows. It looked so neat it might have just left the rental lot instead of almost a week ago. A neatly-folded fawn-colored coat lay on the passenger seat along with two bottles of spring water and an opened box of beef jerky.

"Well, well, well. Let's go find Mr. Carson's keys and see if this belongs to him."

****

"Thank you for a fairy-tale afternoon, Scott," Faith said as they parked outside the Amazing Grace garage. "I know you won't want to hear this, but thank you so much for saving my life, for your friendship, for being a rock in my life. I haven't given you much in return except chaos."

He placed two fingers under her chin and turned her face towards his. She froze as he leaned forward to kiss her. A tender but firm kiss, one that sent a shiver through her from top to bottom. Then he leaned his forehead against hers.

"I'm glad I was here for your chaos. I couldn't imagine going through what you and your family have been through, but I didn't do all that much. Took a few days off to hold your hand." He chuckled. "But I wanted to be with you. I still want to be with you. I hope there's a long-term me and you – and the boys, of course."

She sighed. Beau had been an adrenaline rush but never a comfortable man to be around. Scott was, among other things, easy to be with. Steady, kind, fun, and reliable. Maybe she'd gotten wiser as she'd aged; gained more than some wrinkles, a couple of pounds, and a few gray hairs.

"I hope so, too. But remember, I have to respect the boys and all they've gone through since I was attacked. I don't think Isiah has any objections to me having a boyfriend, but J certainly has indicated that. And, with Gracie coming back, I'll have to decide if we stay here or go back to Texas, I guess. We haven't dealt with any of those things."

Scott straightened and searched her face with his gaze. He tucked a wisp of hair behind her ear and cupped her cheek in his palm. "I'm a patient man, and that's for real. We'll work it out or at least give it a darned good try. You let me know if I've overstepped at any time, fair enough? Always be honest with me, that's all I ask."

She nodded in reply, her heart beating so fast she thought Scott could probably see it. "I will always be honest, I promise," she finally whispered.

Scott got out of the truck, walked to her door and opened it, then helped her to the ground. She steadied herself by holding the door handle while he reached into the back seat and pulled out her walker. He lifted a brow as if to ask whether he should open it for her. She shook her head.

"Let's dazzle them with my amazing progress and the handsome man who made it all possible." She laughed while he rolled his eyes and turned just a bit pink in the face.

"I only responded to the First Aid call, my love. You happened to be the beautiful victim, already safe from the bad guy when I arrived."

"Uh-huh. Bleeding to death and paralyzed, but safe. You did the right things to keep me alive and repairable. That makes you my hero. You'll never talk me out of it, so just get used to it."

"Can we just keep it our secret, then? I'm not heroic. Just doing my job, ma'am," he said with a slight bow.

"I do not promise anything on that one. But we'd better get inside, or Hope is going to bust a gasket trying to figure out what we're doing out here and why we aren't coming inside."

"Gads. I don't want to get on the bad side of your older sister – that could mean big trouble for me. Never know when I'll need an ally." He offered her his arm, and she gladly accepted.

****

Faith walked carefully through the door to the trucking company office unassisted. She cleared her throat and waited for Hope to look up. She knew Scott wasn't more than two steps behind her, though.

"Look at you! You're walking all on your own! That's a major miracle, Sis," gushed Hope, getting to her feet so fast her chair crashed into the wall behind her. "So, I take it you're a physical therapy graduate, now?" She walked around the front of her desk and pulled the client chair out so Faith could sit – and she did.

Faith couldn't contain the joy she felt. The grin on her face almost hurt, but she didn't care. For the first time since the boys disappeared, she felt a genuine relief and happiness that was like shedding a hundred-pound backpack. She looked over her shoulder.

"Scott, come sit a few minutes. You don't have to go yet, do you?"

He placed the folded walker against the wall and sat across from her. Hope sat with one hip perched on the desktop.

"I'm not on until eight, so I've got a little time." He looked at Hope. "You should've seen her. She nearly ran that last fifty feet this afternoon. Just a few weeks ago, she thought it would never happen. She's got to pace herself, though. It won't be good if she falls and messes up all that spinal surgery they did."

Hope nodded. "We'll make sure to keep an eye on her. Her sister Grace is due here next week – says she's got a surprise for us all – but she'll keep Faith on the straight and narrow."

Faith's heart nearly burst. How much good news could a woman get in a day? "Grace is finally coming home! Do you know what the surprise is? Did she give you a hint? I hope she didn't get married or something – but of course, Grace wouldn't get married, right? Not without telling us–"

"Steady, Faith, steady," Hope interrupted her. "Grace didn't give me any hints other than to say she was driving cross-country with a friend. I don't know if that's a male friend or a female friend, but who cares? She's coming home safe and sound."

"Isiah is going to be so excited. Those two have an extraordinary bond. I think it's the math and science aptitude. They're like kindred spirits in some ways," Faith said. She turned to Scott. "This is so exciting. You'll get to meet Grace next week, and then I'll get to meet your family. And no wheelchairs in sight. No sign of kidnappers lurking about. I feel like I've won the million-dollar lottery."

"Family? Scott, your family is coming to Florida? I hope our drama is put to bed before they arrive so we can make a dinner or picnic or pig roast or something special to celebrate all the good news."

Scott nodded. "We'll play it by ear, okay? My parents aren't on a timetable. They just mentioned they'd be in the area in a couple of weeks. So, they will be, but I don't know exactly when."

"I'm hoping that Jack can get Beau's case thrown out at the arraignment. If so, we're well on our way to getting this all behind us. Any more news on the Sherri sighting?" Faith asked her sister.

Before Hope could answer, heavy steps came up the stairs, and Bill stood in the doorway.

Faith turned and noticed the fatigue that had aged him so much in the past few days. "Bill? Where's Jeremiah? Is everything okay?" she asked, feeling her joy ebb away.

He nodded. "Everything went fine. He's up at the house – I think he just needs a little time to himself. Jails are intimidating places, especially for a youngster. He did fine, though."

She stifled a sigh. He'd been through so much, but he wouldn't back down, so what could she do?

"And how's Beau doing? He holding up?" she asked.

"He is. As you know, jail isn't an entirely new experience for him, but never for anything this serious, of course. He's concerned and angry and sorry and all kinds of things. He told me to thank you for letting J visit today."

Either Bill's covering for him, or my ex-husband is growing up. He'd never thanked her for anything that she could remember. She slowly got to her feet and offered Bill her chair. "If Hope doesn't need me here, I'll go on up to the house and check on the boys. Isiah should be home in a few minutes."

Scott got to his feet as well. "I'll take your walker up to the house for you, and then I've got to get going, too. I'm on duty until Friday, so I'll call when I can," he said to Faith.

He nodded toward Bill and Hope. "Just stay positive for Beau. This situation is messy for sure, but it's going to work out okay."

He helped Faith navigate the stairs down to the garage floor, then held the door for her to precede him outside. In silence, they walked to the front-porch door. She stopped and turned around.

She wrapped her arms around his neck and hugged him close. "You be safe, you hear me? Grace would never forgive me if she didn't get to know you better."

He kissed the tip of her nose and then her lips, just a light brush. "If your son looks out the doorway and sees us making out in the yard, he's not likely to think any better of me. I love you. Take good care of yourself."

Without waiting for a reply, he jogged to his pickup, then pulled away.

Hmmm. "I love you, too," she whispered to the wind.

CHAPTER EIGHTEEN

Guess We'll See

Faith let herself into the house and listened for Jeremiah after she shut the front door. Either her son was in the kitchen, or they had a gigantic rodent running loose in there. She navigated through the dining room and was almost to the kitchen when he pushed through the swinging doors.

"Hey, Mom," he said around the nacho chips he had stuffed in his mouth. He took a second look at her. "Hey, no, walker? That's great. Congratulations." He gave her a brief hug and moved to walk past her.

"J, come sit with me for a minute or two, would you? I want to hear how your dad's doing." She took a breath. *Lord, please help me help my son.* "And, whatever else is on your mind."

He shuffled into the kitchen behind her but didn't sit. She went to the refrigerator and pulled out the sweet tea, then poured a glass. "Want some?"

He shook his head.

"So, how did your visit go?"

He shrugged. "Okay, I guess. He didn't kill that guy, Mom. He shouldn't be in that place."

"I know, J. The law is working hard to find the real killer, and they will. We have to be patient."

He snorted. "Easy for you to say – you aren't in jail. And you don't care about him, anyway."

She sighed, then smiled, knowing that smile was probably pretty thin. "That's not true. I can't tell you what's going on, only that when you and your brother were kidnapped, I have never been so scared in my whole life. The idea of you being out of my life forever was such pain I thought I'd die with it. And I've seen your father in a lot of situations over the years, but I've never seen him as terrified of anything as he was of losing you.

"Please try to understand that we may not be married anymore, but we both love you more than life itself. I wouldn't have you to love if I hadn't married your father, and I will always be thankful for that. And I'm still thankful that he's a good dad to you and that your grandparents love us so much."

He looked up at her, his eyes filled with tears. "Then why did you leave? Why did you take us away from him? He still loves you. I know he does."

Oh, dear God, please help me. How do I tell him the truth without crushing him? "J, I didn't leave your father. I–"

"Your father left your mother the first time when you two mites were little more than six months old. Being a father scared him to death," Bill said from the dining room doorway.

****

Faith, Hope, Margaret Ann, and Eddie bustled around the kitchen. The aroma of fresh fried chicken and just-baked biscuits filled the air.

Faith pulled the dishes down from the cabinet, then sat at the counter and glanced out the window to be sure the boys were still in the corral with the horses.

They put Tempe and Magna through figure eights, doing cut

maneuvers around the barrels Hope had set up for them. Both had an excellent command of their mounts, but Jeremiah had an intensity that Isiah didn't have. Isiah let Magna do the work while J worked Tempe hard. Not unlike how his father rode a horse.

She smiled at the memory of how special she'd felt when Beau singled her out of the rodeo Grand Parade. Dressed in her red silk shirt with the mother of pearl buttons, her white hat, and bright blue jeans, she'd carried the American Flag proudly, sitting atop a steel-black stallion who seemed to share telepathy with her. Maybe she should have paid more attention to the horse when it pushed Beau away as he first approached them.

"What do you hear from the sheriff?" Eddie asked her, bringing her back to the moment.

"She says we're in the clear. If the kidnappers were coming back, it would have been before now. I'm going to have to work on this overprotectiveness, though. I find myself fighting panic throughout the day when they're out of my sight."

"I'm no psychiatrist, but I'd think that was pretty normal given the year you've had. If I can help with anything, please let me know." He glanced toward Hope and Margaret Ann, still busy at the stove. "When Grace gets back, I'd like to speak with the two of you, okay? Something I've got planned for Hope, but I want your input first."

Her heart skipped a beat. Was Hope going to get her happily ever after at last? Faith couldn't help wishing for that – she was a romantic at heart. She reached out and stopped Eddie's retreat.

"Would it have anything to do with a special ring and a ceremony?" she whispered.

He looked over his shoulder, then leaned toward her, his voice low. "It might, but then it might not, too." With a short laugh, he sauntered through the doorway to the dining room carrying the plates.

Well, that wasn't fair, she thought. But she'd bet a hundred dollars that was what he wanted to talk to them about. He'd always loved her sister. She knew that. And she knew how sorry he was for the mess he'd made of their high school romance. She rested her chin in her right hand. Hope would accept his proposal, wouldn't she? *If I have anything to say about it, she will!*

Bill and Annie came in through the screen door on the back porch. Faith thought her former mother-in-law looked frail. *Please, Lord, if she's not well, heal her. If she's hurting for her son, please comfort her.* She got to her feet to give them both a hug.

"Thank you for taking care of Jeremiah today," she said to Bill as she wrapped her arms around him and rested her cheek against his chest. She felt his heartbeat and breathed in the fresh scent of his pressed white shirt. She squeezed, then let him go.

Annie grasped her by her forearms and beamed. "Look at you! Walking all on your own! We knew you would make a full recovery, and we're so delighted. Please don't overdo things, though. You don't want to hurt something you've just gotten working, right?"

Faith laughed and held up two fingers in a Girl Scout salute. "Yes, ma'am, I promise."

"That Jeremiah sits a horse just like his daddy does," Annie said with a sad smile. "But Isiah rides more like Bill. Sort of a horse whisperer in Isiah."

Hope interrupted. "Dinner will be ready in about twenty minutes. Bill, would you tell the boys to put up the horses and get cleaned up? Annie, come in and have a glass of wine. Margaret Ann brought something new for us to try in honor of Faith's graduation."

Faith looked around the kitchen and let the warmth of family and friends soak into her soul. What a difference a week could make. For the hundredth time today, she thanked God that she was planning a future and not funerals.

Eddie helped Hope and Faith clear the table while the boys went to the bunkhouse with Bill and Annie, allegedly to get their homework done.

When he'd placed the last of the dishes on the counter by the sink, he put his arms around Hope and held her a moment. It was his favorite place to be – holding Hope. Then he kissed the top of her head and reluctantly stepped away.

"Forgive me, but I've got to get back to the office. Something's come up, and I've got a late meeting tonight."

Hope looked curious, a look he loved on her with her upturned nose and just the slightest frown between her green eyes. But he'd promised to keep this meeting confidential. Even from her.

"Well, good luck," she said. "Call me when you can."

"You bet. Thanks for a great dinner. Sleep well."

Once in his car and out on Main Street, his phone chirped. He glanced at the number and answered it, putting it on speaker.

"I'm on my way, Jack. Be there in about thirty minutes."

"That's okay. I'm bringing someone, and we'll be a few minutes late. It seems that Beau's father has been busy calling in his own kind of markers. Special Agent Pinto has an interesting proposition for us to hear."

"I'll bet they want to make Beau an offer that he can't refuse."

Jack laughed. "Something like that."

****

"Hey, J, was the jail terrible? How was Dad? Aren't you going to fill me in at all?" Isiah asked him as they walked from the bunkhouse to the farmhouse.

Though Isiah couldn't see him in the dark, Jeremiah shrugged. How could he explain how sick he'd felt going there? How glad was he to get outside in the air again?

He scuffed his boots in the dirt. "It's clean and bright and looks like it's taken care of really good, but it's still jail. I couldn't hug him or anything, but it was okay. I told him you were tied up. He didn't want me there, but I'm glad I went."

"I'm glad you went, too. He's going to be out of there soon, isn't he?"

"I think so. Maybe a few more days. That's what G'daddy says, anyway. I left the two of them talking, and I waited in the lobby. The place is creepy as hell, though."

Isiah groaned. "Can't be any creepier than that cabin, J. Are you having dreams about that place?"

Jeremiah slowed his pace. "No, I'm dreaming about Dad going to prison for a murder he didn't do. But you had it way worse in that cabin than me, Ike. Your nose was broken. You could barely breathe, had nothing for the pain, and spent most of your time on the floor." He stopped and turned to Isiah. "Do you need to go talk to somebody? Maybe the Reverend would be good to talk to. He seems to be a good listener, and he wouldn't tell anybody what you tell him."

Isiah looked away for a long moment, then clapped his hand on his brother's shoulder to move them forward. "Nah, I'll just give it some time and see if they go away. If not, then maybe I'll do that. But don't say anything to Mom, okay? She's got enough on her mind already."

"Yeah, like the new love of her life, Scott. I just know this is going to get messy. I don't need two fathers, especially one that doesn't know a thing about horses. I think I'll head back to Texas with Dad when he goes home. Now that Mom's walking okay, she doesn't need us both here."

Isiah was quiet for a few yards. "I can't even imagine my life without you, J. Guess maybe I'll be doing that, too. You think Mom will let us go if that's what we want?"

CHAPTER NINETEEN

Listening

Beau sat in the interview room at the jail and waited for Jack and Eddie to get there. He kept his hands tucked under his thighs to keep from biting his cuticles, which were already a bloody mess. Why had he thought coming to Florida was a good idea?

Now what? Can't be anything good. But I didn't kill Earl, so I don't have anything to worry about, right? He almost laughed at himself. There were more than a few innocent men doing time in prison, he was sure.

He shifted and leaned his elbows on the table. Then he rested his head in his left hand and sighed. His parents were the religious ones, even his sister and, of course, Faith, but it wasn't for him. No. He figured a man made his way the best he could.

How's that working out for you?

Whoa – who was that? The guard stood outside the booth, facing away from him, his broad shoulders as solid as a wall.

Beau shook his head. *Great. Now I hear voices.*

Actually–you're listening. That's different from hearing.

He jumped to his feet and glanced around again as his heart raced. This time the guard was watching him, reached for the door, and opened it.

"Everything okay? You look like you've seen a ghost."

Beau shook his head to clear it. "Are there ghosts in here? I mean, have you seen or heard ghosts in here, yourself?"

The guard raised one brow but didn't laugh at him. "Not me. You hear things you don't understand?"

"Nah, I'm just askin' to pass the time. You brought up the ghosts."

The guard stood well over six feet tall with black hair cut close and dark blue eyes that seemed to look right through Beau. "Son, maybe you're hearing from the Almighty. He can get your attention in a place like this. Nowhere to run if you know what I mean."

Beau looked at him for a long time. "You wouldn't know a guy named Shawn Jackson, would you? Sounds like something he'd say."

"Reverend Shawn Jackson? Sure, I know him. Good man. He comes out here once a week and leads a Bible study for the inmates."

"My sons tell me he did time here. That true?"

The guard closed the door behind him and motioned for Beau to take a seat. "He did. His sentence was sixty days plus a thousand hours of community service."

"So, what's a man of the cloth doing in a place like this?" Beau asked.

"We're all human. Make mistakes. Gotta own those mistakes, pay the price, make changes, start over. Even preachers."

Beau thought about that as he studied his hands. *We all make mistakes.* It's the owning it part that's not for everyone. He looked at the guard again.

"When's he coming back?"

The big man narrowed his eyes. "I'll put your name on his list." At that moment, his radio squelched, and he acknowledged. "Your lawyers are checked in. Be here in a minute."

****

Beau sat across from Jack and Eddie, and they exchanged pleasantries. At least Jack didn't ask him how his day was going. If he had, Beau thought he'd probably scream in his face. *You're letting me rot in here while somebody plays games with my life.* The days were endless and monotonous, and he could almost cry for wanting to be home on his ranch, riding the range with his horses.

"I had a visit from the FBI today," Jack said, looking Beau in the eye. "Can you think of any reason why they might be interested in you?"

Beau swallowed hard. The FBI? *Me? Couldn't be . . ..* "No, sir, can't think of any reason."

The two attorneys waited in silence. As Beau studied them, he realized they'd both make damned good poker players. He, on the other hand, was a lousy one. He sighed.

"You going to let me in on the secret? What was Earl into, anyway? I keep telling you that I didn't even know the guy well. Been years since our paths crossed."

"This is apparently only peripherally about Earl. A group of rodeo fixers owned you, didn't they?"

Beau jumped to his feet. "No, sir. That's a damned lie. Nobody owns me. Nobody has ever owned me." *How did they find out? And why?*

Eddie motioned for him to retake his seat. "You need to control your mouth and your temper in here. Do you need more trouble? We didn't come to jerk you around, but time's up for you. You need to quit running us around, too. The FBI has something on you, and they hold the out-of-jail card."

Eddie looked Beau in the eye. "What was the real reason you came here? And I don't want any crap about you not being able to live without Faith."

Beau felt the air go out of the little room. He shook his head. "I left Faith for Sherri years ago. A big mistake. Anyway, I thought Sherri loved me, but I guess she just wanted money. Things started to go sour with her about six months ago, but I promised myself I wouldn't make the same mistakes and give up. However, she's been running through money like an open dam, so I can barely pay the vet and feed bills right now.

"I found out through my boys that Faith and her sisters were coming into some gas and oil money from their dad. So, I came here to borrow some of that mineral rights money. But the boys got kidnapped before I could talk her through this, and here I am."

Eddie shook his head. "That's a real sad story, Beau. I guess you weren't updated. Those mineral rights the girls were left are only worth a few dollars a year. W. Virginia taxes on it exceed the proceeds by about a dollar. The land leases belong to so many beneficiaries that there just isn't much for any of them."

Now, if that isn't just my luck. "Guess there won't be any help from that quarter, then." And maybe it's just as well.

Jack looked at Eddie, who nodded. "You ever borrow money from the wrong people?" Jack asked.

Beau shrugged. "Yeah, I got into the sharks a time or two. Nothing too serious. I paid them back."

"Do you remember a clown going missing at the Wichita rodeo? Six years ago. A funny guy by the name of Gypsy?" Jack glanced at the report in his folder. "He was supposed to be your clown that day."

"The clowns switch around, and on the travel circuit, we don't know all of them anyway. I remember a clown by that name – his real name was Maury or Maurice or something like that. Rodeo lasted three days, Maury called out sick on day three. It's a rough business, especially for the clowns. I didn't think much of it."

"Did you win at that rodeo?" Jack asked.

"Nope. Got pretty busted up at that one." Beau shook his head and shrugged. "I had to borrow some money to get my horse and me back home."

"Who'd you borrow it from?"

"There's always someone willing to loan you money for outrageous interest. They aren't that hard to find, even if the rodeos run them off the grounds. The sharks just set up in town or out at the campground, the bars, wherever. Someone always knows how to find 'em."

Eddie cleared his throat. "That where Earl comes in? That's the problem, right? Sometimes people can't pay it back, right, Beau? Then they get hurt. Or killed."

"Whoa," Beau said, putting his hands in the air. "I never hurt anyone. I never killed anyone. I don't know who does that stuff, but it isn't me." *This is getting worse by the minute. Oh, God, are we back to Dad's bull?* "Who is Maury?" he asked.

"Was is the proper tense," Eddie continued. "He was found dead, dumped down by the railyards. He'd been stomped to death. He was an undercover FBI agent working to shut down a specific loan shark ring. One tied to influencing rodeo results."

"What, like fixing a fight? How do I figure into all this? I didn't even know the guy was dead."

"Not too long after that, a prize bull was killed. A very expensive bull. Remember that, Beau?" asked Jack.

"Of course, I remember that. And it explains everything," he said, shaking his head, his heart pounding so hard in his chest he was sure it would jump out onto the table. *Sonofa—*

"My father talks about forgiveness and love and all that stuff, but it's crap. Bull crap, to be exact. He went to the FBI about this, didn't he? Had to see me punished for it."

Jack stared at him. "No, sir. The FBI went to him, not the other way around. Apparently, over a year ago. After the lawsuit, your father was given the security tapes for the night his bull went down. He told the FBI that he burned them. Made him sick to watch them. Said he couldn't tell who was coming out of that stall, anyway." Jack leaned forward. "You don't know who it was, do you, Beau?"

Beau looked around, fighting the urge to sob like a brokenhearted child. The silence in the small room closed in on him. The two men working to help him sat expressionless on their side of the table. He put his head down on the table, his hands clasped in his lap.

Are you still listening? Who can hide in secret places so that I cannot see them?

"Dad—" he whispered as years of guilt and shame surfaced and threatened to drown him with tears. He let them come.

****

"Grace, is this really you?" Faith screeched into the phone. "I'm so happy to hear your voice! Hope said you're on your way home – that's not changing, right?"

She listened a moment, barely able to be still. "Wait, let me put you on the speaker, okay? I'm in the office cleaning up some paperwork for Hope." She clicked the speaker button and set the phone back in the cradle. "Okay, talk to me! Tell me what's going on."

Grace's laugh lightened Faith's heart. She'd missed her sister more than she could put into words, but then as twins, they often didn't need words anyway.

"When will you be here?" Faith asked. She could hardly wait to put her arms around Grace again.

"We're in Tuscon, Arizona, right now. I'm making a couple of stops, but I should be there in about three days. I'll call if we'll be any later. Are you walking again all on your own?"

Faith wrapped her arms around herself. "Yes, or at least, mostly. I'm not walking unassisted very far, and the doctor warned me about being in crowds and things without my walker or, at the very least, my cane. I still topple over easy if I bump into things, but I'm doing well. Eddie and Hope are moving my bedroom back upstairs sometime tomorrow.

"Things are getting back to normal, or at least for me physically, they are. The boys will start seeing a trauma therapist on Monday. That should be interesting."

"How are they doing? I hated like hell not being there for you and them. I feel like I let you all down."

"What were you supposed to do?" Faith asked, resting her hip on the desk. "Just up and leave a foreign country and thumb your way home? 'Gee, General, I gotta get home' – The boys and I understand. Everyone does. We're so excited you'll be here soon, nothing else matters, anyway. We've all missed you a lot. The boys will be fine, in time. I'm not so sure I will be, though. Some days the fear just sits in my chest like a late-night pint of cookie dough ice cream, and I want to crawl under the bedcovers and stay there. When I had walking to focus on, I could pretend my life was just about getting my mobility back, but now that's done, the fear's just crashing around me. Hope has to pry the boys away from me to drive them to school. I've become obsessed with keeping us safe."

Grace cleared her throat and hesitated a moment. "Fear is a healthy thing, honey. It ensures our survival. And with you attacked like you were, and then the boys abducted, your reaction seems pretty normal. It's when the fear stops you from everyday living, or you hurt people because you're so fearful, that's when it's out of control. It sounds to me like you might be dealing with some PTSD. Maybe you should see someone, too. How about Shawn Jackson? He knows a lot about living with fear. And he probably knows some professionals in the area, too."

Maybe that isn't a bad idea, Faith thought. Did she want her sons to grow up not knowing how to handle their fear? "I thought PTSD was what soldiers got from being at war."

"It is, but psychologists now feel that anyone who has been through a traumatic event can also exhibit those symptoms. Rape victims, carjacking victims, domestic violence victims, all sorts of people are walking around with it. Soldiers aren't the only ones that experience horrific traumas. Your experience would qualify. And Scott's probably been there, too, being a first responder."

My Scott? Afraid? Angry? She felt foolish for not considering his life in those terms, but Grace was right. "When you get home, we'll talk some more, okay? And I'll call Reverend Jackson tomorrow if I can." She got back to her feet and pulled Hope's chair to the desk. "So, what's this surprise?"

"It won't be a surprise if I tell you, silly. You'll see for yourself soon enough. I think you'll be happy about it, though. It'll be good for everyone." Grace spoke to someone on her end of the phone, then said, "Is the bunkhouse suitable for occupation? I'd rather work out of there for the short term, at least," she said.

Faith's heart rate picked up, and she felt tears building. "Oh Grace, did you and Craig get married without me? I was so sure you'd wait to get back—"

"Whoa, kiddo. I didn't marry Craig or anyone else. I like the guy, but we haven't even talked about that kind of thing. He flew out to meet me and help move my stuff, which was great – and he's driving at the moment – but I've got to get settled, and all of us have some planning to do, don't we?"

"Oh, yes, of course, we do. I'm sorry, I jumped the gun. I've just missed you so much. It feels like it's been months since you left, but I guess it's only been a few weeks, hasn't it?"

"Well, nineteen days, to be exact. But tell me how the boys are doing. Isiah? Jeremiah? Are they sleeping and going to school all right? No fights? Eating, okay?"

Faith smiled as she remembered her conversation in the kitchen earlier. "Hope says they're eating us out of house and home, which is okay with everyone." She sobered. "Isiah isn't sleeping all that well, though, and Jeremiah is almost rude when he and I talk. Bill and Annie are here, but Mary Lou flew home this morning.

"The boys are stressed, that's for sure. Shawn stops by

every other day, and they work the horses almost every day for Hope, so that burns up some energy and brings some routine and normalcy, I hope. But schoolwork is all caught up, and they seem to be okay with that. Not incredibly happy about being chauffeured to school, at least not J."

"I'm sure," Grace said. "Mr. Independence. Well, they are going to adjust for a while. My surprise will help everyone, I think. That makes me happy." She paused. "Hope said the sheriff is closing in on the kidnappers – that's got to make you feel better."

"So far, it's all theories, I think. For goodness sake, they've got Beau in jail for killing one of them. That didn't happen."

"You sure about that?" Grace asked.

Faith felt like she'd been sucker-punched. "Of course, I'm sure. His wife is tangled up in it and some rodeo clown, they think. Piecing it together, little at a time. Two of our drivers saw Sherri a day ago, but nothing since then. I hope they catch her so I can say my piece to her face."

"Well, make sure you wait until I get back. If nothing else, I can help you bury the body."

"Gracie!" Faith exclaimed. Then she began to laugh harder than she'd laughed in many months. Only Grace could help restore balance to her life with a joke.

"See? You haven't lost your sense of humor. It's only a little dented. Hey, are Hope and Eddie making wedding plans by any chance? He asked to see me as soon as I get home," Grace asked.

"I don't know for sure, but I hope so. A wedding here at the farm? Wouldn't that be exciting? I pray for them every night. She so deserves her own happy life, doesn't she?"

"Absolutely. But don't say anything to her about this. I suspect it's on the lowdown, so we'll just wait until Eddie tips his hand, okay? How is she doing after this terrifying and exhausting week? Is she all right?"

"You know Hope. She doesn't say much, but she looked ghastly for the first few days. We probably all did until the boys got home safe. She and Eddie were an amazing team, making sure food, cots, messages all got handled. They even helped the law find them. And of course, Margaret Ann was here, ever the stalwart helper nobody messed with. I'm so blessed to have you all in my life."

"And we're blessed to have you still too, Sis. I have to go. We're stopping for coffee and a bathroom break. Call me if you need me, okay? And don't worry about the fear. We'll get it under control."

Faith exhaled and put a broad smile on her face so Grace would hear it in her voice. "I'm counting on it. Drive safe, and I'll see you soon."

She ended the call, picked up the last of the delivery orders, and put them on the scanner. As they processed out of the feeder, she looked around the office. The boys would calm down, Beau would be freed, and then what? Would she lose her sons to the rodeo as she had her husband? As Annie had almost lost Bill?

CHAPTER TWENTY

Helping Others

Faith leaned on her three-footed cane and took a deep breath. She looked around the restricted area past Bill's back. The Alachua County Sheriff's Office entry area was bright and clean, and she was sure she smelled lavender in the room. Well, if she ignored the bulletproof glass with the tiny speaker in the window, friendly might be how she'd describe it. The chairs were comfortable looking, though few. I sure hope we don't have to wait too long, or my heart may explode.

"The sheriff will be out in a few minutes," the clerk said. His green and white badge said his name was M. Swanson. "Just have a seat, okay? You'll be meeting in that room behind you."

Bill placed his hand gently on Faith's arm, and she welcomed the touch. "You doing okay? You're looking pretty pale for a Florida gal," he said with a chuckle.

She was sure that everyone could see her trembling, so she

sat in the seat against the wall near the water cooler. She took another deep breath and tried to smile at him.

"I'm doing the best I can. I've been having some . . . issues," she said. "Everything makes me so fearful – it's embarrassing, to be honest."

Bill squeezed her shoulder and sat beside her. He leaned forward and rested his elbows on his knees. "I'm sorry, Faith. Would it help to say a short prayer? Annie says that helps her a lot."

"You mean besides the one I'm constantly praying, like 'Please don't let me pass out cold and embarrass myself?'" she asked. Her face felt as though it was frozen in place. She clutched her hands in her lap and looked Bill in the eye.

"Does Annie have this kind of panic, too?" She glanced at the closed door to their right, then back at Bill. "When did that start?"

"She battled it alone for years before I left the rodeo, but I didn't know about it until my last one." He cleared his throat. "That was when I decided I'd ridden my last one. The woman who was my world, the anchor and strength of our family, was having a nervous breakdown when I walked through the kitchen door that night. She was hiding under the kitchen table and had no idea who I was or why I was there. When I reassured her about who I was, she said Bill was dead, killed by a bull."

He shook his head slowly. "I found out later that someone had called her from the hospital and left her a message – or part of one – on the answering machine. Her fears filled in what the call didn't tell her. Unfortunately, she didn't get the part that told her I was going to be late coming home – not that I was dead."

"I'm so sorry, Bill. You don't need to talk about this – it's obvious that it still hurts you."

He shook his head and covered her hands with one of his. "I want you to understand. You aren't alone in how you're feeling. And Beau isn't the only one who put the damned rodeo first in his life – he learned that from me. Talk to Annie. She's asked if I thought she should talk to you, but she didn't want to cause you any embarrassment or pain."

Faith's laugh sounded tinny and strained to her own ears. "I'm stronger than this. I wasn't raised to be a baby or a weepy girl who runs from everything, but lately, running – or hiding–is the first thing that comes to mind." She sighed. Then she realized she almost felt better admitting the fact that she was feeling so out of control.

The door opened, and the sheriff came into the room. She outstretched her right hand to indicate they should convene in the meeting room.

"Faith, it's good to see you under such improved circumstances," the sheriff said. "And who is this?"

"I'm Bill Walker, Sheriff. Faith's –"

"Yes, sir," the sheriff interrupted. "We have your son in custody as a person of interest in the death of Earl Foster, I believe."

"Yes, ma'am," he replied. "We brought you something that we found on the farm. Just outside the door to the trucking company building, near the big azalea bush."

Faith reached into her purse, pulled out a plastic sandwich bag with the bullets in it, and pushed them across the table to the sheriff. "The boys found these a couple of days ago. They don't belong to any of us. We hope they might help you with your investigation – you know, to find the right killer – because Beau didn't do it."

The sheriff took the bag by the top and carefully maneuvered it beside her left hand. "Thank you for this. Maybe they'll be helpful." She pulled a blank pad of paper from the credenza beside the table, used the pen from her suit jacket pocket, and made a note. Then she looked at Faith. "How many people handled these?"

Faith looked at Bill, and he shrugged. "Jeremiah came into the house with them in his hand. He dropped them into my palm. I slid them into the bag. Faith put the bag in her purse. So, three of us, I guess."

The sheriff nodded. "Okay, we've got all of your prints on file. If we find any others, we'll know who handled them when they got dropped. Nice job." The sheriff smiled at them.

Then she put the pen aside. "I know how hard this has been on you. Both of you. All of you. We are not as sure as we once were that Beau is the person we are after, but we have to follow the evidence. He'll be with us another couple of days until his arraignment hearing, unless we determine we cannot proceed. The FBI will be here tomorrow to speak with him."

The FBI? Oh, dear Lord, this is worse than I imagined, Faith thought. Please, please let this be good news instead of bad, she silently prayed.

"What does the FBI want with Beau?" she asked.

"His attorney and Mr. Highspring were here last night. Perhaps they can fill in the blanks for you. It isn't my place to do that." She made another note on the pad. "I do recommend, however, that you encourage him to help them if he can. It's important for him, for you and a wide range of people you'll never meet."

Faith nodded, though her heart began beating so fiercely she thought the sheriff could see it. "I don't understand what's happening, but I spent a whole marriage encouraging Beau to do the right things. What's one more attempt?"

The sheriff let Faith's comment linger in the room a moment, then asked, "Is there anything else that my department or I can do for you today?"

"No, ma'am, we just wanted to get you these bullets," said Bill. "I promised the boys we'd turn them in, and you seemed like the one to take them for us. Thank you for your time."

Faith willed herself to stay calm, though her hands were trembling. She tucked them into her lap. "And I wanted to thank you personally for the support you've given us through all of this. Your deputies have been wonderful, and I'm sure you've had more to do than call me to check in every few days. Just – thank you."

The sheriff got to her feet and smiled. "You can feel safer now, I'm sure of it, Faith. But if anything alarms you, please let us know right away. Nothing is too small or silly that you can't let us know. Remember that." She waited while Faith got to her feet. "We also have the victim's advocates to help you all – they can help you with referrals too if you need that. How are your twins doing?"

"They begin seeing a trauma therapist on Monday, but all things considered, I think they're doing pretty well. Probably better than I am."

The sheriff's smile warmed Faith inside. "You get to a trauma counselor, too. Did you see one when you were in rehab?"

Faith shook her head. "No, I thought I was handling things okay. But almost losing the boys—"

"I understand. Had one of my kids run away from home one time for three weeks. Knowing what I know about human trafficking, you can bet I was out of my mind with worry. It ended well, but so often it doesn't, and no mother worth anything at all wouldn't be beside herself if her kids went missing."

"Did you . . . get a counselor?" Faith asked her.

"I did. It made a big difference for my family and me. Get

someone who specializes in trauma treatment, okay? You are not crazy, and you are not losing your mind." She reached forward and wrapped an arm around Faith's shoulder and gave her a one-armed hug.

She escorted them back to the waiting area and then turned to the right to return to her office somewhere behind that solid steel door.

Faith watched her go and heard the door locks snap into place. *I may never feel safe again, but I'm sure going to give it a try.*

****

"Do you know anything about the FBI, Bill? What could they possibly want with Beau?" Faith asked when they were well on their way back to Merciful. She could see his profile by the light of the dash lights, and his mouth was tense, like a man with something on his mind.

"I might," he said. "I'd rather not say much else about that right now. But Beau is in a position to help people he knows and cares about. The professional rodeo circuit is like family, too."

She sighed. Was it only hours ago that she'd felt so happy in Scott's company? Since her return home from the hospital, her sense of time had become warped as though she'd entered a time-travel chamber. The days were either a hundred hours or ten minutes long.

"I know you two have had your disagreements, but Beau isn't evil or mean-spirited. If he knows something, I'm sure he'll help," she said.

"He isn't mean, but he's selfish, Faith. He's often put himself ahead of everyone else. You, his mother, his sons. He'll help others if he can help himself, that's for sure. Let's just pray that this time he'll learn that life is a lot more precious and powerful when we're looking out for others, not just ourselves."

She sat in silence and digested Bill's words. Lord, please help us. Help Beau. Help Bill. Help my boys— and Lord, help me.

****

Faith was in the kitchen, making red velvet cupcakes when the boys arrived home from school at three-thirty. She knew the smell of food would bring them right to her, so she was staring at the door when they burst into the room.

"Well, how was school today? she asked as she whisked the vanilla into the froth. "Have you heard about your project grade, Ike?"

"We got a B on it, but it should have been an A. Everyone was totally blown away with our video. The teacher thought it was a little short, but we were happy with it."

"I'm glad I don't have to do that stuff," Jeremiah said, coming around the counter next to Faith, where he attempted to nab a naked cupcake.

She swatted the back of his hand with the nylon spatula. "You just wait until they're frosted, young man. You have time to go muck out the horse stalls – if you don't take too long, you can have one after that."

"Oh, Mom, don't tell me about ruining my dinner, okay? I'm almost sixteen, and I think if I want to eat dessert first, I should be able to – at least once in a while," Jeremiah said.

"We're going out to dinner with your grandparents, so we won't eat until later tonight. You can get your chores and your homework done – with dessert – before we go."

Isiah shoved his brother at the shoulder, and the two went out the back door and through the porch at a good speed. Faith turned and watched them through the kitchen window, welcoming a smile to her face. The boys were going to be all right. They had a future and the tools to make it a good one. *And, if I have anything to say about it, so do I.*

She turned back to the window. Isiah was only a stride or two behind Jeremiah by the time they reached the barn door. She could see more differences in them this past year. Jeremiah was almost two inches taller, and Isiah ten pounds heavier. Isiah loved wrestling and basketball, but also science and math. Jeremiah loved all things outdoors, including football, but not much in the way of academics. They'd talked about him going into vocational training after high school, and he was currently in a welding program he liked. Isiah planned to speak with his Aunt Grace about engineering.

Faith jumped at a thumping on the front door. She wiped her sticky hands on a wet paper towel and made her way into the dining room. She peeked out the window and saw Shawn Jackson's car.

"Come on in, Reverend," she called before she began her slow walk back to the kitchen.

"Smells wonderful in here," he said. "Margaret Ann around here somewhere?" he asked with a smile.

Faith laughed and put her hands on her hips. "No, she is not. She went to Atlanta for a couple of days. Be back before Grace gets home. You are smelling my mom's recipe for red velvet cupcakes."

He winked at her. "Well, they smell mighty good, I must say. Any ready?" he asked.

"Want coffee to go with them or sweet tea?"

"Coffee if you have it made. Don't go to any trouble."

"No trouble. I just started a small pot for me – it'll be ready in a few minutes. I've got to get these frosted. So, what can I do for you, Reverend?"

He went to the stove and pulled the percolator off the burner, then took two mugs out of the cabinet and filled them.

"I haven't checked on you yet, and I'm wondering if there's anything I can do for you besides prayers." He placed her cup next to his on the counter. "Come sit with me for a few minutes," he said.

Faith glanced up at the ceiling. *Now you're sending help straight to our kitchen?* She made her way to the stool and settled next to him.

"How did you know?" she asked, stirring her coffee to cool it.

"I have an advantage from the pulpit, you know. I get to see who's in church, who's listening, who's fidgeting, or who's sitting still. It's my job to notice who looks like they might be hurting or struggling with something. I appreciated you being in church with Hope last Sunday, but you look like you're in a lot of emotional pain. Want to talk about it?"

Do I? Can I bear to hear myself whine about the anxiety attacks? About how unfair all this feels?

Shawn sat quietly and drank his coffee, seeming to enjoy the beauty out the back window. "The boys seem to be doing pretty well — at least at the center they seem good. Your Isiah has the patience of Job when he's mentoring the younger ones in math. I wish I had that gift. I can do the basics, but he's got a real gift. I hope he wants to be a teacher someday."

"Engineer, I think. Or at least, that's what he thinks he'd like to do. Yes, he's the patient one. Jeremiah isn't so strong in that arena, but he's young yet."

The Reverent shrugged. "He's good with the kids at the center. He just has different interests than his brother. That's probably healthy. Did you and Grace have all the same interests and talents?"

"No, not at all. I liked dolls and my horses — and making things with my hands, but I wasn't good at math. Grace was a whiz with math, and she was a much fiercer competitor with the horses. She used to behead my dolls if I left one in her room." Faith laughed.

"Ouch," Shawn said with a laugh. He stood, walked to the other side of the counter, and shifted the cupcakes and icing to where he and Faith were sitting. "Let's get these frosted so I can have one before the boys beat me to them."

As they each worked on that task, Faith relaxed in the comfortable silence. She stayed focused on getting the frosting perfectly aligned with the edges of the cupcake. When she'd finished six of them, she asked, "How do I go on with my life without this panic that threatens to suffocate me sometimes?"

"Good question. The simple answer is that we have to trust the Lord to give us strength and everything else we need. That's what faith is. We must believe He'll keep his promise to us about never leaving us alone. About always hearing our cries for help." He reached for another cupcake to frost.

"I've found in my own experience, that having faith is anything but easy. It's a spiritual muscle that takes time and a lot of practice to develop," he said. "We've got to exercise it to strengthen it. Probably best to handle each moment and each day as it comes. You know that I let my fears get so bad that I ended up in prison for my bad decisions. Truth is, when we rely on ourselves, we'll fail every time."

Faith felt the familiar constriction in her throat, the tears building quickly. She took a deep breath. "But what do I do when it comes on?" she asked on a sob. "See? We can't even have this conversation without me becoming a blubbering mess."

Shawn put down his knife and turned to face her. "The priest who came to see us in jail gave me some great advice. He suggested that every time I felt overwhelmed by anything – guilt, fear, worry – that I simply prayed, 'Come Holy Spirit Come' and then take a deep breath, and allow the Lord to take over. I've used it a lot. But now it's my immediate go-to, and the situation calms right down. He told me that fear could not stay in the presence of faith, so I have a new plaque in my office that says, 'Faith over fear' and that reminds me that confidence comes from the Lord, not fear."

She felt her breathing slow and the urge to cry let go. She got to her feet. The boys were making their way back to the house though not at warp speed.

"Thank you, Shawn. Maybe you can suggest a counselor I can talk to for a while? I'll do more praying and try to trust more, I promise, but maybe until I get there, I can find someone to work with me."

He unwrapped the red velvet treat and nodded. "I will do that – I'll make some calls tonight. Reading the Good Word won't hurt, either. That's where God's promises are and if we don't see them – and there are many – we don't know about them. We have to learn that when we ask Him to be first in our life, He won't abandon us to anything – not even fear."

Jeremiah burst through the door first. "Hey, Reverend Jackson! What are you doing here?"

The Reverend laughed. "I came by for one of your mom's great cupcakes."

Isiah reached around Faith for a cupcake while Jeremiah stayed near the door and watched them.

"Are you here to help my mom?" Jeremiah asked.

Faith almost gasped but caught herself and held her tongue, keeping her hands busy rearranging the items that cluttered the countertop.

"I'd be happy to help your mother with whatever I can. What's she need help with, son?"

Jeremiah shrugged and moved toward the rack of treats. "She's pretty uptight these days. Thought maybe you were here to tell her to chill out."

"You don't think she's got good reason to be a bit worried right now?" Shawn asked.

Isiah opened his mouth to speak, but Shawn held up his hand. "Jeremiah, what's on your mind? You don't sound so chilled yourself."

"I'm fine, Reverend. Ready to get back to Texas, that's all."

Faith managed not to let her jaw drop open. *Out of the mouths of babes . . ..*

CHAPTER TWENTY-ONE

Crossroads

Faith was stretched out on the sofa in the parlor reading when she heard the click of a key in the lock.

"Hope?" she called, hearing the keys clink into the bowl on the table in the hall. The pocket doors slid open, and her sister stepped through.

"How are you doing, Sis?" Hope asked. "Have a good day?"

Faith nodded and exhaled. "Talked to Grace, had a visit from Shawn Jackson, and had dinner with Bill and Annie. Boys were okay—mostly, anyway—I think they're anxious about seeing the trauma specialist tomorrow."

"Well," Hope replied, "that's understandable. And they'll be fine. How are you doing with that?"

"I'll go with them, of course. I'm focused on getting the boys through this with the least amount of fear and damage possible." She picked up her tea and took a sip. "I asked the Reverend for a recommendation for me. I need to move on, and I don't know how to do that. Grace thinks I have PTSD."

Hope smiled. "That's our sister for you – hits the nail on the head every time, that one. But we can work with PTSD– there's so much more information on it now than even five years ago. How is Grace progressing on her trip back here?"

She filled Hope in on the tentative route home and got slowly to her feet. "I can't wait to see her! Anyway, how was your day with Eddie?"

"I've got mixed feelings about this house hunting, as you know. But he's got a point. If we're going to have a life together, having our own house will be a part of that. He's not insisting on that, of course, but you and the boys can make good use of this great old house, and you don't need your older sister haunting it."

Faith sat back down. *There's no way to say this except straight out.* "We may not be staying after all, even though I don't want to go back. But Jeremiah is ready to go back to Texas as soon as Beau is released, and if the boys want to go back, then we'll all go back. Not to Beau, of course, but I haven't been gone so long that I can't get my welding business up and running again. At least until the boys graduate high school and get out on their own."

Hope sat quietly for a long time. When she looked at Faith, she smiled. "Whatever you decide, you know I'll support it. But I want you just to consider that perhaps the boys are now where they can make decisions that aren't necessarily dependent on you. You have to decide what you want, too. You have custody, of course, but you never beat Beau up about that. And, for that reason, the boys have a relationship with him. Does Isiah want to go back, too?"

She shrugged. "He hasn't mentioned it, but I can't see him letting his brother go back without him. They're different in many ways, but Isiah still thinks of himself as J's protector.

And I don't want to be so far away from either of them."

"But he thinks of himself as your protector, too, right?"

Faith nodded. "Exactly. And that's why I can't put him in the position to choose which of us to be with. That's not fair. In a few years, they'll be adults and off doing whatever they've decided to do, but that's still two or three years off. I want them to finish high school at the very least, and I can see them both going on with some sort of education. Isiah probably wants to do engineering or architecture, but J wants to go into animal husbandry or ranching, and they'll need degrees for that."

"They can go to college here in Florida as residents, too – don't forget that. And what about you and Scott? Isn't that getting serious? Will he go to Texas or wait for you here?"

"I don't know—I do want a relationship with him. He's such a good man. And he'd be a good influence on the boys, too. He says to take it a day at a time, and we'll find a way to work things out. He says they probably need paramedics in Texas, too." She smiled, remembering the kiss he'd given her after he said that.

"He's a keeper for sure, little sister! He's right though—no sense borrowing trouble. The Lord says to let tomorrow tend to itself." Hope sat and put an arm around Faith's shoulders. "Do you remember what happened when you and Grace were sixteen?"

"You mean besides you not letting us get our driving permits on our birthday?" Faith laughed as she remembered how angry Grace had been – and how relieved she'd been herself.

"It was Christmas Eve Day, you silly goose. We couldn't go until the following Monday. Jeesh. No, Daddy and I planned the big birthday party at the church that afternoon. After Mom's death, we wanted you to have something wonderful to remember for that birthday—and Christmas, too. Grace wouldn't come, remember? And what did you do?"

Faith closed her eyes and thought back to the days when she and Grace were almost inseparable. She smiled and glanced at Hope.

"I stayed here with her for about an hour, but when I couldn't talk her into going, I saddled Toro and went to the party."

"Why did you come without her? Do you remember?"

"I kept thinking that you and Daddy would be sad if we didn't come to the party you'd arranged just for us. We'd have ruined Christmas, too. Or that's what I thought. I think that's when I realized that Grace was going to do whatever she wanted to do, and it had nothing to do with me." She sighed. "It may have been the first time I understood that we were going to have different lives. Being an adult was going to be really hard."

Hope nodded, squeezed her shoulder and got to her feet. "And your boys will do the same. You all do whatever you have to do, but I'll miss you so very much if you leave. God will show us each the right things to do. Remember to listen for His guidance, okay?" Hope moved to the door.

"It's nice to have the reading room back, isn't it?" she asked as she looked at the sofa back in place, and the hospital bed gone.

"Goodnight and sleep well your first night back in your old room. If you need help getting up the stairs, just shout to me, okay?"

Faith again smiled. "I've always loved this room—memories of Daddy with his book and his pipe. And yes, it will be nice to sleep in my real bed. Go ahead to sleep – I'll be fine getting upstairs. And thanks, Hope. I love you."

"Mom?" Isiah whispered from his bedroom as Faith began to close her bedroom door. She moved across the hall and leaned in to see him. Jeremiah's soft snoring came from the upper bunk.

Isiah swung his pajama-clad legs to the floor and joined her. "Can we talk?"

She nodded, and they went to her room, then softly closed the door. She put the bedside lamp on.

"What's up, Ike?" she asked as she reached out to push a lock of hair off his face. They sat on the edge of her bed, side by side.

"Will you let us go back to Texas if J wants to go? Will you come with us?" he asked while looking at the floor.

She looked at the young man so rapidly growing up and yet still her precious child. The sensitive one. "I will. Your happiness means everything to me. Besides, I was only supposed to be here for a few months while you hung out with your father and grandparents this summer – things just didn't work out that way."

"Will that kill what you've got going with Scott?" he asked quietly.

She looked at him for a long moment. *Lord, how I love this child.* "I don't know. I think if what we have is strong enough to be permanent, then we'll find a way to work out the location stuff. It will take compromise and maybe some time, but it's not impossible."

"I don't want you to be sad anymore, Mom. You didn't deserve what that man did to you, and you've fought hard to get well. And you didn't deserve what Dad did to you, either. You should be happy. I think Scott makes you happy and I'm good with that. I don't need another dad or anything like that, but I like him."

"I am happy. Sometimes I struggle with –" she looked away from his wide-eyed hazel gaze. "Sometimes I'm scared, and I don't know how to stop it – can't always get it under control. I can't catch my breath. I can't clear my brain. It isn't about being happy or sad – it's sort of an uncontrollable fear-thing."

He got to his feet, then bent down and hugged her tight. "I kind of know what that is. I close my eyes and hear the gunshot, and I look for J and can't find him. My heart beats so hard that I think it's going to pop out of my body."

She returned his embrace. "I'm so sorry. I would do anything to take that away from you." She swallowed hard to keep the tears back. "I hope the trauma specialist can help you with that. That's why you're going, right?"

She felt him nod in agreement and let him go. He stepped back and looked hard at her. "Who's going to help you?"

"I'm working on that. I promise I'm going to get help, too. Tomorrow, I start." She smiled at him. "We'll get ourselves straightened out, you'll finish school, and then we'll figure out the residence question, okay? You boys can go for your Florida licenses in just a few weeks—if you want to, that is. Maybe you want Texas licenses instead. Either way, you boys driving on the road is plenty scary enough for me."

Isiah grinned at her. "We've been driving for years already, Mom. Road driving will be a piece of cake."

She winked at him. "Having a bull chase you in a battered ranch pickup truck is different from having a thousand multi-ton vehicles aimed at you on a daily basis. But you'll see for yourself, son of mine."

****

Sherri made it to San Antonio and still had nearly

three-hundred dollars in her pocket. She checked into the
Econo-Stay and booked a room for two nights. She wouldn't
stay for both, but it would give her time to relax, soak in
the tub, catch up on sleep, and have two good breakfasts
before she drove the last leg of her trip over the border and
into Mexico. And, to make a good plan. She stopped at the
Walmart outside of town to get some new clothes, some
toiletries, including hair color, scissors, and a new phone.
She'd given up any hope that Denny would call her, so she ran
hers over in the lot and tossed it into the Walmart dumpster
behind the store.

She turned on the television after soaking for nearly forty
minutes and crawled into the white-clad bed that promised a
night's rest beyond any other. *Anything has to be better than
sleeping in that truck –.*

She reached over to the light on the nightstand and shut
it off, then fluffed the pillows and allowed herself to sink
into them, thinking to stay awake long enough to see the
local weather and news – but she was sleepy. Her eyes closed
as the news team droned on about the San Antonia High
School football team's latest success.

"Tonight, we are asking viewers to look carefully at these
pictures of Sherri Duncan or Sherri Walker. Also, authorities
are asking for your help with any information on this man
who is believed to be Dennis Carson. Please call the hotline
number shown at the bottom of your screen. They are both
persons of interest regarding the abduction of two teenaged
boys in Florida last week. She is—"

She closed her eyes and fought back the tears. She was so
tired. *What a horrible mistake all of this has been.* Marrying
Beau, leaving him, getting involved with Earl – all of it. She
gathered her things from the bathroom, including the hair
color box, and tossed everything on the bed.

Then she wrapped it all in the extra shirt, undies, and stretch pants she'd bought and pushed the bundle into the bag.

She dashed back into the bathroom and swiped a fresh washcloth off the counter and began to wipe down everything she saw. *I'll be in Mexico in a couple of hours. A lousy hundred and sixty miles.* She stuffed the cloth in her pack and picked up her keys off the bed.

Damn. I have to get rid of this truck – it was due back two days ago. Even the borrowed license plates wouldn't help if she got stopped. She sat down on the mattress and hung her head. What would she do in Mexico? The whole plan had been based on having a lot of money and Earl. She couldn't even speak the language.

She pulled her wallet out of the backpack and worked the phony credit card out of the slot. Would it work? She could dump the truck at the airport, and with her new identity, she could still get away. Or maybe she should head for Canada where at least they spoke English.

She shook her head. No, she'd drop the truck off at the McAllen airport, get a room and then figure it all out. She looked around the room one last time, pulled the pack onto her shoulder, picked up her purse, and flicked the light switch down with her elbow. She opened the door and stepped outside, looked both ways, and walked on the sidewalk to the truck at a regular pace. So far, so good.

She opened the truck door, tossed in her things, then opened the driver's side door and climbed in. She turned on the truck and pushed the switch for the heat. She glanced toward the office and saw the clerk standing outside the office, speaking with an officer from the San Antonio PD. She needed to move and quickly. *Or maybe I need to sit tight and wait it out.* She was less than one hundred yards from

I35, and then she'd be on her way to freedom.

What do I do? Wait or run?

She slowly turned her head and glanced to the left. The SAPD car and the clerk were no longer in view. Whew, that was close. The relief was so great she almost cried with it. *I'll make it, yet.*

She waited another two minutes, put the truck into reverse, and left the lights off. She drove around the building and exited onto the highway, then got into the lane for I35, holding her breath as she spotted a San Antonio Police car sitting at the light across the intersection. She put on her signal, then made the turn to get on the interstate.

She hadn't gone a mile when she spotted flashing lights behind her, and it was obvious they were meant for her. The game was over. She signaled, pulled over to the shoulder of the highway, and waited. *What's taking him so long?* It was another two minutes before she watched the trooper's approach in her rear-view mirror. She opened the window.

"Good evening, officer. How can I help you?" she asked, turning to smile even as her dinner threatened to come up right there and then.

"You don't have your lights on, ma'am," he said as another trooper pulled in front of her truck.

"Oh, how silly of me. I'm tired, and I guess I just forgot. Thank you for letting me know."

He touched the brim of his hat with the first two fingers of his left hand. "May I see your license and registration, please?"

She had her new license in hand, but the registration wouldn't match. "I'm sorry. Here's my license, but I don't have the registration. My friend rented this for me, and I don't seem to have the paperwork."

The officer took her license, slipped it into his top breast pocket, and opened the driver's door for her. "Please shut off the vehicle, step out, and walk back to my car. I'm sure we can clear this up."

She got out of the truck and walked ahead of him. She was out of time and out of options. "Officer, I'm—"

"Please put your hands behind your back, ma'am, so that I can get you safely in the car. I do believe some folks in Florida want to speak with you. You are Sherri Duncan Walker, I believe?"

CHAPTER TWENTY-TWO

Out of the Valley

Faith glanced around the large picnic table on the back porch at all those gathered for the news. *Thank you, Lord, this is finally just about over.*

Eddie had called and asked everyone to meet before dinner. He was bringing Beau's attorney with him, and they finally had some news for everyone.

Bill and Annie sat side by side with their fingers intertwined. To Faith's right were the twins who were arguing over something to do with school, and Hope had just put lemonade and sweet tea on the table while Margaret Ann finished another batch of fried chicken in the kitchen.

Eddie gave Hope a quick hug when he and Jack came onto the porch. "Have a seat. This won't take too long. Jack and I want everyone to know what happened today."

Faith patted the seat on her left and moved a bit to the

right to make it possible for Hope to sit down. She linked her arm with Hope's and focused on her breath. The doctor said breathing was the key to beating the anxiety. *And I will beat it.*

Jack Edwards looked at the twins. "Boys, your father will be released from jail tomorrow. He's a free man."

Isiah and Jeremiah whooped and hollered for a good two minutes before Faith could get them to settle down again.

"They caught Sherri, then?" Isiah asked.

Jack nodded. "They did, though she's in Texas now, not in Florida. She's not fighting extradition, so she'll be back here tomorrow sometime." He looked at Faith, then the boys.

"Your father is working with the FBI to help them stop the people that Earl worked for. You're going to hear some things about your dad that won't sound good. He's going to tell you what he can when he gets here tomorrow, and that won't be easy for him, but he's doing the right thing now. Remember that, okay? We all make mistakes and we can all make amends."

Eddie nodded. "Faith, Hope, we thought it best that Beau talks with you here, but the FBI has a place for him to stay for a couple of weeks, and he needs to be there, nowhere else. They'll be providing you all protection while he's here. If his coming here causes you all too much stress, we can do it in the law office or even at the Sheriff's Office."

I can't believe I'll be happy to see him, but I will. Faith shook her head and smiled. *It is over, praise God.* "Here is fine, Eddie–as long as the family isn't at risk–but it sounds like that's covered. Jack, thank you for all you've done for my family. We appreciate the hours, the motions, and the rest of it." She looked over at Bill and Annie.

"And thank you for staying until this was settled – and

paying Jack's bill. Beau's incredibly fortunate to have all the support he's got from you. We all are. I hope he realizes that."

Bill nodded. "I think our son has learned valuable things." He looked at Jeremiah. "You and your brother mean the world to him, and he wants to be a good example for you. You be sure to learn, too."

"We will, G'daddy," Isiah said. He looked at Jack. "Will he have to wear one of those ankle monitors?"

"Until he's completed his initial services with the FBI, yes. He asked for it, so there will be no confusion or misunderstanding regarding his whereabouts during that time."

"Can we go see him wherever he's staying?" asked Jeremiah.

Jack smiled. "I'm sorry, son, that won't be possible. He's going to be making statements against some unfriendly people, so this protocol is for safety reasons—his and yours."

Faith's heart skipped a beat. She glanced around the table, then took a breath. "Is there any chance those people will come after us here? The boys at school?"

"We believe it's remote. In this case, we suspect the ring they've targeted is in trouble from more than one direction. The ringleader was running a rogue operation, so his boss is not happy, either. While the government wants to shut them down and protect people from being harmed by the loan sharks, they're more focused on inconveniencing enough of the underlings to make the whole thing unattractive to operate at all.

"The government will never stop it all, but in this case, some bigtime fraud and embezzlement charges are hanging over their heads. Beau isn't the only witness, but he's a particularly good one for what the FBI wants to do."

"What's a loan shark?" J asked Faith.

"It's someone who loans you money and demands a fast payback with extremely high interest. If people can't pay it back, they get hurt, killed, or used by the sharks to do bad things."

Annie spoke up. "In this case, your father paid them back the money he borrowed, but it's almost impossible to pay it back on time. Then they have something to hold over you to make you do things you wouldn't do."

"Oh," said Isiah, "I learned about some cases in our civics class like that. They go after pro athletes a lot because there's so much money involved in gambling on sports games and events."

"Exactly," said Jack. "And now, if you'll excuse me, I'll be heading back to Palatka. I've got to be in court at nine tomorrow morning."

The boys stood and reached out to shake Jack's hand as he walked past them. "Thanks again, sir," said Jeremiah. Again, Faith couldn't miss noticing how they'd matured these past few months.

Jack looked at them hard. "You're welcome. Keep in touch with me and let me know how you are doing, both of you. Just don't call me to get you out of jail – that will break your mother's heart. I think she's already had quite enough."

"Yes sir," they replied in unison.

****

The night was chilly, and Hope and Eddie sat on the wooden double swing Scott had hung for Faith on the front porch. The cicadas sang in the forest behind the property, and off to the south, an owl hooted almost non-stop as the day's light finally extinguished itself behind the trees. The smell of a wood fire tinged the air.

The porch door creaked, and Faith stepped out to join them. She sat on the top step and pulled her jacket tight across her chest. "It's gotten cool. It's so peaceful right now, isn't it?"

Hope settled into the crook of Eddie's arm and pulled her sweater closer, too. "It is. We sure got some great news today, didn't we? And how did your appointment go today?"

Faith smiled. Her sister was ever the mother in their relationship. And she thanked the Lord for that. "I'm very relieved that this is almost behind us, that's for sure. I haven't met Suzanna Kane in person yet, but she called me because Shawn asked her to, and we talked a long time. She's retired military, and she did three tours in the Middle East. She was with the VA in Lake City for five years, too. I learned a lot about PTSD today. Gracie was right. It's not just for soldiers."

"Will the doc want to see us, your cheering section? We may have to relearn things to help, too," Hope said.

Faith sighed. *This is what family is all about.* "She mentioned that it was possible. I told her you'd all be happy to come in. She was glad to know you won't mind doing that."

"Wait a minute," Eddie said, pulling Hope closer. "I don't have to go too, do I?"

Faith laughed. "Yes, you do, almost-brother-in-law. You're part of this family, so if you get a call, you're going, too." She shivered. "Suzanna said it might only be one or two sessions."

"Wait," Hope said, straightening away from Eddie's embrace. "Almost-brother-in-law?" She looked at Eddie with narrowed eyes. "How almost? Does my little sister know something I don't know?"

Eddie's hands went up in front of him as though fending off an attack. "Not at all. But we're looking for a house, aren't we? At some point, we're going to get married and move up the road, right? That's all she means. You'll be the one to set the date, not me, Honey. I promise."

Hope settled back against Eddie and winked at Faith. "Have you talked to Scott today?" she asked.

At the thought of his gentle gaze and patient smile, Faith smiled. "Oh yeah. He called me twice. Tomorrow he's going to the fire academy to help with training some new cadets, so he didn't want me worrying if he didn't call me until late. He knows how nervous I am about the boys starting their therapy tomorrow."

"I'm glad you liked your psychologist. I know the boys will do well, too. And Shawn and Margaret Ann are leading a morning prayer meeting just for our family tomorrow morning. With the Lord on high alert to all we need, I think we're going to be sitting pretty before you know it," Hope said.

Suddenly, Faith got a chill and shivered hard in her sweater. She got to her feet and leaned over to kiss Hope on the cheek. *What was that chill about? Beau? The boys? Scott? Grace?* She tried to shake it off. *Mom would have said someone had just walked over my grave . . ..*

"Good night, lovebirds," Faith said as she reached the porch door. *The Lord is my shepherd; I shall not fear . . . .*

****

Bill and Annie returned to the bunkhouse after the celebratory fried chicken dinner and turned on the television. He pulled their suitcases out of the closet and put them on the couch as Annie had asked. He took a silent breath, put on a smile, and turned to face his bride of almost fifty years.

"You sure you want to leave tomorrow?" he asked.

She wrinkled her nose, then smiled at him. "I am. Our work here is done, I think. There isn't anything we can't do for any of them from home, is there? Prayers and money are pretty portable commodities."

He laughed and pulled her into a bear-like hug. "You are such a magnificent woman, Annie Walker. I love you. You know that, right?"

Without releasing him, she nodded against his chest. "Well, you may be less enamored of me after driving Mary Lou's car all the way home. But it's time for us to get on with our lives."

She cleared her throat and squeezed him tight. "And me with my treatments, too. I have an appointment with the team on Tuesday morning."

Bill put Annie at arm's length and looked into her deep green eyes. How he'd prayed for her change of heart—prayed that she'd work with the doctors about the heart disease.

"Edna Anne, are you sure you want to do this? You were dead set against it when we left home. And you don't have to do it for me. Open heart surgery is no walk in the park from what we've been told." He looked away. "I sure hope to have you in my life for the rest of it," he said quietly.

She placed her palm on his right cheek. "I always have – and always will love you, Russell William Walker, but I'm doing this for me. And for our children and grandchildren. And because I've seen such tremendous courage and grit here with this family that I can't do anything else. If I don't give every day my absolute best effort, what will I say when I face the Good Lord?" She stood on tiptoes to kiss him. "Besides, it's all in God's hands no matter, right? So, I'll give Him the chance to fix this old ticker."

He blinked back tears and swallowed hard. Thank you,

Lord, he prayed as he pulled her to him again. She clutched him around the waist and held him tight as he silently sobbed with relief.

His son would come home a man of integrity, and his wife would fight for her life. Isn't the light of grace all that much brighter coming out of the dark valley?

CHAPTER TWENTY-THREE

Perspectives

"Hey, J, are you nervous about this stuff?" Isiah asked his brother as they sat in the school office, waiting for their mom to pick them up. His stomach was hatching butterflies by the hundreds, but his brother seemed almost unfazed. The office secretary smiled at them from the counter and then went back to her desk.

Jeremiah shrugged. "Nah, I don't know what the big deal is. We got away from them, right? We got home safe and unhurt – well, except for your nose, that is." He punched Isiah lightly on his upper arm. "Girls like that rugged look, Dad says. They'll be chasing you all over the place."

Yeah, right. Until they find out I almost throw up when someone comes up behind me. Isiah kept his voice low. "I had a horrible dream last night."

"Listen, Ike," J said, "these dreams are crazy. I told you, I'll never be so far away I can't get to you. Stop worrying."

He shifted on the bench, glanced out the office windows, and lowered his voice to a whisper.

"It wasn't about you, this time. It was Mom. She kept calling for me, and I was answering her, but she got further and further away and never heard me. I started running to her, and she kept going further away. Then I heard her crying–and I woke up."

"We're all okay, Ike. This stuff is going to go away, you'll see." Jeremiah looked around to be sure no one was listening to them.

"Look, don't give the shrink anything to work with, or we'll be doing this for the rest of our lives. Like that girl at the church. Jenny?"

Isiah swallowed hard. *Will the shrink think I'm crazy?* He was sure feeling a little crazy this past week. "Don't be mean, J. She can't help it–and she's nice enough. You have to admit she's had a pretty messed up life. At least our parents didn't kill each other – that has to be pretty horrible to live with."

Jeremiah nodded, then shrugged. "Yeah, in our case, it was only our step-mom trying to kill us. But Jenny's on so much medication she's a zombie. You want to live like that?"

Nope, absolutely not. "I'm hoping that talking might avoid all that. No pills or booze for me, buddy. Dad's life makes that pretty clear for me."

"Hey, Dad's fine," J snapped. "He drinks a little, that's all. Men do that stuff, get a little wild. Nothing to get upset about."

"He beat Mom up. That's not okay. Do you remember that, or do you have selective memory? He hurt her bad. That's why we left."

"Hey, keep your voice down. Of course, I remember. That was over six years ago. And it was only once. She was yelling at him. He got mad. I get mad at her when she's yelling at me, too. I wouldn't hit her, but I get plenty mad."

"She's just really stressed out right now, that's all. She never really yelled at us except when you jumped off the farmhouse porch roof. You have to admit, that was dumb. You could've broken your neck."

"I knew what I was doing. Stuntmen do it all the time," Jeremiah said. "That's what I want to be – a stuntman."

Isiah shook his head. "I'm very sure they get a lot of training before they do that stuff. You were lucky to end up with a broken ankle and not a broken neck." He glanced at the doorway and saw Aunt Hope standing there waving at them.

"Let's go. Our ride is here."

Jeremiah swung his backpack over his shoulder and muttered, "Going to be so nice to be able to drive ourselves where we want to go."

Isiah followed him out of the office. *I'm probably not going the same direction as you, brother of mine.* The realization that they were somehow parting ways almost stopped him in his tracks. He suddenly felt like crying.

****

"Hey, Mom, good to see you driving again," Isiah said when he opened the back door of the truck and climbed inside.

"Good to be able to drive again. At least on the short drives, anyway." The seatbelt alarm sounded, and she glanced in the rearview mirror at them. "Buckle up back there, please."

"You know, Mom, in Texas, you don't have to wear seatbelts if you sit in the back seat," said Jeremiah.

"Oh, yes, you do, my son. But, once you're over eighteen in Florida, they're not required. However, being ejected from a vehicle regardless of the seat you are in is not a good thing," she said while praying for patience. "Scott is always responding to calls like that, and sometimes it's kids your age he's trying to save by the side of the road. Life has enough risks, J. Silly to take more than you need to."

"Right," he snapped.

She glanced in the rear-view mirror again and noticed his arms crossed over his chest. *It seems like I can't say anything to him these days.* She fought back a sigh and concentrated on getting them to the Family Behavioral Center.

Faith made the turn into the driveway of the two-story Victorian house and parked. She followed the boys to the sidewalk that led to the covered porch. Hope got out and hugged Faith, then moved to the driver's side and got in. "I'll get the groceries and be back here in about an hour. Take your time."

"Let's go, boys," Faith said. She watched their long legs take the steps two at a time. She found the stairs just a bit more of a challenge than they did, but she managed without any assistance. *Another win for me. Hurrah!*

Jeremiah swung open the heavy eight-paned glass door, and they all stepped through into the empty waiting room. To either side of the desk were long hallways with gleaming wood floors.

She signed in at the desk and motioned for the boys to do the same. The receptionist gave them each a warm smile, handed them a business card, and asked them to take a seat. "It'll only be a moment, Mrs. Walker."

"You okay, Ike?" she whispered. He nodded but reached out and squeezed her hand as though to reassure her.

She swallowed hard as the first signs of the panic attack began. As the beads of sweat formed on the back of her neck and along her hairline, she took a long deep breath and slowly exhaled. *All is well with my children and me.* She repeated the breath and the thought. Her stomach calmed down. She looked at her other son. Jeremiah seemed fascinated by the giant fish tank in the wall, where a variety of brightly colored fish swam lazily in and out of dark green grasses and shipwrecks. *What's going on in that macho mind of his, I wonder?*

She turned her head at the sound of footsteps and looked up into kind eyes the color of dark chocolate. The woman's smile was infectious, and Faith smiled back.

"Come on in, Ms. Walker. Isiah, Jeremiah."

They followed the heavyset woman into a room that was full of sunshine and books. On the floor near the windows was a colorful rug that looked like a small town. Perfect for small cars and trucks to run around on.

"I'm Mary Tellor," the woman said, shaking Faith's hand, then doing the same with Isiah and Jeremiah. "Jon Loprete is not going to be able to meet with us today. We had an emergency, unfortunately. Can I get you all something to drink? I've got pop, coffee, and sweet tea."

"I don't want anything, thank you," Isiah said.

"Me either," echoed Jeremiah.

"I'll take some water if you have that," Faith said. *My mouth feels like cotton – maybe that's my angel telling me to listen and not talk.*

Mary went behind her desk, opened a cabinet, produced two cold bottles of water, and handed one to Faith. "Let's sit over here and get acquainted, okay? That's what today is about, so we could meet, talk some, and see what –if anything – is needed going forward, okay?"

Faith took a good swig of her water and put the cap back on. She sat at the large round table in the chair to Mary's left. *Here we go . . ..*

The boys sat beside one another opposite them. The doctor pulled a blank yellow pad in front of her.

"What's that for?" Jeremiah asked Mary, pointing to the play rug on the floor.

"We have some very young patients. Allowing them to play helps us to discover what's bothering them, or sometimes, they just need a safe place to be little kids for a while."

She smiled. "I'm a psychiatrist who specializes in child trauma therapy. While you are young men, not children, the victim's advocate office though we should meet anyway. I'm familiar with the legal file on this case, but I don't have any idea what may or may not be bothering either of you."

She paused and turned to Faith. "Are you comfortable being an observer of this session?"

Faith looked at her sons. *The doctor is right – they're young men, not boys.* She could show that old anxiety a thing or two by letting go a bit.

"I'm okay to stay or to go outside and sit on the porch. Boys? Would you be more comfortable if you spoke with Dr. Tellor without me sitting here?"

Jeremiah's nod would be unnoticed by anyone other than Faith. She winked at him and saw the pink begin to creep into his cheeks. Isiah looked at her and nodded openly.

Okay, then. "My boys are growing up, and that's a good thing. I'll wait for you two on the porch, okay?" She stood and clutched the bottle of water in her hand. When she closed the door quietly behind her, she took a deep breath. I'm so glad they're alive to grow up is more like it.

The first step is always honesty, she'd been told. She'd face her demons and give her sons the tools to do the same with their own.

****

"Well, boys, what did you think of Dr. Tellor?" Faith asked

them on the drive back to the farm.

"She's nice. And she's got a good sense of humor," Isiah said. "She said we have a lot of courage and thinks we'll be fine, but if we don't feel good about something, we're supposed to call her."

"Jeremiah, how about you? Are you okay?" she asked with her heart in her throat.

He shrugged. "She's cool. But I'm fine. Ike may need a chill pill, but I'm good." He looked out the window for a minute. "What time is Dad coming over?"

Ah yes, the confessional dinner. *I almost forgot. Good thing I asked Shawn Jackson to join us.*

"After dinner. Around seven. Do you have a lot of homework?" she asked them both.

"No," said Isiah, "got mine done in school today. One of my teachers was sick, so we had a study hall. I want to ride this afternoon if I can. Magda doesn't get so stiff if I work her every day. I thought I'd set up a couple of barrels."

"She's old," Jeremiah said. "She's what, close to thirty, Aunt Hope?"

"Oh, no," Hope answered, taking the turn to the farm. "Magda is actually the filly of your mom's mare. Magellan was her sire. She's just twenty-five."

"Well," Jeremiah said, "that's not young."

Isiah smacked his brother. "It's not that old, either. Tempe isn't any youngster, you know," he said.

"He's only eighteen. Got plenty of life in him. He –"

"Boys," Faith said through gritted teeth, "that's enough. There's value in age as well as youth. You'd be well advised to remember that."

As she pulled into the long drive, she saw a deputy's car parked near the truck barn. *Oh, no, now what?* Her heart rate picked up, and she felt that familiar tightening in the center of her chest.

Hope parked near the back porch. The boys unbuckled their belts, grabbed their backpacks from the back seat, and scrambled from the truck. Faith followed close behind.

Deputy Taylor walked about halfway to the house and greeted them. "Hey, boys. How are you doing? Everything going okay?" She gave Faith a wave.

"Yes, ma'am," said Jeremiah. "Are you here about our dad?"

"No, I came to talk with your mom for a minute. That okay?"

He smiled and nodded. "Sure. See you later."

Isiah lingered and stood next to Faith. She looked at him and gave him a wink. "You go ahead and get that ride in, and I'll meet you at the house. Just be careful, please."

"Are you sure? I can wait for a few minutes."

My defender. She shook her head. "Not to worry. I'll catch up with you later."

The two women watched the boys disappear into the back porch. Then Faith took a deep breath and looked at the officer who'd become a friend.

"What's up? I know that they picked up Beau's wife in Texas, and she's coming back here, right? And we're expecting to see him later tonight. I hope that hasn't changed – the boys would be heartbroken."

The deputy shook her head. "No changes that I know about. I did want you to know that they've identified the other kidnapper and he's dead. There's no threat left."

Faith gasped. "Dead? How? Sherri?"

"Doesn't look like foul play – but the autopsy results weren't in yet when I went on duty. He was in a motel room on the outskirts of Atlanta. The cleaning lady found him still in bed when she went to clean. He was dead for around seven hours, according to the coroner."

"How did they connect him with our kidnapping?"

"The rented Jeep keys were found in his room, in the microwave. The Jeep was rented to Earl just like the Ford F150 was. From the description the boys gave, right down to the cowboy hat and bandana, it seems this Denny Carson was the second man." She looked at the boys as they raced from the house to the barn, their long legs tearing up the distance quickly.

"I don't want you worrying anymore. It's all over now, Faith. You, your boys, your family – all safe. It's okay to move on, now."

Faith nodded, unable to speak around the lump in her throat. It was finally over. She took a breath and held it a few seconds, willing her legs to hold her up. The relief was immense. The deputy reached out and patted her shoulder.

"Thanks so much," Faith whispered as she exhaled. "Thanks for coming all the way out here to let me know."

"That's what we're all about here in Alachua County. Service with a smile." She laughed, then turned away to walk back to her car, opened the door, and settled in to begin her rounds.

Faith began to walk toward the house to give Hope the good news and maybe even carry in a light bag of groceries. She'd taken a half dozen steps, feeling as though she was walking on air, when Deputy Taylor called out to her.

"Faith, are you still seeing Scott Byrnes, the paramedic?"

She couldn't help but smile at the sound of his name. She turned around. "I sure am. Why?"

The deputy walked back to her and put a hand on her arm. "I just got a call. There's been an accident at the fire academy.

It will be on the five o'clock news, for sure." She cleared her throat. "There are two men unaccounted for."

Faith couldn't get her breath. The roar in her ears was so loud it hurt, and she pushed Taylor away as she gulped for air. Shaking her head furiously, she clasped her hands over her ears.

"No, no, no!!"

CHAPTER TWENTY-FOUR

Almost Free

Beau, Jack, and Eddie were twenty feet away from the door of the jail's reception area when Beau stopped in his tracks on the sidewalk. He looked around as though seeing the outdoors for the first time. *If you can hear me, thank you for my freedom.*

"Everything all right, Beau?" Jack asked.

"Better than all right, I think," he replied, feeling a smile tug at the corners of his mouth. "I've never been so happy to be outside in the fresh air!".

Eddie pointed at his car. "Your boys are excited–I can tell you that. Did you see your parents before they left this morning?"

Beau nodded and remembered their sobering conversation, one that had brought him to tears. "I did. Mom has to have open-heart surgery, did you know that? I hope I can be home before she has to go in. But I promised to do this, and I mean to see it through." He looked at Jack and cleared his throat.

"My father says he's proud of me. Can you imagine a man my age caring that his father is proud of him?" He shook his head. "It's more important to me than I knew, I guess."

As he opened the back door and tossed in his small duffle bag, there was a loud commotion in the next parking lot, near the prisoner transport doors. He cocked his head and straightened up.

"That's Sherri. I'd know her voice anywhere. She's having a meltdown."

"Beau? Get in the car," said Jack sternly. "She's not your concern at the moment."

He stood looking in the direction of her voice another few seconds. "Well, she is, but I understand your point." Before he could get into the car, he heard his name being screamed. It was the only word he could make out clearly.

He got in and shut the door. "I do want to talk to her, though. I've got a lot of questions." He settled in the back seat. "She's going to need someone to stand by her. She's got no one." He shook his head. "She's never had anyone."

Eddie started the car, then pulled out of the parking space. He glanced into the rear-view mirror. "Let's just do one day at a time, okay? Likely, you'll both be in the same courtroom at some point, so you'll get your chance. Just don't mess up your freedom deal because there won't be any second chance."

I know that and no more jail for me. "No problem, counselor. Let's see those boys of mine. I've got some explaining to do – I promised my mother I wouldn't wait on that, either."

****

Jeremiah led Tempe out of the barn and climbed into the saddle. As he adjusted his hat, he watched his mother collapse like a rag doll. The deputy was kneeling beside her.

"Isiah," he shouted over his shoulder, "something's happened to Mom." He spurred his horse across the yard and dismounted in a leap to her side.

"Mom? Mom? What's wrong?" *Is she paralyzed again? Why isn't she moving? Is she dead?*

Deputy Taylor reached over and gripped his arm. "She's okay, Jeremiah. She got upset over some news and passed out. I caught her before she hit the ground, so she didn't hit her head or back. I've called for First Aid to come and check her out." She looked him in the eye. "Go let your Aunt Hope know, okay? Maybe she can come outside and give us a hand."

"Maybe call Scott–" he began, then stopped. "He'll know what to do, right? He helped her the first time," he said.

The deputy looked at him, then checked her watch as she held her fingers on Faith's pulse. "Scott's been at the academy for a training week, and there's been an accident. We don't have confirmation on who's missing, but two men were trapped in the building collapse."

He felt like he'd been thrown off his horse. *Oh, no! God! I didn't mean any of those things. Please, God* – "He's an EMT, he wouldn't be in the building, would he?"

Taylor shook her head. "I don't have any more facts than what I told you – or your mom. Now please go get your aunt."

Faith moaned, turned her head and blinked a few times. "What's going on?" she muttered.

"It's okay, Mom. You're okay. Scott's okay. I know he is. Just don't worry," Jeremiah gushed in a single breath. He took her hand in his. "The ambulance is coming, so just lay still." He looked at the deputy.

"I'll be right back."

He got to his feet and ran to the porch door. "Aunt Hope, Aunt Hope, come quick! It's Mom. She needs you," he hollered as he burst into the kitchen. He looked around. Hope wasn't there, but the grocery sacks were on the counter.

"Aunt Hope?"

He ran through the dining room and found her standing in the parlor, her eyes glued to the television. The scene was hard to make out with all the pitch-black smoke pouring out of the building.

"Scott?" he whispered. *Mom's heart will just break beyond repair–.*

Hope shook her head but didn't take her eyes off the screen. Then she turned to him. "Are you okay? What's the matter?"

"Mom passed out in the back yard. Deputy Taylor called for help. She wants you to come out, too."

"Oh, Lord, what happened, do you know?" she said as she followed behind him.

He gave her the abridged version over his shoulder. When they cleared the back-porch door and rounded the side of the house, he almost stumbled over his own feet. His mother was sitting on the ground, leaning against Isiah. The deputy and the first aiders were on either side of her.

"Mom?" he asked as he knelt by Ike. "How's she doing?" he asked his brother.

The deputy got to her feet. "I've got a call, so I need to go. I'll check back with you later."

"Be safe," Hope said.

The first aid captain answered Jeremiah's question. "Her blood pressure is a little low, but this reaction isn't uncommon with anxiety disorders. I'd like to get her inside the house, get some coffee or sweet tea into her, and see if her BP doesn't come up. No injuries that we can tell."

Faith waved her free hand in the air. "I'm fine, really, and I'm so sorry. You need to be helping at the academy. Go, I'll be okay. My sons can help me get inside."

Jeremiah squeezed her hand. *That's my mom, who never*

wants any attention. "You need to listen to these people, Mom. Not every unit can respond to the academy accident. Anyway, the sooner you do what they want, the sooner they can leave." He glanced up at the captain, who smiled at him.

"Smart boy you have there," the captain said. "Come on, up you go, pretty lady."

Jeremiah lifted his mother under her arms and put her on her feet. The boys each supported an elbow. Hope kept the porch door open, and Faith motioned to sit in the rocker.

"Thanks so much, boys. Gracious, I've got a headache," she whispered.

"I'll get you a tea, Mom," Isiah said.

Jeremiah sat next to her. "No names on the news yet, Mom. But you know Scott—he'll be fine. Things are probably crazy there, that's all. Like this place was when we came home, remember? Hard to tell what's going on, probably."

The first aid responder put the arm cuff on again and checked Faith's blood pressure. "Coming up with you moving around. You drink that tea, then get something to eat – and relax." He glanced at Hope, then Jeremiah.

"We'll make sure someone calls you as soon as we know what's going on out there. We're upset about the accident too, but 'unaccounted for' means they haven't all checked in, that's all. We're praying for good news all the way around. You do the same, you hear?"

Jeremiah nodded and moved aside so Isiah could hand their mother the sugary drink. "We will. And thanks. Scott's pretty special to us here, too," he said.

Faith covered his hand with hers. "Yes, he certainly is. I think we need to let these good people get on the road so they can assist someone who needs them."

The team began to pack their gear back into the hard cases. The captain offered Hope his hand. "If you need anything else, don't hesitate to call, okay? And don't worry."

Jeremiah watched the tears fill his mother's eyes. *As if she can do that...as if any of us will be able to do that.*

****

Faith prayed as those around her sat watching the news feed for updates on the academy accident. *Lord, you've given me every sign that things will be okay for us all. Please get Scott and the firefighter out safely and help me to feel your peace, not this terrible dread.*

"Anybody home?" called a familiar voice from the front hallway.

Oh, my Lord, thank you, thank you, thank you. Faith got to her feet as fast as she could without falling on her face. "Grace! Is it really you? Get in here!"

Her twin sister, dressed in her signature jeans and a desert tan sweater, peaked around the pocket door frame. "I have a visitor that's come to meet you," she said with a grin on her face.

"Of course, bring Craig with you. We've—"

Around the corner of the doorjamb walked a German shepherd who then sat at Grace's feet and looked up at her.

"Oh, Mom, can we keep him?" cried Isiah, rushing to hug his aunt and pet the big dog. He looked up at Grace. "What's his name? How old is he? Is he yours?"

"Whoa, partner, slow down a minute. Let me get the lay of the land here. What's going on?" she asked, looking Faith in the eyes.

She could always do that. She always knew when I was in trouble. Faith swallowed and waved at the television.

"Scott's been involved in some kind of accident at the fire training academy. It's taking forever to find out what's happening and who else was involved. We're just sort of waiting. Waiting for news, waiting for Beau, waiting for you—"

Hope got to her feet. "I'm going to make some coffee – I'll be in the kitchen. Eddie should be here with Beau any minute now." She looked at Reverend Jackson. "Shawn, come give me a hand, will you? Boys, you give your Aunt Grace time to catch her breath, okay?"

"Yes, ma'am," they replied.

"Grace, I'll put a bowl of water out in the kitchen for the pup. Craig with you?"

Grace took the lead off the dog and hung it around her neck. "I left him at his place a little while ago. He'll be by tomorrow in the afternoon." She knelt in front of the dog.

"Go, play." And with that, the dog looked at Hope and fell into step with her.

Faith nearly fell into Grace's open arms. "I wish I could tell you how I've missed you," she whispered. "I love your civilian haircut. Looks great on you."

"Thank you. I've missed you, too. It was sure terrific to see all of you here in the parlor together like a Hallmark Christmas card." She hugged Faith and stepped back.

"Now, tell me what this new disaster is about." She led them to the front porch, where they sat on the swing.

Breathing through the tightness in her chest, Faith gave Grace a recap. *I will not cry about this. Not yet.* "So, Beau's due any minute to have a heart-to-heart with the boys, and I'm losing my mind waiting for news on Scott."

"Well, you've got the Rev here for Beau's visit. Good idea. How's the idiot-ex doing, by the way?" Grace asked.

Faith shrugged. "I think he's gotten a serious dose of how reality works, this time. His nonsense contributed to the kidnapping – not a straight-line chain of events, but all related. The FBI's now involved, and he's working with them on some aspect of this. And his mom has got some serious heart trouble, too. Open heart surgery is around the corner for her. I certainly hope that this discussion he wants to have with the boys is for real. That's why I asked Shawn to be with us tonight. And now there's Scott to worry about."

Grace glanced over her shoulder and spotted the dog watching them through the front door. "Isn't he a beautiful animal?" she asked as she let him onto the porch to join them. He sat down next to Grace's left leg.

"He sure is," Faith said, smiling as she looked at him. "What's his name? How long have you had him?"

"I've had him for about a month. He's part of my new civilian-life business plan. As for the name, well, I adopted him from a kennel that called him Clarence, but that's a dumb name for a dog. You may want to give him a better name than that," Grace said, her dark-blue eyes twinkling.

"Me? Why would I name him? And what's this business plan about? Are you staying here in Merciful?"

To Faith's delight, Grace tossed back her head and laughed. "I'm going to be working with dogs who can help humans with anxiety to manage life better. And yes, I'm hoping to make this place home base. That's why I asked about the bunkhouse situation.

"But as for his name, well, I've been training Clarence to be your dog. Someone you can keep with you to help with the panic when it gets to be too much."

"Mine? I don't know if I can manage a dog, Gracie. I have no idea how my situation will look in a month from now."

"All the more reason for a companion who is not emotional or needy, then. Honestly, Faith, this dog is amazingly astute and will make a lot of difference for you. We can talk later about all of that. Let's go get a cup of coffee."

"As if you haven't already had a gallon of the stuff today," Faith said, turning toward the door. The dog got up and turned, too.

She looked over her shoulder at the sound of the car tires on the driveway. "Showdown at the OK Corral," she muttered. "Beau's here. Lord, give me the strength to be calm and polite."

"Amen," Grace added. "And, that failing, I could just choke him to death for you."

Faith elbowed her sister. "While you could, and I love you for being willing, he is the father of my boys, and I don't want to make them choose, you know?"

Grace nodded. She stood shoulder to shoulder with Faith as Eddie and Beau walked to the front porch. The dog stood beside Faith and made a low grumble.

"Quiet," Grace said softly, and the sound stopped.

"Evening, ladies," said Beau. "Grace, I didn't know you'd be here, but good to see you. Great dog. Everything all right, Faith?"

Just peachy, but here goes nothing. "Yup," Faith said, forcing a smile. "Boys are in the front parlor, and coffee's on in the kitchen. Nice night to sit on the back porch if you'd like."

He looked at the ground, then back at her. He cleared his throat. "I appreciate what a great job you've done raising the boys. And I'm sorry about all the pain I brought you—I know it was a lot. I hope you'll forgive me someday for it."

Faith couldn't speak, so she held his gaze for another moment and nodded. "I've been working on that, Beau. You just be the best man and father you can be to our sons, and you and I have no quarrel. Now, they're waiting for you. Go on."

Beau moved past the women and entered the house. Faith could hear the boys clamoring to greet him, and her smile became genuine. They really loved him no matter what.

"A dog?" asked Eddie as he walked up the steps to follow Beau. He looked at Grace with one raised brow, then at Faith.

"Why not?" asked Grace. "Everybody needs somebody."

"Mom," Isiah said from the door, "there are no updates on the accident yet."

She nodded. "Thanks, Ike. You go visit with your father. He's got a curfew, so he can't stay all that long. I'll be okay."

Faith looked at Grace, then at Clarence. He let out a low whine and sat close enough to touch Faith's leg.

"You thinking what I'm thinking?" Grace asked.

"If you drive, I'm ready to go," Faith said.

CHAPTER TWENTY-FIVE

Up in Smoke

Faith held onto the dash and the door with a white-knuckled, two-handed grip as Grace navigated the Jeep over the rough pavement to the fire academy grounds. Never a smooth-riding vehicle, it got them where they needed to go, and Grace skidded to a halt a bit away from the incident command unit, spraying gravel in all directions.

Grace hopped out, helped Faith down, and told Clarence to wait. He hopped into the front seat and looked out the partially open window, ears forward, eyes alert.

"Bleib," Grace said again as she used her remote to lock the vehicle.

"Do I have to learn German to communicate with the dog?" Faith asked as they worked their way to the command center.

"No, but that means 'stay' and he's used to that one," Grace said. "Don't worry, you'll be a great dog mommy."

Faith recognized one of the K-9 deputies and began to walk toward him. *Thank you, Lord –*.

"Deputy Rogero," she called.

He turned and saw her, then waved and moved to meet them. "Ms. Walker. Good to see you." He nodded toward Grace. "Ma'am."

Faith touched his arm. "I'm here about Scott Byrnes. Is there any word? I can't just wait at home for news—I'm losing my mind."

He glanced toward Grace again.

"I'm so sorry," Faith said, realizing he didn't know who was with her. "This is my sister Grace. She's just retired out of the Army. She trains dogs, too."

His eyes seemed to light up. "Nice to meet you, Grace. And, to meet another K-9 person, too." He turned back to Faith. "We got word about ten minutes ago that the two missing men have been located. Both are alive. That's about all I can tell you."

"Did you have to go in?" asked Grace, nodding at the canine.

He shook his head. "That's why we've been on standby, but it was a firefighter team that located them. They're pinned under a steel beam." He looked away.

"There are injuries. We don't know how bad. The first guy was injured on the first floor when a burning beam came down and caught him wrong—compound fracture to the leg at least. That's when Scott went in. Then, the second collapse happened, and we lost contact."

Faith looked around. News trucks were being kept behind the fences of the academy, but reporters and mini cameras milled around the command center like ants at a picnic. She felt the pressure building in her chest. *He has to be all right, Lord, he just has to be.* She forced herself to breathe in through her nose and slowly blow it out through her lips.

Grace tapped her arm. "Let's go wait with Clarence," she suggested with a nod toward the Jeep.

"Good idea," Faith said. She turned to Rogero.

"We'll wait over by the Jeep and keep an eye on things from there, okay?"

He placed his hand on Faith's shoulder. "We've got the best responders there are, so try not to worry, okay?"

"I know you do, but one of them is injured, and worrying is something that seems to be out of my control these days," she replied with a wry smile.

"You've had plenty of good reason to worry, Ms. Walker. But we've got a lot of prayers working on this. You just believe they'll get out of this."

****

Faith leaned against the front door of the Jeep, arms crossed on her chest, one foot tapping the ground. Clarence whined softly behind her right ear from the front seat.

"It's okay, boy. He's going to be fine. And so are you," she whispered as she reached in through the window and gently stroked his head. She took a deep breath and swallowed, working to lessen the knot in her throat.

Grace came to her right side and pushed a bottle of water into her hand. "Drink this. It will help with the tightness in your chest."

She still has it, that uncanny ability to read my mind. Faith smiled at her and took the bottle. "Thanks. Am I that easy to read, or are you just that talented?"

"You're easier to read than you used to be. Don't forget I know a little about what you're experiencing too, so I'm looking for signs – ways to help," Grace replied, watching the smoke thin out to an opaque gray color. "Fire's almost out."

"Thank God for that," she replied. "Grace, I don't know if I can do this. He's always on the front lines, always going to be in the position to be injured – or worse."

231

Her sister nodded. "Do you love this guy?"

Faith met Grace's gaze. "I do. I didn't plan to and never thought I'd trust myself to get involved again, but somehow, he made it so easy. He didn't push me or demand anything, and he's not showy in any way, but before I knew it, I was hooked. But now I don't know if I can commit to all this fear. I swear, I'm losing my mind half the time."

Grace reached up and wiped a tear from Faith's cheek. "Listen, little sister. I don't give advice on love, and you know that. And Beau was – maybe still is – a real jerk. But we're not kids now, working through grief and parent issues. The genie is out of that bottle – you've learned a lot since then. Maybe, at last, we're just ready to make decisions that will bring us happiness. And until you've got a handle on the panic attacks, maybe you shouldn't make such life-changing decisions."

At that, Clarence rested his paw on the opened window edge and touched Faith's shoulder. She closed her eyes and felt some of the tension drain out of her body. "I agree about his name, though. Clarence is terrible," she said. "What's Clarence in German?"

Faith opened the door and let the shepherd jump out. Again, he stood by her side, just touching the side of her left leg.

"Kutsche. But he's your dog. You name him whatever you want to name him. He answers to commands, not so much his name. And he's already decided you need him, so there's no turning back. You'll see, he'll make an amazing difference in your life. I've seen some astonishing recoveries with the people who have PTSD–among other challenges–when they get a dog. That's why I decided that's what I want to do with my time now. There are too many people in need of dogs and too few trainers and providers."

Faith heard her name being called and looked toward the

voice. Rogero was jogging toward them. She began walking forward, stopped, looked down at Clarence, and said, "Bleib." He sat and looked at her, ears forward.

Rogero reached them. "They're bringing them out of the building now. Come on up if you want to – or you can meet us at the University Hospital in Gainesville."

"No, I'm coming right now," she said. With Grace beside her, they hurried to where the ambulances waited.

She held her breath until Grace reminded her to breathe. The first man out was soot-faced and unconscious as they levered the backboard onto the gurney and slid it up into the ambulance. It wasn't Scott. Her shoulders slumped with relief. *Dear Lord, please help this man to be healed and back with his family soon.*

She fixed her stare back at the building entrance and worked her jaw back and forth. Her whole body trembled. *Where is he? Where is he? Why isn't he out of there already?*

"Here they come now, honey," Grace said as she wrapped her arm around Faith's shoulders. "Looks like he's talking – that's a good sign."

Faith closed her eyes in a silent prayer of thanks, then blinked back tears of joy. When the stretcher was almost alongside her, she pulled away from Grace and dove at Scott's body.

She looked down at his closed eyes and blackened face and bent to hold him. "Scott? Scott, please look at me. Please tell me you're all right," she begged.

He turned his head, opened his eyes, and squinted. "Faith?" he croaked.

She nodded several times fast and then dropped onto his chest and sobbed. "Please, please don't ever do anything like this to me again, okay? Not ever, do you hear me?" She let go and straightened so she could look at him.

His smile was tired but there. The smile he always gave her. Then he winked. "You ready to talk about forever, are you?" he whispered.

Faith looked at him for ten seconds and then shouted, "Yes, yes, yes! Will you marry me, Scott Byrnes?" She stared at him and then realized they had a large audience. "I mean, not right now, like today—but someday?"

He tried to laugh but it sounded like it hurt. "I'd be honored to marry you, Faith Blessing. But maybe not today," he said just as he began to cough hard.

His comrades smiled at her. "We gotta get him to the hospital. He got a lot of smoke. But he'll be okay. We'll make sure he calls you later, all right?"

CHAPTER TWENTY-SIX

I Do

The Blessing Farm was alive with people of all ages. The large white tent set up between the garages and the house sported two Happy Birthday banners and provided shade for the people, and multiple tables of food set out.

Beau, Eddie, Hope, and Margaret Ann sat together at one table, eating as they watched Jeremiah and Isiah throw the football around with Scott. Faith, Craig, and Grace sat behind them with Reverend Jackson and a group of parents from the church youth ministry. Hank Williams Jr. sang in the background about all his rowdy friends.

Faith twisted the new diamond ring on her left hand and smiled as she watched the twins dive for the ball. "Next week they'll be driving. I cannot believe it's been sixteen years, already," she said.

Clarence, who'd recently been renamed Percy, laid beside her with his shoulder touching her calf. His snout rested on his front paws. She knew he wasn't sleeping at all.

Craig tapped Faith on the wrist with a finger. "How did a dog named Clarence end up being renamed, Percy?"

She shrugged. "Well, no one seemed to like the name Clarence, and we weren't calling him anything most of the time—he's so well trained he just about does what you tell him to without much fuss. But one night, I was in the library holding Dad's picture, and Clarence put his nose on the glass and did a little woof. So, I told him, 'This is Percy.' And then he barked and wagged his tail.

"So, then I asked, 'Do you like the name, Percy?' and he wagged that tail again." She laughed and dropped her hand to stroke the shepherd's head. "The boys have been calling him that ever since, and he responds quite well, so Percy it is. A fitting tribute to Daddy, I think."

Shawn Jackson looked at her and nodded. "Indeed, it is. Percy would protect you with the same devotion your four-legged friend has. The boys are doing well, aren't they?" he asked.

She nodded. "They sure are. No lingering effects from what I can tell. Even Isiah seems to be sleeping and eating well again. I'm so very thankful for trauma counseling. Jeremiah doesn't seem so angry anymore, either."

Grace pointed toward Beau. "That may have more to do with Beau coming clean with them than the therapy. He fessed up, huh?" she asked.

"From what I was told, he did. J was noticeably quiet for a couple of days, but he seems to be coming to terms with it all now. Scott asked him and Ike if it would be all right to propose to me." She laughed. "I'm sure glad they both said yes—especially since I'd already proposed and didn't ask anyone! With cameras rolling no less." Everyone chuckled.

"You still planning on heading back to Texas?" Craig

asked.

"Not right now," she answered, shaking her head. "I plan to go out to visit with Annie after her heart surgery, but it will only be a week, maybe. The boys want to go, too, so we're planning a trip around Thanksgiving. Beau's plan is to stay local to see Sherri through the trial, anyway.

"The boys are content here and, even when Beau goes back to Texas to take over Bill and Annie's place, the boys can eventually drive out and visit." She pointed at Isiah. "I also think there's a pretty little church gal in the mix as well."

Faith ate a spoonful of potato salad, then picked up a piece of fried chicken before she turned to Grace. "How are the plans for the dog kennel coming along? When do we break ground on the building?"

"We're just waiting on the okay for the permits," Grace said. "Should be this coming week, I think. Or at least, that's how it sounded at the last planning meeting. It helps that we own the land, but it will be a business open to the public, so the county is going over the plans with a fine-toothed comb. Parking, bathrooms, all that kind of thing."

Eddie got to his feet and called everyone to the tent. Faith noticed the look of dismay on Hope's face and tried not to smile. She and Grace knew what Eddie was up to, but Hope didn't. Would they finally get one over on their older sister?

"Everyone, can I have your attention for just a couple of minutes?" Eddie called a second time.

"Isiah, Jeremiah, Scott – come on over," yelled Beau in his deep bass voice. The ball ended up in Isiah's arms, and the three joined everyone under the tent.

"Ladies and gentlemen, thanks for joining us today. We have so many things to celebrate, and so many people we're thankful for that we thought this the best way we could do all that." He moved toward Hope.

"And, I want to do something today, in front of God and all of our friends, that I should have done forty-two years ago."

He got down on one knee in front of Hope and looked up at her. He reached into his jacket pocket and pulled out a ring box. Faith prayed that her sister wouldn't faint with embarrassment.

"Hope Blessing, will you be my wife? I will never be complete without you. I promise to love you and honor you all of my life."

No one moved or made a sound as Hope stayed silent. She nodded, slowly at first, then let out an old-fashioned rebel yell. "Yes, I will, Eddie Highspring!"

Percy jumped to his feet, tail wagging furiously, as Faith and everyone else under the tent whistled and cheered and clapped with joy.

Faith looked around and caught her twin's gaze. She pointed her finger at Grace and silently mouthed the words, "You're next . . .."

THE END

Don't miss the first book in this inspirational series:

Hope, Faith and Grace Blessing return to their hometown to bury their beloved father, sort out his troubled trucking business, and save their family's Merciful, Florida homestead from foreclosure.

Separated by distance as well as memories and emotions, the estranged Blessing sisters are forced to find a way to live and work together before time runs out on their last chance to save it all.

But when their number one enemy ends up dead, Hope is suspected of murder while she, Faith, and Grace battle an unknown adversary bent on destroying everything their father left behind.

With little else to turn to, the sisters turn to the God their parents taught them to trust and lean on when things go wrong.

But will prayers and faith be enough to set things right?

And who's behind the dangerous sabotage that threatens not only the family business, but the sisters' very lives?

MERCIFUL BLESSINGS, winner of a Royal Palm Literary Award, a Silver Award-winner in the Florida Authors and Publisher's President's Awards, and Foreword Indies Honorable Mention.

Print ISBN: 978-1-62390-075-5

Ebook ISBN: 978-1-62390-076-2

Get to know the Blessing family and the residents of MERCIFUL at their Facebook Page – Amazing Grace Trucking Company

https://www.facebook.com/ Amazing-Grace-Trucking-Company-Series-100394514983813

About Daria Ludas

w/a D.K. Ludas

 D. K. Ludas is a retired elementary school teacher, a New Jersey Realtor, and a short fiction writer. She's usually working on ideas for the next book in their Amazing Grace series and is becoming quite adept at attending Zoom meetings. When not writing or selling homes, she's involved in town politics, church organizations, Liberty States Fiction Writers, and Sisters in Crime. Email: DLLudas@verizon.net

About Nancy Quatrano

w/a N.L. Quatrano

N. L. Quatrano is a short fiction and mystery writer, and a neighborhood columnist for the St. Augustine Record. When she's not working with Rotary or her church, she does developmental editing, copywriting, and press releases at her business, On-Target Words. She and D.K. Ludas released an electronic short story collection in July of 2020, titled Always Chasing 'Em, available for Kindle, Nook, Apple, and other eBook platforms. She's a member of Liberty States Fiction Writers, Sisters in Crime, and Florida Writers Association. Email: Nancy@NLQuatrano.com